FLAT BROKE IN PARADISE

PATRICK LIVANOS LESTER

The events that take place in this book are entirely fictional. The names and characters depicted in this book are of the author's imagination and any resemblance to any persons living or dead is purely coincidental.

Flat Broke in Paradise/ Patrick Lester—1st ed.

Book painting *Palm Shadow* by Patrick Lester

ISBN: 978-1-948992-01-5

6.2

For Kim, the love of my life–and the perfect pearl.

Thanks to Eugenia Lester for her never ending support and encouragement, and to Sandy Boucher and Ruth McDonnell for their superb editing.

C'est Quoi la Vie?
(What's Life About?)

Part One

ENDINGS

Chapter One

"What do you mean the account is empty?"

Nick Thomas had been working at his desk for about an hour when the phone call came from the bank.

"Would you like to activate the company's line of credit to cover the incoming checks, Mr. Thomas?"

"I don't understand," Nick said.

"There isn't enough in the account to cover the checks."

"There must be a mistake. A bank in New York transferred thirty-two million to the account this morning. It should already be there."

Nick shifted through the pile of papers on his desk. "I have the account number right here. Let's double check." Nick read the number. He heard a typing on the line.

"Could you please repeat that?" the banker asked.

He repeated the numbers, tapping his pencil on the antique desk as he waited. He heard more keyboard clicks on the line.

"Mr. Thomas?"

"Still here."

"I entered the information into the database."

"So it's all clear now?"

"Well, no. Thirty-two million dollars was transferred from New York on Friday evening."

"Friday evening? The funds weren't going to be sent until this morning."

"The funds were transferred Friday evening just before five and then a few minutes later transferred out to the National Commercial Bank Jamaica Limited of the Cayman Islands."

There was silence on the line while Nick took it in.

"An offshore bank," Nick said.

"It looks that way."

"How much is left in the company account?"

"Well, uh..."

"The account really is empty, isn't it?"

"Yes, well, nearly."

"I'll get back to you." He hung up the phone and slid deep into his high-backed leather chair.

Nick's wife, Jody, had been in Washington, D.C. visiting her sister for the weekend. He had returned late the previous evening from a trip of his own, spending the weekend with college friends, taking snowmobiles on Friday afternoon to a remote cabin in the Sierras, off-the-grid and out of touch for more than two days.

He dialed Lance's mobile phone. Lance, Nick's best friend and business partner, was supposed to be in New York closing the biggest deal the company had ever had. The call went straight to voice mail. The last time he heard from Lance was the previous Friday. It was a text message:

The deal is signed. Monday the $ will be wired to the company acct.

Nick dialed Lance's home number. Lance's wife answered.

"Hi, Katherine. Have you heard from Lance?"

"No. I called him last night, but he didn't answer his mobile. I tried him at the hotel, and they said he had checked out. I thought that was because he was going to stop in Boston and visit a friend from college. He said he would return tonight."

Nick felt a twinge in the pit of his stomach.

"That's what I thought, too."

"Do you think something's wrong?" Katherine asked.

"I'm not sure. Would you have him call me if you hear from him?"

"Of course."

There could be only one explanation. The money was gone with Lance, no doubt now in the offshore account, or elsewhere. Nick could picture him—tanned to a golden hue, margarita in hand, beautiful woman at his side. Perhaps he was at the tables in Monte Carlo. What did it matter now?

It was over; Nick knew it. The company had grown and Nick had leveraged his own assets and securities for working capital. He didn't feel as though there was much risk. It had never occurred to him to distrust Lance. The thirty-two million was a loan expand the company's markets. Twenty million of it was to pay off Nick's notes coming due at the end of the week. The company was reputable and would have been solvent. Why would Lance throw away what they had worked so hard for?

Nick's mind raced at the ramifications of losing the money. He wiped a bead of perspiration from his brow, leaned back in his chair, closed his eyes and took a deep breath. When he opened his eyes, he let out a laugh. The sound surprised him.

He lifted his phone and punched the autodial button for his attorney.

It was after 3:00 a.m. when Nick fell asleep. He dreamed he missed the cable car and was late for an important meeting with his bankers. The underground cable pulling the car snapped with a loud bang, and the car careened down a steep San Francisco hill. The next thing he knew he was pranging his plane into the ground, flames were everywhere, the cockpit filled with smoke. He was coughing as he crawled from the wreckage of the plane and onto the deck of his sailboat, where he stood helplessly at the helm, the orange towers of the Golden Gate Bridge looming above him while waves beat the boat to pieces on the rocks.

The alarm blared and jarred him awake, soaked in perspiration, his heart beating palpably. "What the hell was that about?" he asked himself, reaching to turn off the clock.

Nick usually woke up without an alarm; now all he wanted to do was sleep. He rubbed his eyes and rolled over; the bed beside him was empty. He got up and walked to the bathroom where he stood at the sink and looked in the mirror. Jody had returned from her trip the previous evening and moved into the guest room. She had grown distant in the past months and Nick had no idea why. When he broached the subject, she became angry and ended the conversation by leaving the house. He would have to go it alone.

Any other day, Nick would go for a morning run, but now nothing was normal in his life. It was all he could do to drag himself out of bed. He showered, dressed, grabbed a banana from the kitchen and walked the three blocks to the cable car on California Street. Nick waved and the car braked to a halt. He climbed on next to the grip man.

"Good morning, Charlie. How's the foot?" Nick glanced down at the taped ankle. Charlie had sprained it playing Frisbee golf on the Marina Green.

"Hey, Nick. Getting better, thanks." He looked Nick up and down "You don't look so great, though."

"Yeah, I had a rough night."

Charlie clanged the bell; the cable hummed below them. He pulled back on the grip. The cable car lurched and moved forward as the grip took hold of the cable beneath the street. Nick took a firm grasp on the handhold above him, and recalling the dream that morning, felt a shudder run through him. The car vibrated and the wheels shrieked as they shot along the street.

The cable car, like most of the city, was awash with diversity. Charlie had dreadlocks and wore a Bob Marley button on his uniform. There were pinstripes in camel-hair overcoats, two nurses in colorful scrubs and a doctor in a lab coat coming from San Francisco Memorial Hospital, a couple of aging 1960s era hippies, and a guy sporting a 1980s spiked Mohawk. The car smelled of patchouli. Nick thought the only common element among them were tattoos. It seemed that all the passengers on the cable car had visible tattoos, even the doctors and nurses. There was a Mickey Mouse, a "Mom" and a portrait of Che Guevara. There were crosses, flames, and naked women—even on the women. Everyone had tattoos but Nick. He felt like a foreigner in his hometown. Nick rode the car to Powell Street and walked the rest of the way to his office.

He sat at his desk thinking about his options. He spent the next couple of hours going through the accounts, trying to formulate a plan. By midmorning, he had come up with nothing. Joan, Nick's secretary, came in and set the mail on his desk.

"Any word from Lance?"

"No," he said, lobbing a dart at the board across the room. He hit Lance between the eyes. It was a photo from the company website, with Nick standing beside Lance, Nick edited out, and Lance taped to the dartboard. That was the one piece of work he had accomplished in the morning.

"There's a letter addressed to you. It looks like his writing." Joan gestured to the envelope on the top of the stack. She looked at the dartboard. "Your aim is getting better. May I?"

"Be my guest."

She picked up a dart and threw it, hitting Lance in the nose. "Huh," she said and left the room.

Nick examined the letter. It was a simple white business-size envelope with a San Francisco postmark, no return address, and a single first class stamp. Nick used his pocketknife to open it.

Nick-
By now you have realized that I am gone and so is the money.
All of it.
Your plan for the company was near perfect. There was only one fault.
When you were doing the risk analysis for the business plan you didn't consider that your business partner would make off with everything.
You shouldn't be so trusting, Nick.
No hard feelings, eh?
Someone has to lose.
L.

"Someone has to lose." It was Lance's mantra, something he spouted during strategic planning sessions. Nick, being more of a win-win guy, had always been put off by the comment.

"What an ass," Nick said aloud.

There was a knock on his office door.

"Nicholas Thomas?"

"Yes, I'm afraid so," he answered without looking up.

"Special Agent John Mitchell, FBI. I've been assigned to investigate the case of your missing partner." He took a notebook from his breast pocket and opened it. "And a missing thirty-two million—and change."

Nick glanced up to see a man standing in the doorway holding out his badge. "Please come in, Agent Mitchell." He stood up, shook hands.

"May I see your identification, please?"

Mitchell held it out across the desk. Nick looked at the badge and the ID card and then at Mitchell.

"Thank you. I've never seen an FBI badge." Nick motioned to the chair.

The both sat down. Nick slid Lance's letter across the table to him. Mitchell leaned forward and read the letter. He reached in his breast pocket for an evidence bag and slid in the letter.

"An envelope?"

Nick slid it across to him. "It came in the morning mail—San Francisco postmark, no return address."

Mitchell added it to the bag. "Maybe forensics will come up with something interesting."

"Perhaps."

"Did you know him well?" Mitchell asked.

Nick walked across the office to a credenza and coffee maker and poured two cups of coffee. "Until yesterday, I thought I knew him very well. We were best men at our weddings. We were best of friends; he was my top executive and advisor."

"Not so much now, I see," Mitchell nodded at Lance's skewered picture on the dartboard.

"No. Not now." Nick held up a cup. "What do you want to contaminate it with?"

"Excuse me?"

"How do you take your coffee?"

"Cream and two sugars, thanks. Do you have any idea where he could be?" Mitchell again checked his notebook. "You knew him for what, eleven years?"

"Almost ten. Now I don't feel as though I knew him at all." He handed a cup to Mitchell. He looked out the window at the shoppers in Union Square. "The south of France, New Zealand? He had guidebooks of those places in his office."

"Do you think he would be that obvious?"

"No, I don't."

"You sound sure. Why?"

"Lance was a master-level chess player. He always thought five steps ahead. It was amazing the way he outmaneuvered our competitors. He's nowhere near those places, or he left a trail to lead anyone following him off his track."

Mitchell took a sip. "Good coffee."

Nick could feel Mitchell sizing him up.

"Before the letter, the last time you heard from Mr. Grabowski was in a text message on Friday?" Mitchell asked, referring to his notebook.

"Yes. We received a loan from a bank in New York City, formalized the deal, and he was in New York to sign the papers and shake hands." Nick picked up his mobile phone, scrolled through to the message, and handed the phone to Mitchell.

"Why didn't you go?" Mitchell read the message, took a picture of it with his own phone and made an entry in his notebook. He handed the phone back to Nick.

"Lance put a great deal of effort into making this deal happen. He found the bank and worked with them. I didn't want to hog his glory."

"So he has a three day head-start. That's bad. The first forty-eight hours can be critical in finding someone. He can be anywhere on the planet by now, but it will be easier to find him if he's still in the states. If he goes abroad, it gets a lot harder."

"So what's the plan?"

"We're working closely with our New York Office. They have interviewed the staff at the bank. No one has heard from him and none of their people have disappeared. It looks like Grabowski's in this by himself, but we will continue to monitor the company. They are very unhappy."

"I talked to the manager of the bank yesterday. I asked them why they transferred the money on Friday and not as scheduled on Monday. He told me Lance had all the paperwork ready and there was no reason to wait, so they went ahead and funded the loan."

"Our New York office has been scrambling since you called the bank yesterday morning. They are connected at high political levels. I'm glad I'm on this side of the country."

"Do you have any idea where he is?"

"No, but we're tracing Mr. Grabowski's cell phone, e-mail and credit cards."

"How is that going?"

"Nothing on his phone or e-mail, but one of his credit cards was used at an electronics store in New York City on Saturday afternoon. The clerk who recognized him said he was well dressed, had on a suit and tie. King chess piece lapel pin."

"Chess piece. Yes, that sounds like him."

"The clerk said he didn't know much about computers," Mitchell said, looking at his notes.

"Yeah, that does not sound like him. That makes no sense."

Mitchell made a note in his book, drew a star next to it.

"We're searching the airport departure records and the borders. Nothing has turned up. Yet."

Nick looked into his coffee while Mitchell looked around the office.

"Does he think of himself as clever?" Mitchell asked.

Nick thought for a moment. "I think he is aware of his capabilities. This was not a spur-of-the-moment thing. He had to have been planning this for months, years even. Yes, he thinks of himself as clever. And he is."

"In my experience, the ones that think they are clever are the ones that don't get away."

"I'd be very surprised if you found him," Nick said, balling his fists.

"It's hard to hide these days. He'll make a mistake and we'll find him."

"That could take a while."

"That's true, but I'm a patient man."

"I don't have the luxury of patience. Unless you find him and the money by the end of the week, there's no real point."

"Why is that?"

"Twenty million was to pay back a blanket loan on my personal holdings and have twelve million left for the company. I signed over everything I have as collateral. Not only will the company go under, so will I."

For a month Nick had been on a slow burn. At first it had appeared his life had taken an absurd, even comical path. It was certainly surreal. His weeks had been filled with lawyers, accountants, bankers, creditors, and more lawyers. Competing companies materialized with low offers to buy the business. Each was analyzed by the creditors, lawyers, and Nick.

Nick approached it as he did any other project—focused, prepared, professional. He was not willing to let Lance get the better of him and he didn't consider failure; he stayed focused. Despite his best intentions, below the calm exterior Nick seethed. His secretary, Joan, could see it was taking a toll on him. The FBI interviewed everyone in the office many times and the company was in chaos. She knew Nick wanted to make things happen and she knew he was told to stay out of the investigation, to let the authorities do their jobs. She could see it was driving Nick mad, being told to sit on his hands, not go after Lance, just stand at the helm as the ship slowly and agonizingly took on water and sank.

Seated at his desk after an entire morning in the conference room at his attorney's office, he looked up from his desk at the dartboard. Lance's face was all but obliterated. Most of the staff had come in at one point and taken a few shots. It seemed to help them in some way, made them part of the process.

Besides the stress of trying to save the company, Nick had to dismiss most of his staff. He felt a great responsibility to them. To a person they had been supportive, realizing he had been trying his best to save the company and their jobs. They focused their anger at Lance, the common enemy.

Now only a skeleton staff worked at the office and the

place felt barren. The slightest sound echoed. An accountant was using Lance's desk. Nick worked sixteen-hour days, taking breaks only for exercise and meals. His home life was in shambles; Jody was growing more distant.

Joan popped her head around the corner of his office door. She took a long look at him before she spoke softly. "It's seven-thirty and I'm going home. You should, too," she said. "You look haggard."

He shook his head to clear it, ran his hand through his hair. He stood and put on his jacket. "You're right. Come on, I'll walk you out."

It had seemed promising for awhile. He had been negotiating with one of his company's competitors to take on his company's debt for ownership of the company and all of its patents, software, and other assets. After three weeks of intense discussions, it turned out to be a dead end. The other company tried to obtain valuable processes during the talks; they had no intention of paying for anything. The deliberations ended in a whimper.

By the time Nick returned home he was exhausted. The first thing he saw was Jody's matching set of luggage. The second thing he saw was Jody, his wife of twelve years, arms outstretched, hands holding papers and pen. It was a legal document, blue paper on the first and last pages. Nick took it from her and read the title.

"Whatever happened to 'for richer, for poorer'?"

"Get real."

"Jody, what's going on? I don't understand. I'm doing everything I can to save the company, our home, and our lifestyle. I know you've been distant in the last couple of months, but it started before Lance stole our money, killed the company, and put our staff out of work. We can work this out."

"No, we can't."

"What did I do to make you want to leave?"

She stood in front of him, jaw set, arms still outstretched with the papers and pen. "You know."

Nick was perplexed. "I've wracked my brain trying to figure it out, and when I've asked you, you walk away. No, I don't know what I've done. Please tell me."

"I'm not going to play with you Nick. I'm leaving. Nothing you say will change that."

"You're not going to tell me?"

"Look, Nick, you can sign the papers now or we can do it the expensive and hard way in court with lawyers. With the FBI camped in your office do you really want another legal proceeding?"

Nick winced. He looked her in the eyes and recognized the expression on her face. It was the one he had seen many times before; the unresolvable Jody. She had made up her mind and she wasn't going to change it. He took the proffered pen, walked to the table, sat down and signed the papers.

"Good luck," she said, grabbing her suitcases and walking out the door. A taxi had pulled up to the curb. "The divorce should be final in six months," she said over her shoulder.

Nick could feel things slipping away. He had held out hope. He had lists of possible solutions. Of course, finding Lance and the money would solve his problems, but that wasn't progressing at the speed he needed. He poured himself a finger of rum and sat down at the piano. His shoulders dropped and a sensation of total defeat came over him.

"Oh, well," he said aloud to the empty room.

He started playing and tried to lose himself in his music.

Chapter Two

Six years earlier, Nick and Lance were sitting at Café International in San Francisco's Haight-Ashbury district. It had been months since they had seen each other and Nick had been hearing about Lance's mystery girlfriend. He had never seen his friend so happy.

"So when am I going to meet Katherine? You've kept her to yourself for too long."

Lance checked his watch. "She should be along any time now."

"She's joining us for lunch?"

"Here she is now." Lance jumped up to meet her. Nick rose and turned to see the woman walking toward them. He smiled as the woman approached.

"Hi, Kathy," Nick said.

"You know each other?" Lance said, sounding shocked.

"We spent time together one summer when we were in college," she said giving Lance a kiss on the cheek. She turned to Nick, "I go by Katherine now."

"You spent time together?" Lance asked.

Katherine reached for Lance's sleeve. "I'm starving. Have you ordered yet?"

"She's a real catch. She's smart, beautiful, and comes from a good family. And she likes me." Lance had told Nick earlier. Katherine came from one of the more established San Francisco families. Lance was later to learn that she had such a solid trust fund that a prenuptial agreement would have been superfluous and a waste of attorney fees. Katherine's trust income, home, and investments would allow them to live comfortably, with no income from Lance. Lance's dream of rising above his parents' station and making it on his own talent would not happen with Katherine, and he wasn't comfortable living off his wife's wealth.

Katherine found Lance to be bright, handsome, funny, and driven. He was trying to rise above his roots, on his own, with nothing handed to him, and he differed from the suitors her parents expected her to choose among.

NICK AND LANCE HAD MET THEIR SENIOR YEAR IN college after Nick had returned from a year abroad in France. They had a few classes together and endured required group assignments. The two of them did most of the work while the other students parked themselves in the campus pub and drank beer. Nick earned a degree in engineering with a minor in business; Lance graduated in business and computer science.

Lance's introduction to Nick's world was somewhat of a shock. Nick had never alluded to his family's wealth, and he drove an old and well used hand-me-down BMW. When Lance entered the tony Pacific Heights neighborhood with foreign consulates and private schools and walked through the carved front doors of Nick's hundred-year-old family home and into the marble foyer with the sweeping staircase and the crystal chandelier above, he was stunned by the opulence. He knew it was the life he wanted, one he had always wanted. Lance was raised in a working class neighborhood north of San Francisco. He both desired the life Nick had and resented it, although he gave Nick no indication of his feelings.

Born prematurely, Lance was small in stature through high school. Being smaller than the other boys and many of the girls made life difficult for him. He tried to find something that would set him apart from his peers. He worked at a local grocery store, and from an early age he became obsessed with money. He would get ahead by finding a loophole, or breaking the law. He felt that if the rules didn't say he couldn't do something, it was acceptable to do. Lance didn't worry about ethics; it was all about winning. He felt that the rules didn't apply to him and he had been clever enough not to get caught. It was the way he was wired. One night he noticed a coworker skimming from the till at the store. He collected the evidence and built a solid case against her. Instead of telling her superior, he blackmailed the woman for months, increasing the money she paid him each week. One day she disappeared, leaving no trace. Lance stepped into her position at the store with an increase in pay.

After high school, from seventeen to nineteen, he grew seven inches, topping out at six feet tall. He embraced his new height and went to great lengths to get into and stay in peak physical shape. It added up to making Lance a competitive person with a strong work ethic and a flexible moral code. That competitive ethic drove a desire to win at any cost. It cost him friends, girlfriends, mentors, what extended family he had left, and it was taking a toll on his marriage. He was careful to not alienate those he found useful to him—or those with more wealth, fame, or power. Those were the things he admired most. He put Nick into one of those categories.

Nick was generous with his possessions and included Lance in the use of his cars, vacation home, plane and boat. But it pained Lance that Nick had them and he didn't. Nick had even known Katherine before Lance did. Katherine had never talked about her time with Nick, and Nick never mentioned it to Lance. Lance watched them closely when they were all together. Nick and Katherine were comfortable and acted like old friends. As far as Lance could tell, there was no undercurrent one often sees in former lovers. Still, he couldn't be sure and Lance saw it as another point in Nick's favor. When Lance quit his job and Nick offered him the CFO position, Lance saw it not as a level of respect for Lance's abilities, but as charity from Nick. His insecurity grew. He obsessed about how to beat Nick. He made plans, mapping out his campaign. It took years and became the focus of his life. He had file after file of encrypted notes on his computer. With his obsession came paranoia. It evolved from winning the game of having more than Nick to needing to destroy Nick and taking him for all he had.

As CFO, Lance suggested Nick leverage his personal holdings to take the company to the next level. He presented the well thought-out plan. In fact, it was a good plan that would have worked well. Nick didn't even see it as a gamble. Nick's money was his own. His father wanted Nick to do with it what he wanted, not to be burdened with the complications of a trust. Nick's father had no interest in controlling his son's life from the hereafter. On his deathbed Nick's workaholic father told him, "Spend it. Enjoy life. Don't do what I did. Live." When both of his parents had passed, Nick settled into the family home in Pacific Heights.

Had the money not disappeared with Lance, Nick would be able to keep his homes, cars, boat, plane, home in Tahoe, and a sizable cushion of cash. The company would have paying customers and would be growing quickly and steadily. But that was not going to happen now. No, Lance set out to destroy Nick and went at it with focused determination.

It was June of his freshman year in college and Nick was staying at his family's home for the weekend. One evening his parents asked him to join them at a local charity function. Nick knew it meant a lot to them, so he dusted off his dinner jacket and black tie and joined them. It was an overpriced event of the sort his parents frequented. There would be dinner at a hotel, a longish speech with bad jokes, and lots of polite chitchat and talk of politics and money. The men would be in evening attire, their wives would be dripping in their finest jewels. Many would buy new dresses for the occasion.

Nick stood with his parents making conversation near the bar, his father, Peter with his single-malt scotch and his mother, Helen with her vodka gimlet. Nick sipped a martini and surveyed the room, checking out the elite crowd. Most of the women were wearing dresses in a shade of peach with their hair unswept. Sheep, thought Nick. His mother was elegant in a sapphire blue. She always bucked the trend and dressed as she pleased, a free spirit. Unlike Nick's father, she didn't come from wealth; she was an outsider. It was the same with Nick's grandmother.

"I see Kathy is back from Switzerland for the summer," Helen said, gesturing with her glass across the room.

Nick turned and followed her gaze to a young woman

dressed in a long black dress with a single strap, like a toga, but form-fitting with a slit nearly to the waist. Her long black hair flowed down her back. She wore a single Tahitian pearl around her neck with matching pearl stud earrings.

"Yum," Nick said.

"Yum, indeed. She does have nice lines."

"I love it when you talk like a sailor, Mother."

"Why don't you go talk to her?"

He kissed her on the cheek. "Don't wait up."

"Play nice," she called as he headed across the room.

By two in the morning Nick and Katherine were walking hand-in-hand down the dock to *Icarus*, the boat that had been in Nick's family for generations. His black bow tie loosened, his jacket over Katherine's shoulders.

That evening was, in fact, the start of an intense romance for Nick and Katherine. Nick spent the days at his father's law firm and evenings and weekends with Kathy. They took road trips to Big Sur, Mendocino, and Tahoe, and managed a two-week trip to the Caribbean where they chartered a sailboat and anchored in deserted turquoise-water coves in the Grenadines. In San Francisco, they spent much of their time on *Icarus* because they were both staying at their parents' homes for the summer and the boat afforded them privacy.

Nick and Katherine had known each other for years. Their families had attended the same gatherings and were both in the *Social Register*, that odd bastion of old money and power. They ran in different crowds within the same group. Katherine had spent much of her education abroad, A Levels in London, college in Switzerland.

NICK SPENT THE SUMMER AT HIS FATHER'S LAW FIRM, AS

he had many summers before. Peter had never pressured him to do anything in the area of law. He liked Nick's quick and analytical mind and as he told him, "I'd rather keep the money in the family and pay someone I know I can trust." He figured if Nick liked the law enough, he would go into it of his own accord.

For Nick, working for his father meant flexible hours, good pay, and knowledge that would help him later in life. Peter kept a small firm with little turnover in employees. Nick had been going to the office all of his life; it was like another home because the staff treated him as part of their extended family.

His father did not have an original Monet in the lobby as did his nearby legal competitor, nor did he constantly remodel or feel the need to expand and grow. He had a simple, yet elegant office on Union Street in the Cow Hollow district of San Francisco, left to him by Nick's grandfather. Peter paid his employees well. He chose his clients carefully, he didn't pad his hours, and gave them a fair price. His clients, in return, were very loyal. It was a badge of honor to have Peter as one's personal attorney.

IT WAS A FOGGY WEDNESDAY SUMMER AFTERNOON IN San Francisco. Peter was at a client meeting and Nick had finished his work by noon. He called Kathy to see if she could get away. Her mother had set her up with a summer job at a local museum.

"We have an electrical problem at the museum. The power is out and the fire department is here checking on it. I was about to go home."

"Want to meet me at *Icarus*? I can be there in twenty."

"Don't you have to work? Or is this a nepotism thing—boss's son gets to leave early?"

"Hey, I worked late last night and I'm done for the day. My father will be at client meetings for the rest of the afternoon."

"Oh, goody. I'll see you aboard in a half an hour."

Nick was delayed from leaving by a call from his father. As they finished their business Nick said he was going to meet Kathy, unless Peter needed him to stick around.

"Love before business, Nick. Always. See you tomorrow?"

"Thanks, Dad."

"Give Kathy my best," his father said, then rang off.

It was a reunion of sorts. Nick had been away for the week making repairs to the family Lake Tahoe home. He was excited to see Kathy, and happy that she had made *Icarus* a second home. She had brought in extra pillows and fine sheets and while he was gone had recovered the well worn settee in the main salon with blue and white striped fabric. It brightened the boat up and made it homey.

Nick stopped at a local gourmet shop and bought two bottles of champagne, some French cheese and bread, some fruit, and a bouquet of Gerbera daisies, Kathy's favorite. He saw a green bottle on the shelf of the shop. It was a 12-year-old Venezuelan rum he had been looking for. He had introduced Kathy to rums, and this was one of the best. He added a bottle and a bag of ice to his basket.

"I have to make a point of ordering more of that rum; I sold a bottle only ten minutes ago," the woman behind the counter said.

By the time he arrived at *Icarus*, he could see a warm glow coming from the portholes. He hustled down the dock as a summer squall started to pour. Climbing aboard, he opened the companion way hatch and looked down into Kathy's smiling face. He reached down and handed her the flowers.

"Ah, my favorite daisies."

He climbed below. Kathy had turned on the heater and had some music on the stereo. She looked though his shopping bag and made approving noises as she pulled out the cheeses and Bollinger champagne. As she looked into the bottom of the bag, she let out a laugh.

"What's funny?"

"I did some shopping, too. I found this." She pulled a green bottle of rum out of the cupboard. "And we have enough champagne for a month."

As the San Francisco summer of fog and sun continued, Nick and Kathy spent many nights on *Icarus*. The boat hadn't left the dock in more than a month.

One day Peter stopped off at the boat to pick up a wrench he needed for some plumbing at home. He dropped into the companionway and saw the cabin. There were empty champagne and wine bottles, clothes, magazines, and books. Nick's CD collection had migrated to the boat, stacked up by the stereo.

Back home during dinner that evening with Helen he said, "I dropped by *Icarus* today to pick up a tool."

"Still afloat, is she?"

"She's taken on some extra cargo and is riding a little lower in the water."

Peter told her about the condition of the cabin.

"I guess they need the privacy. I had figured Nick had been staying at Kathy's."

"Well, they built their own little love nest on the boat," Peter said.

"That's nice. I like Kathy."

"They do seem happy—and inseparable."

BY LATE JULY, BOTH NICK AND KATHY'S PARENTS WERE ecstatic about the couple spending so much time together. By August they were dropping not-so-subtle hints about marriage. At first Nick and Kathy laughed it off, but soon it grew to a point that could not be ignored. One sunny August day as they sat on a bench on the edge of Stowe Lake in Golden Gate Park feeding ducks that wandered by, Nick decided it was time to talk.

"We should talk about our parents' plans for us," Nick said with a sigh. Dinner conversation the previous night with Kathy's parents was laced with inquiries about their future together. It had made them both squirm.

"You realize that our union would be more of a merger between established San Francisco families than a marriage. Well, more than that, of course. I really enjoy our time together," Kathy said.

"I enjoy being with you, too," Nick said.

Nick tossed a piece of bread to a passing emerald green mallard. The drake pecked it to shreds, lifted his head and shook his neck to swallow it. Other ducks made their way to the couple in search of a handout, squawking and fussing to get Nick's attention.

"I want something different. Our children would end up going to the same schools, the same colleges, the same cotillions. They would be members of the same clubs as we and our parents. If we're together there will be expectations and pressure to do that. I don't want that. I love San Francisco; I don't like the crowds we run in," Kathy confided.

A couple in a paddle boat shaped like a swan passed in front of them. They, too were feeding the ducks and had a trail following them. The ducks in front of Nick and Kathy abandoned them for the couple in the boat, leaving them in silence.

"Well, that makes it easier," Nick said.

"What do you mean?"

"It seems we both have the same opinion. I don't want to be a clone of my parents. Look at us. We're only half-way through college; we've been together two months and our mothers are picking out china and designing wedding invitations. My father has probably already drafted a prenuptial agreement," Nick said.

"My father told me last night after dinner that the trust his attorney wrote was so tight I wouldn't need one. I think he should call it a 'mistrust' instead."

"I'm sure they mean well. They worked hard and want to make sure we're taken care of." Nick tossed a piece of bread to a newcomer.

"I'm sure they do, but it's a little early for them to start," Kathy said.

"Our parents are pushing us away from each other by pushing us together, kind of like Romeo and Juliet in reverse. Neither of us like to be told what to do," Nick said, turning to her.

"Maybe we're too much alike." Kathy shot him a rueful smile.

A man in a park uniform who had been eavesdropping came and stood beside them as they looked down at the ducks. He turned to Nick and Kathy and said, "I think you two kids ought to finish school and then decide if you want to be together. A lot can happen in two years."

"Yeah, that's for sure," Nick said.

"It's a big world out there and life is short. Make your own decisions. Don't let someone else make them for you." He walked off, leaving them to ponder his comments.

Things cooled between Nick and Katherine after that, although they continued to see each other through the summer. At the end of August Katherine headed back to Switzerland and Nick accepted a year abroad at a university in France. They were across the world from their home, but less than 400 miles apart. They e-mailed a few times and talked less. It would be a few years before they would see each other again.

THE SILICON VALLEY CAN BE AN UGLY PLACE, especially for a bright young person wanting to get ahead. It is said one has about ten years after graduating from college before being surpassed by the next generation coming along. Lance had moved his way up the management chain, soon in line to be Chief Financial Officer at Global Paradigm, a custom software company. He studied the stock options he was to be offered, analyzed the cash flow of the company, the existing and promised contracts, ran the numbers. He figured with the promotion and a five-year vesting program for his stock he would have enough to cash out, retire, do anything he wanted—and with his own money, not Katherine's.

The first sign that his future was far from certain came when he was called into the office of Glenn, the CEO, also the founder and majority stock holder.

"You wanted to see me?" Lance called from the doorway

of Glenn's office. The size of the office always amazed him. There was a massive desk, a conference table with seating for twelve, a lounge area with a sofa and chairs, a wet bar next to a small kitchen, a bathroom with shower and bathtub, and the largest flat screen television Lance had ever seen.

Glenn turned away from the huge monitor of his computer. "Chris will be joining us full time. I'd like you to get him up to speed on the financial end of the business." He turned back to the monitor.

"Chris?" Lance asked.

"Yes, my son Chris," Glenn said, keeping his eyes on his work.

"Oh, right. Chris."

Chris had been interning at the company for six months, showing up at various meetings, sitting in the back, taking notes. He wasn't engaged in the discussions or even acting interested. Lance noticed him looking at him with an odd expression. Creepy kid, he had thought.

Glenn turned to Lance and leaned back in his chair, annoyed to be talking to Lance. "He's about to graduate from Wharton and I want him to learn the business."

"Okay, I'll show him the ropes."

"Thanks." Glenn turned back to his computer, dismissing Lance.

Lance looked at him, tilting his head in wonder. Glenn rarely showed social skills, but that was extreme even for him. He turned and walked out of the room and back to his office where he sat at his desk and dropped into a funk. It disappointed him that he hadn't seen it coming; knowing the next move was something on which he prided himself.

Two weeks later when the CFO position was presented to Chris in a management meeting in Glenn's office, Lance wasn't surprised. Glenn didn't even have the decency to tell

Lance before the announcement. Lance was sure it was coming, but that wasn't the point. There was a stifled gasp of disbelief from the staff at the announcement. Eyes shot to Lance, who was standing against the wall next to the wet bar. They all knew he was the one in line for the position.

Lance wasn't about to play the victim. Smiling, he walked forward and offered Chris a handshake and congratulations. "I'm sure you'll make your father proud," Lance said, turning to Glenn. "And I want to thank Glenn and the rest of you for the experience I gained at the company. I enjoyed working here."

There was another, louder gasp from the staff. Even Glenn seemed shocked at Lance's announcement. He's probably angry I upstaged him. This guy doesn't think things through, Lance thought.

After the meeting the parade of shocked co-workers and well-wishers stopped Lance in the hall. Taking the easy-out of "I signed a non-disclosure statement," he avoided the questions of "Where are you going?" and "What are you doing?"

Later, back in his office, Lance thought of the time he had invested in the company. His plans for financial success had dissolved and he was now five years behind in his ten-year plan. He thought about sabotaging Chris and the company before he left. He realized he didn't have to. While Chris now had the financial picture, Lance was the one who negotiated with the clients and built one-on-one relationships with each of them. By studying their industries, he knew what they wanted and anticipated their needs. It kept him ahead of the competition. There was no one available to replace him. He had been asking for staff to share the load, a plan to train his replacement, but Glenn had been more interested in going on to the next new thing than producing or selling the product. Chris had focused on the numbers and not the alliances.

There would be a gaping hole left by Lance. It would take time to find someone qualified to take the job and months or even years to build up the relationships.

The phone rang. It was one of Lance's customers. He heard Lance was leaving and wanted to know where he was going and who would replace him. Lance received three similar calls before Glenn appeared in the doorway. Lance gestured to a chair and Glenn closed the door and sat down.

"My phone has been ringing," Glenn said. He was puffed up and peeved.

"Mine, too." Lance sat back, smiled. At one time Glenn had intimidated him. Now Glenn was coming to see him. He didn't feel intimidated; he felt contempt for the guy. By quitting Lance removed the power Glenn had over him.

"What's it going to take to keep you here?"

Lance had played out this conversation in his mind. He didn't hesitate. "The CFO position." He didn't frame it as a question; he spoke it as a demand.

"My wife would kill me," Glenn said, a pained expression on his face.

"I didn't realize Stella ran the company." Lances's mobile phone rang and he pushed a button to send it to voice mail.

Lance's comment hit home and Glenn winced. "I just can't."

"No, you just won't," Lance said, leaning forward and looking him in the eyes.

"Would anything else keep you here?"

Lance reached into his desk and pulled out a piece of paper. The paper had the salary and stock options that he would have received with the promotion. He grabbed a pen and added a golden parachute in case Glenn agreed and later wanted to fire him. There was no way Lance would trust him now. He slid the paper across his desk to Glenn.

Glenn read the paper. "The board will never go for it."

"You are the majority shareholder. You control the board. You ARE the board."

Glenn looked around Lance's office. It was cleaned out, nothing personal left, ready for the next occupant. He seemed to regain some of his hubris. He shrugged. "How long have you been planning this?"

"Since you told me your son would be CFO."

"I never told you that."

"Yes, you did. You just weren't listening to yourself."

After Glenn left, the phone rang again.

"Lance, it's Nick. I returned from a few weeks of business travel. I received a call that you'd quit your job."

"Hold on a second." Lance rose and closed his office door.

"Yeah, I gave my notice today. A lot has happened since you left."

"What's going on? With your CFO leaving, I thought you were next in line."

"Well, Glenn's son is about to graduate from college. Glenn gave the position to him."

"The CFO position? That's ridiculous for a recent graduate with no experience. I heard through the grapevine you have plans you can't talk about."

"Glenn broke the news of his son's promotion at a staff meeting about an hour ago. I announced my departure about 10 seconds after offering my congratulations to his son. I had to tell people something. I don't have any plans."

"Well my meetings went well and we need to move away from accountants and auditors to a full time financial staff. How would you like to be CFO?"

Lance didn't hesitate. "You're on."

"Great. By the way, I always thought 'Global Paradigm' was a stupid name for a company."

Chapter Three

"Jody left."

Nick was sitting with Katherine at her kitchen table one morning in March. Katherine's home was in the Sea Cliff district nestled between the Presidio and Lands End on the Northwest tip of San Francisco, overlooking the mouth of the Bay and the Golden Gate Bridge. The area was even more exclusive and expensive than Pacific Heights where Nick grew up.

He looked dejected and Katherine had never seen him like that.

"You ran out of money," she said. "She married you for your money and she's tragically insecure."

Nick sat back in the chair. "I'd like to think she married me for more than just my money."

"Well of course she did, but money played a huge part of it."

"I suppose." Nick looked around the room. There was a show of money in this room, albeit subtle. The place felt rich, much like Nick's own home. Katherine, as much as she tried not to be like her parents, ended up being surprisingly similar.

She spent much of her time on boards of nonprofit organizations and arranging fund raisers, just as her mother did. Katherine had received her university degree in art history and that led, with her family's money, to a spot on the board of various museums in San Francisco and around the Bay Area. It kept her busy and somewhat fulfilled. Like Nick, she did not have children.

"If it weren't for the shopping, she'd have nothing. How many times did she redecorate your home?" Katherine asked.

"Well, she seemed to enjoy her life. But it seemed more than just me losing my money. She was angry with me, and it had been going on for some time. I tried to talk to her about it, but she wouldn't say what was bothering her. I don't know what I did to upset her so."

"That woman is not satisfied with anything. You managed to make her reasonably happy for a considerable period of time. You need to move on, and the sooner the better."

He glanced across the table at Katherine and he knew she was right. "What about you? Did you see this coming? I sure didn't. I was completely blindsided."

"I've thought about it a lot." She took a breath and continued, "Lance loved money, Nick. Think about it. If you had a conversation with him, he brought up money within a minute or two. He graded people's success by how much money they had. He would get on-line in the morning and study his accounts, moving money around from investment to investment. He had spreadsheets that he constantly fiddled with. He was always running numbers. He also couldn't stand to lose. He would win at all costs and if he couldn't win he sulked and was unbearable. You've played tennis with him haven't you? He makes noises to distract you when you're serving the ball. He does the same thing with chess. He badgers you until you move a piece. On vacation, we played golf with some friends. It was embarrassing."

"I never played golf with him."

"Well, don't."

"There's a good chance I won't."

"He is obsessed with winning and he is obsessed with money."

He pondered her words, let them sink in, thinking back to how Lance acted in the past. He knew she was right.

Katherine broke the silence. "You seem blasé about Lance."

"Blasé?"

"Yes, you don't seem angry."

"I need to figure out how to salvage the mess of my life he left behind. I can be angry with him later; I don't have time for that now."

She poured more coffee into their cups. "Lance was jealous of you, Nick."

"Me? Why?" Nick scratched his head. "What did he have to be jealous of?"

"I'm sure he was jealous of the time we had together. Although he often tried to get me to talk about it, I never did."

"That was a long time ago and I never talked to him about it either."

Katharine looked across at Nick, held his gaze for a moment, a smile in her eyes and a slight smirk on her lips. "That was a great summer, with you, on *Icarus*."

Nick met her gaze and smiled. "Yeah, it was."

They sat at the table, their thoughts retreating to a summer long ago.

Katherine composed herself. "Lance was envious of your family, the houses, the plane, the yacht, your wealth, the whole package. He wanted all of that. Oh, I know you were generous and shared much of it with him, but it wasn't the same. Your largess was an affront to him."

"You had money, why did he need his own?"

"He didn't want my money, his ego wouldn't stand for it. He wanted to make it on his own."

"If he waited six months, he could have had it all, too."

"He's an impatient man. Besides, he has it all, Nick, and now you don't."

Nick sat back in his chair as if someone had punched him. "Huh," he muttered. He thought back to buying the cars, the plane. Lance had been with him each step of the way, helping him decide on what to get, the options, the colors. Nick never thought of Lance as a jealous man. He seemed to get as much pleasure from Nick's purchases as Nick did. Nick often loaned Lance the use of the cars, boat and home in Tahoe. Now he felt like a naïve idiot.

Katherine projected a relaxed air about her. He thought of his time with her and felt a pang of loss. "How are you?"

"I'm not all that happy with having my husband run out on me. But I have always kept my family's money separate from my marriage. It's a requirement of the family trust. My attorney says I'll be fine, at least financially, and that I should be thankful for my parents' foresight. As for our marriage, we were drifting apart and had been for a while. In fact, I am lucky. I file for abandonment and it's done. No hassle, no battles in court." She leaned forward and grabbed his hand. "I'll be fine, Nick, but I'm concerned about you. How is it going?"

"Rather badly. Lance did a thorough job. I have to admire that." He looked across the room at an original Picasso above the fireplace. He knew Katherine's grandfather had known the artist. He also knew few people outside the family had seen the work.

"Is there anything I can do for you?"

Nick laughed. "I took a cab here. Do you think I might borrow a car?"

"Lance's BMW is in the garage. You can use it as long as you'd like."

Nick smiled at Katherine. He was grateful for the long friendship, one that made it easy for him to accept her help.

Chapter Four

Nick spent the month being put through the ringer by a bankruptcy judge, Detective Mitchell, and forensic accountants. They drilled into his accounts, holdings, and anyone with whom he had ever done business. They made it clear he was a suspect believed to be conspiring with his missing partner.

When did he last talk to Lance?

When did he last see him?

Did he know where Lance was or where he was going?

The investigation team asked these and other questions. The forensic accountants—a trade he had had no idea existed, tore through his and the company's financials and asked more questions. The company had a full audit each year because working in a post-Enron era required ever more paperwork. The company was clean; it was Lance who was dirty. It was a talking point Nick hung on to. He made every effort to remain grounded, to not let the process make him crazy. Occasionally he succeeded.

The reaction of Nick's creditors was swift. They froze his

assets. There was a *For Sale* sign on the front lawn, but he was allowed to stay in the house until it sold.

He saved the leasing company the cost of repossession by dropping off Jody's Mercedes Benz and his BMW. The plane was impounded. He was insolvent and living off cash he kept in his safe at home. It was not the exit strategy Nick had envisioned for him or his company.

Nick realized the inevitable; he would never save the company, and he would lose all he had worked so hard for, and everything his father and grandfather had worked for. He set his jaw and looked up at the dartboard, saw a shadow out of the corner of his eye.

"Detective Mitchell. What can I do for you?" Nick asked.

"There is no sign of your partner," Mitchell said from the doorway.

"I wish you'd stop calling him that. When will I no longer be a suspect?" Nick asked. He had been a suspect for many months and it still bothered him to be looked at that way. He felt defensive, but it was just a part of his daily life.

He dumped a marketing folder into the trash.

"When we find your part—Lance—and he admits that you were not involved."

"Why would I stay around and put myself through this? I'd have to be out of my mind." As an afterthought he added, "I'm not there, yet."

"If I've learned anything from this job, it's people do things for all sorts of reasons. I've learned not to be surprised by any form of human behavior."

"That must be a horrible way to live."

Mitchell shrugged. "I was in the area and I thought I'd drop by, see how the negotiations are going."

Nick let out a sigh. "The company is doomed."

"You gave it quite an effort."

"Now I want to let the lawyers and accountants fight it out. There's nothing I can do."

This guy has been taking a beating, Mitchell thought.

"I'd like to try something else," Nick said.

"So what do you have in mind?"

"I want to change my focus. I want to find Lance."

In reality, Mitchell no longer thought of Nick as a suspect, mainly because he could find nothing connecting him to the loss of the money. Maybe he would slip-up and reveal something, but Nick's motive to take the money was a weak one. Sure, it would have increased his fortune, but assuming he would have split it with Lance, it made little sense for him to do so. But there was always some doubt and years of experience telling him to press on with his investigation of Nick.

Nick's blasé approach to being a continued suspect Mitchell attributed to fatigue and not arrogance.

Mitchell walked to the credenza and helped himself to a cup of coffee. "Well you've been wanting to find Lance since he disappeared," Mitchell said, gesturing with the pot to ask if Nick would like more. "I guess it's time we try to do that. Together."

It was an odd pairing. Mitchell, the hunter, and Nick, still a suspect. Nick had nothing to hide, and he wanted to find Lance as much as Mitchell, so why not team-up with him? And Mitchell? He made sure the information was flowing in one direction, from Nick Thomas to him.

Mitchell took another sip. "I'm trying to get a bead on Lance. He will have slipped up somewhere. Even though there is no sign he has left the country, I've contacted Interpol and given them his description. It's still not that difficult to get a passport, especially with today's new technology."

Nick researched his records, journals, and searched for anything that would lead him to Lance. Mitchell was still in full interrogation mode, pulling as much information from Nick as he could. Did Lance have any homes or apartments he knew about? They reviewed each of Lance's friends that Nick had met. There weren't many. Lance was a workaholic, athlete, computer geek, and a chess player. His friends were Nick and a couple of guys he met in college. His marriage, it seemed, was at the end of a long list of other priorities.

Mitchell filled a notebook with information and contacts. Reading it over, he occasionally called Nick for clarification on an item. Nick started his own notebook on Lance. Told by Mitchell that no detail was too small, Nick dove into the task with gusto, driven by the frustration of doing nothing for too long. He called Mitchell whenever he thought of something, regardless of how trivial. He let Mitchell read his notes in the morning as they were drinking coffee in Nick's kitchen. Then Mitchell would drop Nick at his office and Mitchell would follow up on any leads they had generated.

One afternoon Mitchell poked his head around the corner of the door to Nick's office.

"Want to go for a ride?" he asked.

Nick thought about the stack of paper he had to review and looked out at the blue sky peeking through the buildings of Union Square.

"Why not? This stuff can wait."

"So this friend of Lance is working in Paris for another couple of months. I tracked him down and he told me that Lance was looking after his apartment while he was gone. I told him Lance was missing and asked him to call his landlady to let us in to his apartment to look around. After he had his attorney check me out, that is," Mitchell said.

"Smart guy. You could have been anybody," Nick said.

"It was faster than getting a search warrant," Mitchell added.

"What's his name?"

"Blake Morris, He was at school with Lance."

"I remember him. He was a good guy."

"He has a clean record and a serious job, but I'm checking him out."

The building was narrow and deep like many in San Francisco. This one was ornate and upscale. It was in the Marina District near the bay. In the fall of 1989, the Loma Prieta earthquake collapsed part of the Bay Bridge and made a mess of the area. The building had been repaired; however, the land was still the same unstable fill from the huge 1906 earthquake. Nick guessed that the next big shaker would do the same thing the last two did. It was a nice spot though, with the San Francisco Bay and the Golden Gate Bridge nearby. The earthquake didn't seem to have an affect on the home prices.

Mitchell pushed the buzzer and announced himself.

"Please come up, detective. I'm in 2B," the landlady said. She buzzed them in, and they climbed the polished mahogany stairs to the second floor. The landlady stood waiting for them on the landing.

"Mr. Morse said I should let you in, that his friend looking after his apartment was missing."

"That's right. Thank you for letting us look."

"May I see your identification, please?"

"Of course." Mitchell showed her his badge and photo ID.

She put on her glasses, peered at the ID, took off her glasses and looked him in the face.

Mitchell smiled at her.

"It's 3A. We need to go up a floor," she said turning her back and starting to climb.

"If you give me the key, I'll save you the trip," Mitchell offered.

She stopped and turned on the stair and stared down over her glasses at Mitchell and Nick. "I think it would be best if I came along and locked up after you."

Mitchell met her eyes. "As you wish."

They finished the climb and entered the apartment. It was classic upscale bachelor quarters: neat, sparse, and expensive; the furniture was ultra modern and imported from Europe. There was a stack of mail on the table. Mitchell ambled around the room, looking for clues. Nick did the same in the opposite direction. They met in the middle, the landlady keeping a watchful eye from the doorway. They continued on to the stainless steel kitchen.

"Mr. Morse's friend brought a woman with him. They always stayed an hour or two, if that's any help," the landlady said, a downturn on the corner of her lips.

Mitchell and Nick exchanged glances.

"That's a big help. Let us look around a little longer and then we can talk. Would that be okay?" Mitchell said.

"I suppose."

Nick continued into the bedroom while Mitchell checked out the bathroom. Later, his face rigid, Nick walked out to the living room and looked at the landlady.

"That woman Mr. Morse's friend brought with him. Was she about five seven, brown hair, blue eyes, a great dresser?"

"That sounds about right. Do you know her?"

"I think I might."

When they were outside, Mitchell asked, "What did you find?"

Nick held up an earring. It was a sterling silver hoop with a pearl suspended in the middle. "I found this on the bedside table. I had these made for Jody for her birthday."

"You realize this changes everything," Mitchell said, parking in front of a coffee house.

"Well, yes. It's a good thing she already filed for divorce. 'Irreconcilable differences', my ass," Nick said. He wondered if Lance had left the earring on purpose, wanting him to find it, rubbing in his victory. Or maybe Jody left it on purpose. Either way, it had made the point.

"Sorry about your wife. You want a cup of coffee? This place roasts their own beans. Best coffee in town."

"With all the cream and sugar you put in your coffee, I don't see how you can taste the difference."

It was the first testy thing Nick had said since Mitchell had met him. It was out of character and made Nick appear more vulnerable and human. Minutes ago he discovered his wife and best friend were having an affair and acting together they took everything Nick owned. He had every right to be testy. Mitchell let the comment pass.

They took their coffee and sat in the car. Nick was deep in thought, and Mitchell let him think.

Nick had thoughts going in all directions. He felt as though someone had punched him in the stomach. Jody and Lance?

His brain was parroting the interrogation he had been through with the FBI and others:

How long had Jody and Lance been at it?

How long had Lance been planning it?

Where are Lance and Jody now?

Where is the money?

Nick's head was spinning. He took a deep breath then blew it out. He turned to Mitchell. "You knew, didn't you?"

Mitchell, eyes straight ahead, took a sip of coffee. "I had an idea. I wanted to question your wife and she seemed to have dropped off the map. In this job coincidence is not something to be taken lightly."

They sat drinking their coffee. The windows were steaming up. Mitchell started the car and pushed the defrost button on the dashboard.

"I'm kind of glad you found the connection to Lance and your wife. I wouldn't like to have been the one to tell you."

"Coward."

"Well, yeah, about some things," Mitchell said, setting his coffee in a cup holder and starting the car. "By the way, I need the earring. It's evidence."

Nick reached into his pocket and dropped it into Mitchell's palm.

"Sorry about the coffee comment."

"Forget about it."

"Where to now?" Nick asked.

"I'm going to drop you back at your office. Then I'm going to go to work looking for your wife."

"Soon to be ex-wife. And I will be happy to help."

Chapter Five

After college Nick pursued an aerospace career where he was promoted to management and groomed for a job at the company headquarters. His coworkers and the next tier of management saw him as a threat, but they need not have worried. After eight years he had had enough. He had tired of the politics, appalled by the waste of money and resources, contemptuous of the inefficient bureaucracy, and exhausted from the never-ending airplane rides, taxis, and rental cars that took him to lonely hotels that all looked the same. The money was good, but it was not the way he wanted to continue living.

It was a trip to Houston that made up his mind. It started out with a contentious meeting he had to sit through. Managers from competing firms were arguing their merits. It became more heated. Words were exchanged, and the government manager, instead of ending the meeting, wanted both parties to hash it out, shake hands and be friends. It was like some schoolyard scuffle with immature little boys. The meeting dragged on and in his notebook Nick doodled a stick figure parachuting out of a flaming space station landing on a palm tree-studded atoll. He looked at his watch and realized he might miss his flight home. He rose to leave.

"We're not done here," the government manager said.

"Well, if I don't leave now, I won't make it back to my office to complete a deliverable due on Tuesday." Nick knew it was the right thing to say. The guy hated it when someone missed a deliverable.

Nick stepped out of the offices and into the June Houston air. It was in the mid nineties with the same humidity and the air smelled of the recently paved parking lot. By the time he reached his rental car a hundred feet away, he was drenched with perspiration. He dropped the car at the rental return and climbed aboard the bus to the airport. Glancing at his watch he saw it was going to be close. He was the first one out the door of the bus at the airport, running to the security checkpoint with his garment bag, computer bag and trench coat. He took off his belt, watch, and shoes and stood in stocking feet with the rest in line. They were all business travelers and he sailed through. He ran to the gate and saw the flight was to JFK and not San Francisco. He approached the counter and inquired.

"Gate change. It's in the other terminal. Here I'll draw you a map." The gate agent took a pad of paper and began to write.

"I know the airport pretty well. Which gate?" Nick asked.

"Oh, okay." The agent smiled. "Gate 23. You'd better get moving. I'll call ahead and let them know you're coming. Last name?"

"Thomas."

"Go now, Mr. Thomas."

His trench coat hanging over the fold in his garment bag, his computer case in his other hand, Nick turned and ran.

He was moving at quite a clip, dodging passengers coming

toward him. He came to an open area and fell into a solid run. He glanced to his right and a man dressed in a suit was running beside him. "United to San Francisco?"

"Yep," Nick said.

"Follow me," and the man sped off, his attaché swinging in rhythm. Nick poured it on and followed him.

The guy turned and Nick followed him past gate after gate to the end of the concourse. Nick could feel his trench coat falling and then the shoulder strap on the bag gave way, the clip breaking. He stopped and grabbed the handle, throwing the trench coat over his shoulder. The man in front of him was at the gate showing his ticket to the agent. Nick grabbed the handle on the case and ran. He arrived at the gate as the man was walking to the plane out on the tarmac, 50 yards away. He could see the waves of heat radiating from the surface.

"Mr. Thomas?"

"That's me." Nick handed her his ticket; he leaned against the counter to catch his breath. His clothes were soaked through.

"Here you go. Better run." She said, handing the ticket back to him.

"Thanks." He grabbed the handle of the garment bag, turned, and ran to the door. The handle came off in his hand.

"Uh oh," the agent said.

Nick hoisted up the bag and clutched it to his chest with his trench coat. He began an awkward run out on the tarmac to the plane. It was then that the zipper on his garment bag broke. Clothes exploded onto the ground. He leaned forward, picking them up as a hand appeared and shoved his clothes into a black trash bag.

"I think it's time for a new garment bag," the gate attendant said.

"Lifetime guarantee. Thanks for the help," he said..

She tied a knot in the bag and handed it to him.

"Now go."

He ran to the plane and up the rear stairs. A flight attendant with tall blond hair was waiting at the cabin door. She took the garbage bag and the remains of his garment bag.

"Well look at yoooou, Mr. Thomas," she said in a strong Dallas accent. "Sugar, you sit right down. We're about to take off." She reached behind him to raise the stairs and secure the door.

"Thanks for holding the plane, Darlene." Nick plopped into a seat. The aircraft started to move before he buckled his seatbelt. He had flown the route so often he knew most of the crew by first name.

Up in the cockpit they had seen the bag explode on the tarmac.

"I think that guy's gonna need a new garment bag," the captain said.

"Yessir, I believe you are correct," said the copilot.

Once the seatbelt light was out Nick left his seat and headed to the lavatory. He stared at the face in the mirror. Perspiration plastered his hair to his head, his tie was sideways, and his shirt was soaked through and clinging to him. He washed his face and straightened his tie. "I have to find another way to live," he said to himself.

In the following weeks Nick's discontent grew. He didn't want to be like many of his colleagues—not separating their career from their lives. He searched for an opportunity to get out, to do something else. He had been in an ongoing series of meetings trying to solve a problem. The company was building satellites for telecommunications, the military, and NASA. The satellites used large solar arrays and radioactive isotopes to power the electronics, but there was a problem with the software controlling the panels. Kludged together from various other systems, it was horribly inefficient. Their competitors were killing them and as far as Nick could tell, their own control software, while better, wasn't efficient, either. He saw the opportunity. After returning home from a trip, he read his employment contract. There was nothing in the agreement stating the company owned the rights to something he had not produced on company time and not at the company. He dropped the contract off at his attorney's office the next morning, just to be sure.

That afternoon his attorney called to tell him he could go ahead with his plans without repercussions. He advised Nick to leave the company to avoid future conflicts of interest. Nick hung up the phone and sat back in his chair. He had a foot-tall stack of documents on his desk, a pile of receipts and expense reports to fill out, the weekly status report due the next day and the timecard requiring him to charge his time to multiple accounts depending on what meeting he was in. There was a safe bolted to the floor beside his desk. He had long ago avoided keeping classified documents in his office. He couldn't go to another office without locking every classified document in the safe. He found it hard to believe some people in the office thrived on having the files. He figured it made them feel important; to him they were an unnecessary burden.

"Blah," he said to his empty office.

Deciding it was time to choose uncertainty over the corporate grind, he opened his laptop and began to write a letter of resignation, sure he could find a better way to run a business.

Chapter Six

The boat was Nick's father's and his grandfather's before that. She was a 57-foot yawl, with a royal blue hull and a deep red stripe. Designed by the famous naval architect John G. Alden and built in the 1930s, she was a comfortable craft, wide in the beam with a full keel and fitted out with the best of her day. Nick's Greek grandfather, Nick Thomas, used the Anglicized version of his middle name as his last when he immigrated to the United States. Nick's grandfather had called a bluff and won the boat in a spirited poker game after the end of World War II. He christened her *Icarus*. The Greek myth of *Icarus* is one of the hubris of man and, Nick's grandfather thought, the perfect name for a boat won in a game of chance.

Being Greek he made sure that when he renamed the boat he did so according to nautical lore. That mythos states that every vessel on the sea is recorded in the *Ledger of the Deep* by Poseidon, and any vessel not properly recorded in his ledger would suffer his wrath.

The renaming ceremony, steeped in tradition, was somber and serious. For the occasion, Nick's grandfather had assembled an audience of local politicians, judges, attorneys, doctors, and family and friends. As word got out, the crowd grew.

The ceremony calls for three bottles of good wine, but substitutions are common. Nick's grandfather had added dozens of bottles of champagne on ice in a huge locker near the stern of the boat.

Nick's grandfather and his son Peter looked out at the crowd on the dock. The faces showed a range of expressions: some curiosity, some bewilderment, some happy to be out of the office on the sunny San Francisco day. Standing above them on the stern, Nick's grandfather took a silver ingot out of his waistcoat pocket. He had written the previous ship's name on the ingot in water-soluble ink. That, too, was part of the ceremony.

He leaned down into the cockpit and rang the ship's bell twice to quiet the crowd on the dock. He welcomed his friends and colleagues and gave them nautical history about the seriousness of the day, and, glancing at the huge container of champagne bottles on ice, the rewards to follow.

He explained how first came the de-naming ceremony. All physical references to the original name of the boat had been removed, including the name on the transom, the boat's logs, the life rings, and the name of the boat on the forward bulkhead. As long as there was reference to the name of the old boat on board, the name would remain in Poseidon's ledger. He reminded the guests that this was a solemn occasion and they must save talking and celebration until after the ceremony. He also asked the old name of the boat not to be mentioned, as once the boat is de-named, she is clean and nameless and homage has been paid to Poseidon.

Thus he began. He had a strong and powerful voice, one of timbre and pitch that required no amplification.

> Poseidon, o powerful and potent God of the Sea, whose boundless realm we and the all ships daring to breach must pay tribute, I humbly beseech you to obliterate for infinite and unending time from your log and memory the name Bar Tab which has no further existence, future or past, in your domain. In confirmation thereof, we offer this silver bar inscribed with her name to be erased through your authority and to be forever washed from the sea.

He pulled the ingot from his waistcoat pocket, showed it to the crowd, and then tossed it over the stern into the San Francisco Bay.

> In thankful recognition of your magnanimity and execution, we offer these libations to your exalted self and those who worship you.

He took a bottle of champagne he had beside him and poured half of it from east to west into the bay. The de-naming ceremony completed, he set the bottle down and moved to the bow, his son and First Mate, following him. The crowd remained in respectful, if awed silence.

Once on the bow, he picked up the second open bottle of champagne, poured two glasses, and handing them to his son, he again began to speak.

> O powerful and potent God of the Sea, whose boundless realm we and all ships daring to breach must pay tribute, I humbly beseech you to record in your log and memory this righteous vessel hereafter and for eternity to be known as *Icarus*, protecting her with your trident and your power over the seas and storms, securing her safe and swift passage during her travels throughout your dominion.

> In thankful recognition of your magnanimity and execution, we offer these libations to your exalted self and those who worship you.

He poured the rest of the bottle, east to west, into the bay. He took a glass from Peter, looked at him with a look that only they shared, one reserved for times when they got into trouble together and had to face "Mother". They drank down the champagne in the glasses.

Moving quickly, to keep the guests from diving into the bottles of champagne, Nick's grandfather took a third open bottle and poured a glass while expounding:

> O powerful and potent regents of the winds, under whose benign protection our fragile vessels make passage across the savage and endless deep, we beseech you to accord this righteous vessel *Icarus* the advantages and enjoyments of your generosity, granting us your attention to our needs.

He turned and flung the wine to the north.

> Great Boreas, winged majestic regent of the North Wind and Bringer of Winter, we beseech you to use your great authority to spare us the forceful curse of your violent hyperborean breath.

He refilled the glass, turned and flung the wine to the west.

> Great Zephyrus, winged majestic regent of the West Wind and God of Spring, we beseech you to use your great authority to spare us the forceful curse of your untamed breath and bless us with your gentle breezes.

He refilled the glass, turned and flung the wine to the east.

> Great Eurus, winged majestic regent of the East Wind, we beseech you to use your great authority to spare us the forceful curse of your destructive warmth and rain.

He refilled the glass, turned and flung the wine to the south.

> Great Notus, winged majestic regent of the South Wind, we beseech you to use your great authority to spare us the forceful curse of your obscuring fog and mist.

Coming to a crescendo, Nick's grandfather puffed himself up to his full height and stature and thundered:

> To the powerful Aeolian guardians of the winds that blows before them, we ask your beneficence to grant us fair winds and following seas as we respectably make passage through your realm.

By then Peter had made his way to the stern and at his father's signal, removed the bunting from the transom.

"Ladies and gentlemen, I present you *Icarus*; may she sail on smooth seas with steady winds."

There was a roar of applause. There always was when Nick's grandfather was in front of a crowd. He was never one to disappoint.

"Please join me in a toast to *Icarus*." There was a rush to the waiters who had been opening bottles and pouring glasses.

He turned to his son, who had joined him at the companionway, and patted him on the back.

"Well, that ought to keep her off the rocks."

"Great boat, father. But Bollinger Champagne? Isn't that expensive to pour into the bay?"

"We don't want to offend the Gods. It's the champagne of the British Royal Family, so it's good enough for us."

Later that night, while the party continued in a tent that Nick's grandfather had rented for the occasion, he was standing on the dock looking at his new acquisition. He was approached by the man who lost the boat in the poker game. The man was drunk and weaving. Nick's grandfather eyed him.

"The upkeep on her was costing me a fortune. I would have liked to have sold her and not lost her in a poker game, but from what I can see you will take great care of her. That was the best damn show I have seen in years. Best of luck to you, sir."

They shook hands.

"Here, let me refresh that glass for you," Nick's grandfather took the man by the elbow and steered him away from the edge of the dock and back to the tent on the Marina Green.

The party continued with music and food, and guests remained until the early hours of the next day. By midnight it was completely out of hand and even the police gave up trying to calm it down. The event made it to the front page of the morning newspaper, helped by the editor and his photographer who were friends of Nick's grandfather and invited to the celebration.

THE UPKEEP ON AN OLD WOODEN BOAT CAN COST A SMALL fortune with the yearly haul-out. There was lots of sanding and varnishing and brightwork and brass to be polished. Nick kept her in fine condition as did his father and his grandfather before him.

His father had upgraded the boat as technology changed, and Nick continued to do so when he took ownership. The Loran had been removed and a modern GPS added, the weatherfax and charts were replaced with a laptop computer. The charts and old brass sextant remained on board; Peter insisted Nick know how to navigate when the power went out.

The boat had been Nick's father's pride and joy. Year-round he and Nick sailed on many Saturday mornings. Nick learned to sail in the San Francisco Bay with all its currents and wind shadows from the islands. When Nick was young his father told him, "If you can sail in San Francisco Bay, you can sail anywhere." He shared his father's and his grandfather's passion for the boat, learning how to maintain and repair all the systems and how to sail in all types of weather.

Chapter Seven

One Saturday morning several years ago he had been at the dock examining the boat, checking the stanchions and rigging. In his hand were the keys on the chain with a small sculpture of that winged mythical Greek, *Icarus*. Not expecting anyone, he was startled to hear his name.

"Nick!" Jim called. Nick turned and smiled at the carriage of the self-assured form walking down the dock toward him.

It had been months since they had seen each other, but Jim was practically a member of the family and appreciated *Icarus* as much as Nick did.

Nick had been an engineer working on the Space Station program, assigned to test a new satellite repair tool; Jim Fujiyama, a retired astronaut and Air Force colonel, worked as a consultant training new recruits for a future space shuttle flight.

The men had met in a "working group" meeting in Houston. They had both been on the same delayed flight from California and arrived late and sat together in the back. As the meeting droned on, Jim kept Nick amused with anecdotes about the various people sitting at the table at the front of the room.

"I don't know why they call these 'working group meetings'. Nothing ever gets done," Jim told Nick during lunch.

After the meeting Jim suggested that he and Nick get together for drinks that night. They made their way to the Flying Dutchman down the road from Johnson Space Center in the gulf town of Kemah. There in the smoky bar drinking beer and eating a mound of crawdads they became friends, finding that they both lived in the San Francisco Bay Area and were both sailors and aviators. They kept in touch and Nick often visited Jim at his remodeled cabin home in the wooded Santa Cruz Mountains where Jim lived alone. He was a rare astronaut, one who had outlived his wife. She had died four years earlier in a car accident while Jim was on a Space Shuttle flight. An independent and adventurous woman, she had been driving south on Highway 5 to Los Angeles when a trucker fell asleep and took the lane that held her and her Lexus. Maggie's car had prescribed a near perfect arc as it flew through the air, reaching toward space where Jim orbited overhead.

"It's hard enough to land a shuttle when life is going well. We want nothing to impair his piloting skills. We'll tell him about Maggie when they get on the ground" had been the edict from mission control.

Jim often joined Nick and his father on their Saturday sails, coming to know *Icarus* nearly as well as Nick. It had been Nick, his mother, and Jim who had taken *Icarus* thirty miles out the Golden Gate and to the Farallon Islands to spread his father's ashes. Jody, as usual begged off. She, as did Lance, became seasick standing on a dock.

That fall morning they headed out under the Golden Gate Bridge, staying south of the potato patch where silt builds up and the water gets shallow, and to the north of Mile Rocks where an odd little lighthouse sits. An engineering feat in the early 1900s, the lighthouse sat on a blasted and flattened 30 by 40 foot slab of rock. When it was built it resembled a three-story wedding cake. The Coast Guard decapitated it to a single blunt story in the 1960s when the lighthouse was automated.

About halfway into the twelve hour round trip, Nick's mother declared, "Your father couldn't be satisfied with being twelve miles out, he had to go another eighteen." She moved forward from the wheel and used the winch to trim the main sail. They had moved out of the fog and into clear air.

"Yes, but he wanted it that way," Nick said. "The ride back should be nice, and we'll be back at the dock in time for cocktails."

They arrived at the islands a few hours later and found a spot sheltered from the wind. It was a brief ceremony, Nick's mother taking the lead.

"You were a fine husband and a good father," she said, sprinkling a handful of her husband's ashes into the water. "I'm glad you are finally out of pain." She dropped more ashes over the side. "But I miss you, dammit."

She wiped a rare tear from her cheek. "Here," she said, handing the container of ashes to Nick.

Nick held the jar of ashes and looked at the horizon. He took a handful and tossed them into the water.

"As you know Dad, the current heads south and then takes a right turn to the tropics. I figure in a few weeks you will be scattered about the Pacific, clinging to the hull of ships traveling the world, and lapping up on white sand beaches. I miss you, Dad. Go in peace." He poured the rest of the ashes over the stern.

Jim reached into his seabag and pulled out four glasses

and an elegant wooded case. He opened the box and extracted a bottle of rum. It was an expensive Appleton Exclusive, Nick's father's favorite. He knew Jim had gone to some trouble to find that rum; it was sold only at the distillery in Jamaica.

Jim handed a glass to Nick's mother and one to Nick and set the other two on the tray on the binnacle. He opened the bottle and poured a shot into each of the four glasses.

"You were a fine man, a good friend and like a father. You treated me as a son. You were quick to give advice, and it was always sound. I'd like to send you off with your favorite toast with your favorite rum."

They all raised their glasses.

"One for you, one for me, and one for the old man in the sea." They all drank and Jim poured the fourth shot over the stern. Nick's mother upended her glass and tossed it over the transom. Nick and Jim watched her and followed suit. Two more glasses hit the water. They all stood for a while and looked back at the island. Nick moved forward and raised the sails while Jim took the helm and pointed *Icarus* east back toward San Francisco and home.

Chapter Eight

Six months before Lance brought the company down, he and Jody were lying in bed in Blake Morris's apartment. Lance had offered to keep an eye on the place, take in the mail, change an occasional light, make the place look lived in. Blake didn't want the attentive landlady rifling through his belongings.

It was a weekday afternoon in late summer. Nick was in Atlanta at a trade conference; leaving CFO Lance behind to mind the books, or as Lance thought of it, to mind his partner's wife. Lance had slipped away from the office in the guise of an afternoon at the local gym.

Jody was curled up on Lance's chest. It's coming together nicely, Lance thought, looking around the stylish apartment. He had jazz playing on the stereo.

"What do you find most attractive in Nick?"

Jody looked at Lance quizzically.

"Well, in the beginning he was fun. Now he just works all the time."

"So why do you stay with him?"

"He gives me what I want."

"What if he couldn't?"

"Couldn't or wouldn't?"

Lance thought he might have gone too far. "Either way."

"Do you know something I don't?"

"I'm just making conversation," Lance said, "getting to know you better."

Chapter Nine

Icarus had become a home for Nick, but living on an old wooden boat in the winter in San Francisco Bay can be a challenge. The city frowned upon live-aboards, and Nick couldn't afford to move the boat to Sausalito or across the bay to Alameda or Oakland where it was less expensive. Nick had paid the non-refundable charge for the slip in advance, so he left the boat where it was. Nick sneaked onto *Icarus* in the evening and off early in the morning, showering at the bathroom in his office. Cliff, the Harbor Master who had known him all his life, looked the other way when Nick took a duffle bag and moved aboard. He had heard what Nick was going through, had read it in the papers, and as long as Nick was discreet, he was happy to help him out.

The cabin was roomy for one person. The smells of the wood, varnish, and oils gave Nick comfort while he was aboard. In the large salon there was a small framed photograph of the three generations of owners of *Icarus*: Nick, his father, and his grandfather. Next to the photograph of the men was a framed picture of Nick and his parents, the three of them swimming in the water, laughing, with *Icarus* tied to a wharf in the background. There was another of Nick's grandmother, strapped into a parachute harness, coming into a landing on a beach, cocktail in her hand. It was one of Nick's favorite pictures. After his grandfather died, Nick's grandmother joined the other widows in her group and traveled the world. The others had bet her a mai tai she wouldn't get towed around Acapulco Bay in a parasail and one of them snapped the photo.

Nick camped on the large double berth in the bow. He had brought thick mattress pads from the house and his best sheets and pillows, a thick down comforter, and a small space heater. Years before he had installed a good stereo system and there was even a small flat screen television and DVD player. His grandfather had painted the interior white and installed prisms through the deck to get more light into the boat. The previous year Nick had added lighting to brighten it even more. The boat still showed signs of his time on it with Kathy, the upholstery the same blue and white stripes with the matching pillows.

Nick spent his evenings aboard making simple meals in the galley, listening to music, and reading in his bunk. He read books on sailing and islands. He started with *Sailing Alone Around the World* by Joshua Slocum, who rebuilt a derelict wooden oyster sloop and in 1895 set sail, logging more than 46,000 miles circumnavigating the world before returning home three years later. After devouring Slocum, Nick dug into *The Blue of Capricorn* by Eugene Burdick, a book filled with tales, reminisces, and essays on the geography, flora, fauna, stars, water and people of Oceania. He had read both of the books when he was a boy, and he enjoyed them as much the second time as the first.

He made a point not to bring work home and *Icarus* became a sanctuary from the madness of his daily life. He realized that even among the turmoil he was happy, savoring his time alone on the boat. He knew he had to enjoy it while he could.

A WEEK LATER NICK WAS IN HIS OFFICE EARLIER THAN usual. That morning a sea lion had parked itself at the end of the dock. Maybe he was lonely or looking for his mate, but he started barking before 5:00 a.m. and didn't stop until Nick got up, undogged the hatch above the forward berth and poked his head out. He looked at the sea lion and said, "What's the matter?"

The sea lion stopped barking and looked back at him. They stayed like that for a minute or so, having a staring contest until the sea lion backed off the dock and slid into the bay. He popped his head out of the water, took another long look at Nick, gave him a forlorn last bark, and turned and swam toward Alcatraz.

Wide awake, Nick bundled up and took an early morning run.

Later, back in his office, he was emptying his desk, closing down the company for good. Detective Mitchell stood in the corner, watching him.

"You're not going to bark, are you?" Nick asked.

"Excuse me?"

"It's not important."

Nick picked up an unassembled cardboard file box from the carton beside his desk and folded it into shape. He didn't have to look at the box to do it; he had assembled so many he could do it with his eyes closed.

"So you don't have any leads to his whereabouts?"

Nick set the box on his desk. He picked up a framed

photograph of himself and his parents. It was taken at the party the night he and Katherine started seeing each other. The three of them were standing by the bar. His mother had an odd smirk on her face, and Nick and his father had their heads thrown back in laughter. Nick took a long look at the picture, thinking how much he missed his parents.

Nick's mother was forty-five when she had Nick and his father was eleven years older than she. Nick's birth was a difficult one resulting in Nick being their first and only child. His parents told him he was born laughing, that a nurse called out to the other nurses and they had come running, expecting more problems with the delivery. They were met with a gurgling, smiling baby boy.

"Look. He's laughing," one nurse said.

"Hah, it's just gas," said the matronly head nurse.

"No, he's definitely laughing," another nurse said.

That's how Nicholas John Thomas came into the world.

As a family they were close, and Nick was comfortable being with both his parents. They were a strong team before Nick arrived and they made him part of it. A nanny had not raised him as were many of the children in his social set. His parents could afford and had help, but Nick always came first in their lives. He wasn't viewed as an accessory.

Nick took the silver-framed picture and its stand and placed it in the box.

Mitchell watched the entire scene as they talked. He was struck by the obvious sentimentality in Nick. Mitchell had become convinced that Nick was not involved in Lance's scheme and was more of a Boy Scout than an embezzler. His record was certainly clean. The guy didn't even have a parking ticket, not an easy feat in a city like San Francisco.

"Lance covered his tracks well. The accountants traced the funds to three different offshore banks. He used banks in countries that value their clients' privacy, so we didn't get far. That, and the money has already been moved." Mitchell wandered to the bookshelves that lined the walls.

"I've been reviewing his travel schedule for the last couple of years. The guy's been around the world. I've been going country by country, seeing if I can get a lead on where he could be."

"How is that going?"

"Nothing yet. He doesn't show up anywhere. Other than spending money at hotels and restaurants, there is no sign he did anything else. No banking, no property purchases, nothing."

Nick continued to pack up the pieces of his life. There was a Space Shuttle tile given to him during one of his many trips to Washington, D.C. There was an ancient Charlie McCarthy hand puppet that was his father's when he was a young boy. He packed those and other mementos into the box. He then assembled another box and turned to the bookcases where Mitchell stood perusing the shelves.

"What about passports, social security numbers, and the rest?" Nick asked, moving to a shelf next to Mitchell.

"With that kind of money he can be anyone he wants to be." Mitchell took a Mark Twain first edition from a shelf. "You sure have a lot of books."

There were a lot of books. Books on sailing and astrophysics, dictionaries of every kind in more than two dozen languages. There were dictionaries defining art, engineering, astrology, and dreams. There were collections of Hemingway, Twain, and Steinbeck, sections on existentialism, South Florida fiction, art and artists, pirates, and a huge section on the South Pacific and its islands and the Caribbean and its islands.

"You can blame it on my parents. We could never walk

past a bookshop without stopping in. Used book stores were our favorite, still are for me. My parents had a television but it was rarely on. If it was, it was an old movie. I spent a lot of my youth reading with my parents."

Mitchell replaced the Twain and moved to another bookcase. "It seems you have a book on just about any subject."

"My parents encouraged that. They wanted me to be able to talk to anyone about anything. My father said it was why he was successful in life."

Mitchell was looking at the travel section covering Hawaii, the South Pacific, Asia, Europe. "You don't have the slightest idea where Lance could be?"

"Of course I've been trying to figure that out. My guess would be Europe somewhere. He does speak Polish."

"We know that. Nothing has turned up."

"So where does it all stand?" Nick asked.

"These cases can take years, but we could very well find him. The world has become a small place."

"Years." The thought made Nick's head hurt. He rubbed his forehead.

"You look kind of pale. Do you feel okay?"

Nick sighed. "Nothing that getting back to my boat wouldn't make better."

THE NEXT MORNING, AFTER A NIGHT OF FITFUL SLEEP and tumultuous dreams, Nick awoke in his bunk. He lay there thinking about the day ahead when he realized there was something wrong. He had known the boat all his life and *Icarus* didn't feel right to him. The smell was wrong and the boat felt heavier than normal. He rolled out of the bunk and put his feet on the floor of the cabin, shocked as cold water sloshed up to his ankles. He waded through the water to the instrument panel and checked the circuit breaker for the bilge pump. It was switched on, and he toggled it twice. He hustled back to his bunk, got dressed and ran to the Harbor Masters office to see if Cliff had a spare pump.

"She's taking on water? You sure have had a couple of months of it," Cliff said. "How much time do we have?"

"She took on more than a foot overnight."

"Okay, follow me."

At the storage shed Nick and Cliff wrestled out a big gas-powered water pump fitted to a large cart with balloon tires.

"Let's hope it starts. With your luck lately—sorry. Let me give it a pull."

Cliff primed the gas and adjusted the choke and pulled hard on the starter pull-cord. As the engine sputtered and coughed, he reached forward to adjust the choke until it idled smoothly. "Let's go."

Four hours later the big pump had done its job. Nick and Cliff were down in the bilge trying to find the source of the leak.

"I bet it's the stuffing box," Cliff said, pointing his flash-light behind the engine. "When was it upgraded?"

Nick looked at him blankly.

"You have the original stuffing box?"

"Well, yes, but I've maintained it and have never had a problem before."

"Well, I'd bet it's a problem now."

Two hours later, they found the leak, and it was indeed the stuffing box, the part that keeps water outside the boat where the propeller shaft penetrates the hull. The bilge pump problem was a faulty wire that just needed reattaching.

Nick sat down on the wet floor of the cabin, thinking about his options. "I don't have the money to haul out the boat. She's not taking on that much water. Now that it's re-attached, the bilge pump should keep up with the leak."

"That's going to cost you even more when you have to hoist her out of the bay when she sinks." Cliff said.

"Not recommended?"

"No. But I read about a guy in the UK who replaced a stuffing box—they call them stern glands there—while the boat was in the water. I think we can do it, but we'd better have that big pump idling on the dock."

"You're a lifesaver, Cliff."

Three hours later after a run across the bay to a chandlery in Oakland, they had a new, updated seal and set about their work. Nick had insisted on doing the job. If anyone was going to sink his boat, it was going to be him.

At 2:00 p.m. there was a voice from the dock asking to come aboard. It was Mitchell.

"I've been trying to find you since this morning," he said, looking down, talking to Nick's feet. He was pretzeled around the engine, his feet the only part visible.

"He woke up to *Icarus* taking on water," Cliff told Mitchell.

"Your boat was sinking? Man, you have the worst luck."

"That's what I said." Cliff reached down and handed Nick a wrench. "If we don't do this just right, we're going to send her to the bottom. So if you don't mind, let's let him concentrate."

"Good idea. The name's Mitchell. Have him call me when he gets back on dry land."

Mitchell got off the boat shaking his head, wondering what was next for Nick Thomas.

AFTER DAYS OF RUNNING A DIESEL-FIRED HEATER, *ICARUS* was fully afloat and dried out. Nick walked through the offices taking stock. The rest of the staff had been dismissed. There was dust in the corners, marks on the walls where artwork had hung. The place was a ghost town, just a shell now, and the quiet unnerving to Nick. He thought of the hard work and excitement he had there of producing something vital, working with a team. As he walked through the halls he wondered who the next tenants would be.

He made his way back to his office and through the glass front door saw Detective Mitchell. He opened the door to let him in.

Mitchell handed him a cup of coffee as they walked to Nick's office. It was piled high with boxes, ready to be moved. The only furniture remaining was his desk, two chairs, and an empty filing cabinet.

Mitchell looked at Nick's hands, his knuckles raw in some places, three fingers were bandaged.

"What does the other guy look like?" Mitchell asked.

"What? Oh. Boat bites," Nick said, looking at his hands.

Nick had exchanged his attaché case for his old favorite leather day pack, complete with an ink stain on the outside pocket from his fountain pen. It sat on the edge of his desk with a small pile of papers.

"I'm out of time. Friday I see the lawyers for a final assessment of my situation. Do you have anything you can tell me?"

Mitchell shook his head. "I wish I did. The trail is cold. Our only option now is to wait for Lance to slip up, make a mistake."

Chapter Ten

In months following the start of their affair, Lance continued to drop hints to Jody, giving her the impression that Nick had grown tired of her, that he was about to make a drastic change. Lance was vague, letting Jody come to her own conclusions. Jody fell for the ruse and convinced herself that Nick was seeing someone else. She did a better job of inventing a mistress for Nick than Lance ever could. She needed to rationalize her affair with Lance, a way to ease her conscience. Then her imagination got away from her and she built the case in her mind. In detail she dissected her relationship with Nick, his time away, any woman he had ever met. Lance listened to Jody rant, impressed by her ability to make a case where Lance was certain there was none. Lance acted the concerned ear and made sympathetic noises.

Motivating Jody to leave Nick was all too easy. The hard part would be trusting her to not give away his plans.

One November afternoon at the apartment, lying in bed, Lance sat up and looked down at Jody.

"If you could be anyone you like, use any name you like, who would you be?"

Jody thought for a while, twirling a strand of hair around her finger.

"I always loved the name Antoinette. I'd be Antoinette Duval."

"Antoinette Duval," Lance repeated. "It has a nice sound to it."

"And, of course, I'd be French. I still speak French quite well, you know. It came to me easily and I never lost it."

"French, eh? Speak to me in French."

Jody cocked her head at him and said, "*Rien ne pèse tant que un secret.*"

He knew enough French to get the gist, but played that he didn't. He raised his eyebrows in question.

"Nothing weighs more than a secret," she translated. "Jean de La Fontaine. I studied French poets when I was at school in Lyon. It seems appropriate for our circumstances."

Chapter Eleven

Nick's family home, being in a desirable neighborhood, sold quickly. The stark reality of his future was sinking in. While the home was in escrow, Nick began to search for places to store the rest of his belongings. He called storage companies, first in San Francisco, then further south on the Peninsula and then in the East Bay. The prices were outrageous, and the discount for long-term storage didn't help much. To top it off, his cash was running low. He closed his laptop and sat back in his office chair. An hour later he was having lunch with Jim in a nearby café, telling him about his morning search for a place for his possessions.

"I'm going have to get out of my house soon. I might as well face it and get my affairs in order."

"Why don't you try out of the area? Get on Highway 5, go north for a while. Some of those little towns have storage places right off the highway."

"I hadn't thought of that. I'll make calls when I get back to the office."

That afternoon Nick found a secure storage facility in a small ranching community about two hundred miles north of

San Francisco. It was a long way away, but the price was right. He called Jim to thank him for the idea.

"So when are we going?"

"We?" Nick asked

"Sure. We can use my truck and rent a trailer. You can hire college kids to pack your things and we can take a road trip. We should be able to do it in a day," he paused, "a long day."

NICK AND JIM LEFT SAN FRANCISCO AFTER THE morning rush hour and drove across the Bay Bridge toward Oakland.

"I checked the traffic. There's a big wreck on the Bayshore Freeway. I'm going to head east and go across the Benicia Bridge. It will add miles, but it should be faster than sitting in gridlock," Jim said.

"I'm all for not sitting in traffic," Nick agreed.

Once across the bridge they continued north along the Suisun Bay.

Nick looked out the window at what most people but the navy calls "the mothball fleet." To the US Navy, it was the *Pacific Reserve Fleet*, groups of ships rafted up in the bay and kept in working order, ready to be activated if needed. When Nick was growing up, many were Liberty Ships used in World War II to ferry service men to Europe and Russia. The *Glomar Explorer* had been docked there. The Explorer was built to extract manganese modules from the ocean floor, but that was only the cover story. It was built for the CIA to raise a sunken Soviet submarine lost in 1968.

The reserve fleet had been reduced in the past twenty years with many of the ships being deactivated and scrapped.

Nick was brought back to his thoughts of *Icarus*. Too bad he couldn't put her in mothballs there.

They rode for another hour, passing through the ranch lands west of Sacramento.

"Gas, Beer, Bait, and Bullets."

"Pardon me?" Jim turned down the music.

"Gas, Beer, Bait, and Bullets," Nick repeated. "It's the name of the store we passed."

"Gotta love the country."

Nick watched the countryside go by outside the truck window. He looked at his mobile phone; there was no reception. They were passing the rice fields just north of Arbuckle.

"It's beautiful in the winter. There are so many colors of green in the fields. Speaking of country, when did you get into this music?"

"What, because I'm Japanese?" Jim asked with a laugh.

"No, because I've never known you to listen to country music."

"It seems to go well with the truck." Jim turned up the music again. George Strait was singing about getting to Amarillo by morning.

"I like it, and it seems to go with the truck. I wonder if I would enjoy living out in the country."

By the time Nick moved out of his family home, it was not much like it was when he grew up. Jody had remodeled when they moved in and took over the house from Nick's parents. They repainted the walls, had the hardwood floors sanded and refinished and the kitchen and baths updated. Nick had insisted many of his family heirlooms be kept, which comprised family portraits and pieces of art, some furniture, and books. Those, and other items were all packed in the trailer being towed behind Jim's truck. The rest he was planning to sell for money to live on and pay to store his possessions. He found it hard to believe all of his worldly belongings had been reduced to the contents of the trailer in tow.

"I hate to be the one to ask, but have you made any plans?" Jim had been watching Nick's life move in a continued downward spiral. First it was losing the company, then being betrayed by his friend, then Jody leaving, then Jody and Lance's affair, *Icarus* nearly sinking, then continuing to have his inheritance, everything, taken from him. With a measure of awe and disbelief, Jim watched his friend fight on without complaint, waiting for the next axe to fall. It made him wince when he thought about it.

"Have I made any plans? What sort of plans?"

"You know, when this is over?"

Nick thought about it. A double-trailer truck blew past them, rocking their own truck with its wake.

"I guess I'm not sure what 'over' is."

Jim didn't pursue it and a few miles later pulled off the highway and into a truck stop to fuel the tank. Nick paid for gas while Jim waited for a pump. They filled up and rode in silence for another hour.

"I have been offered a couple of jobs," Nick said.

"Yeah?"

"One in Houston and another from our competitor trying to buy the company's assets."

"And?"

Nick paused for a minute and looked out the window. He saw a plane flying low across the highway about a mile ahead. As they approached he recognized it as a crop duster. The pilot was doing aerobatic maneuvers above the fields. Nick thought about his impounded plane and wondered if he would fly again. Of course he would, he could always go up with Jim. He let out a sigh and sat back in the seat. He was determined not to feel sorry for himself. Nick had had the privilege of experiencing things that most people never would in their lives.

"That's quite a show they put on," Jim said.

"They sure do." They watched the plane land on a frontage road beside the highway.

"Taking the job in Houston would feel like I was going backwards in life, and I can't imagine working for a competitor. I get the impression that as soon as they got all the intellectual property out of me they would let me go. I can't sell myself out like that."

"So where does that leave you?"

"Option C, I guess."

Nick never thought of life being binary. When faced with two choices, it was his habit to think of a third. It had driven his wife crazy. Whenever Nick, Jody, Lance and Katherine were together, Lance and Jody teased Nick about his "Option C." Jim was no stranger to the concept, or the teasing. He also knew it was not the time to make light of it.

"So what is your option C?"

Nick turned to look out the side window again. A moment later he turned back to Jim.

"I don't have an option C."

A little more than two hours after leaving San Francisco they came to the town of Maxwell. Nick recalled when years before on a college ski trip to Bend Oregon, a wheel bearing blew out in the friend's car he was driving. With a smoking front axel, he had pulled off the highway and into the little town. Back then, there was nothing but a general store, a mercantile, the kind of place that had anything one could need. It was also the local auto supply. The guys got out of the car and entered the store. They were driving an old Chevrolet Monte Carlo, and yes, the store had a wheel bearing in stock that would fit the car. They also had a sign above the counter in the parts department which read in foot-tall letters:

WE DO NOT LEND TOOLS!

Nick paid for the replacement wheel bearing and walked out to the car to give his fellow travelers the news.

"I bought the part but they have a big sign saying they don't loan tools. I don't know how we will change out the wheel bearing."

Jeanette, Nick's girlfriend at the time said, "We'll see about that." She pulled her shirttail out of her tight jeans, undid two buttons, and tied her shirt into a midriff top. She then unbuttoned another button on the top of her shirt and pushed up her brassiere. The two other girls on the trip watched her and then followed suit.

"Come on girls, let's go get those tools."

Less than five minutes later the girls came out with their arms loaded with tools and drinks.

"Men are such boys," Jeanette said.

Nick laughed, and shaking his head in wonder, opened the trunk and pulled out the jack to lift the car. In less than half an hour they were back on the road driving north to Oregon.

A HUGE FLOCK OF STARLINGS INTERRUPTED NICK'S thoughts of the ski trip. They were flying in perfect formation. There were thousands of them and they changed direction as if they were a single bird. Nick and Jim had their heads pressing against the windshield watching the birds perform their aerobatics.

"And I thought the crop duster was amazing," Nick said.

It was a clear day and later they could see the snow-covered peak of Mount Shasta, still more than a hundred miles away.

They crossed the Sacramento River and its many creeks, and drove by several signs advertising Indian casinos before they got to their exit. Jim pulled off the highway and they drove a few miles to the East, passing railroad tracks, a general store and café, a cattle stockyard, a two pump gas station, and a cowboy bar before Jim pulled into the driveway of a new modern-looking storage facility. They parked and got out to stretch their legs.

A woman came out of the office and asked, "Are you Nick Thomas?"

"Yes I am."

"I have your paperwork ready. Come on into the office; it won't take but a minute."

After Nick signed the papers and paid for a year, he and Jim unloaded the trailer into the storage unit.

An hour later, sweaty and dusty, they drove the truck towing an empty trailer and stopped at Cody's Stockyard Café for a bite to eat. The parking lot was filled with trucks of all sorts from pickups to semis, some hitched to horse or cattle trailers.

They walked in and hung their coats with the others on a row of horseshoe hooks on the wall.

"Well that's done," Nick said, taking a seat on a red vinyl barstool next to Jim at the counter. The restaurant was filled with ranchers and cowboys, the real deal, dressed in Wrangler jeans, flannel shirts, and muddy boots, some with spurs.

There were cowboy hats and hats with Purina Feed and John Deere logos. There was a table in the corner with four old ranchers drinking black coffee. The sign on the wall advertised locally-grown dry-cured meats, and there was a set of horns about six feet tip-to-tip above the cook's window. Covering the walls were wood plaques with brands of ranches from Canada to Mexico. Nick glanced around and noticed that the portions were large, just what one would need if he were going to spend the day running cattle. When their meals came the food was fantastic. The place wasn't a greasy spoon, and the waitresses and the customers all knew each other, just as you would expect in a small cattle town.

"Any news of Lance?" Jim asked between bites.

"No. It seems that he's completely disappeared."

"I never had any use for that guy," Jim said. "He always seemed like he had a chip on his shoulder."

Nick shrugged.

On the way out of the restaurant Nick stopped and looked at the framed pictures of the ranchers on the wall. There must have been hundreds, and judging by the people in the pictures, they went back to the time photography was invented. The people were all in ranch attire, seated in an oak chair in front of a white wall. Nick studied the expressions on the men and the few women in the photos. They were like Grant Wood paintings. He walked along looking at the photos, he and Jim pointing out the more interesting shots. One man had his head thrown back in laughter, another looked like some desert rat who had just crawled out of a mine, another wearing a straw hat had a huge cigar stuck in his mouth and another four in his shirt pocket. Nick noticed the oak chair in front of a white wall in the corner.

"Jim, hand me your phone and sit down," Nick said.

"Okay." Jim sat and Nick shot a picture of him. "One more, now look like a rancher."

Jim sat up straight and put on a serious expression. Nick took another shot.

On the way out Nick stopped and perused the bulletin board near the door. It was full of hand-written ads. One note tacked up with a black plastic pushpin read "Wanted — Winter Pasture for 50 Pairs" Another scribbled note read "3 young working cow dogs — free to a good home. Call Lisa." "Another read: "Mighty Damn Fine Hay For Sale — 3-Way"

"I wonder what 3-Way means," Nick said, gesturing to the note.

"It means it's a mixture of oats, wheat, and barley."

Nick looked at his friend. "You have a scary depth of knowledge." He glanced down at Jim's feet. "You're wearing cowboy boots."

"Just trying to fit in."

"Astronaut cowboy," Nick said.

"Something like that."

"Space cowboy," Nick continued.

"Gangster of love," Jim offered.

"Maurice," they sang in unison. They stood there laughing until Nick noticed an old rancher standing off to the side looking at them.

Checking his watch, Nick saw it was getting late. They needed to drop the trailer off in a town an hour south before the place closed. When they walked out to the huge parking lot behind the café and climbed into Jim's truck, Nick felt like he could fit in to the little community.

On the way out of town they saw a small sign with an arrow pointing to the right. It read:

Lake California
A Private Community

Nick was intrigued by the idea of a community so remote. The drive back was quiet until they came into the Bay Area and its traffic. Rain was starting to fall and the sun was setting by the time Jim dropped Nick off at the harbor and *Icarus*.

Chapter Twelve

The evening before his "treachery" as Lance thought of it, he was on a tight schedule. He was in New York City where he had timed the meeting with the bank for late afternoon on Friday, just before closing. He had moved the meeting up from Monday morning, giving him some time before Nick would discover his actions. Nick was still under the impression the transfer of funds would occur the following Monday. Lance knew Nick was traveling until late Sunday, so he was confident Nick wouldn't learn of the change until sometime Monday when it would be too late to do anything about it. The meeting was just a formality to complete the transfer from the bank to the company. Well, not to the company, to Lance. Once deposited, he would have full control of the funds.

At the completion of the signing, Lance shook hands all around and left, telling them he needed to catch an evening plane back to the West Coast. Once out of the building, he walked to a coffee house and sat at a table in the back.

Lance had made elaborate plans to move the thirty-two million. While he was traveling abroad for the company visiting customers and suppliers, he opened accounts and set up drop boxes. He formed corporations within corporations. He never opened accounts in the country he was visiting on business; he did it in neighboring countries with a quick day trip via train, car, or if necessary, plane. He was meticulous about not leaving a trail. He had account numbers and addresses encrypted and stored on self-destructing computer flash drives. He had copies of the drives hidden in different cities.

Then he logged into a secure virtual private network. It had taken him months to build the program, an automated process for moving the money from bank to bank, account to account. The program broke the money into different-sized portions so anyone searching for the funds would not see similar amounts being moved. The program was not something one would outsource and Lance had done a trial run before the big day.

He glanced up from the computer and around the coffee house. There was classical music playing, the smell of fresh ground coffee, modern art on the walls, and people spread about the shop working on laptops and reading books. A couple closest to him seemed like they were on a late afternoon date, heads close, talking intently. Maybe they were plotting something. It was just another late Friday afternoon in a big city.

Lance thought of what he would do. How a slight movement of his finger would change the path of many lives, and certainly his own. His pulse quickened and he turned back to the computer and tapped the enter key, sending a command to his software that started the transfer of funds that would wipe out Nick, shut down the company, and make Lance rich. He watched the process for a while, making sure the program was working. He waited for it to make the first transfer. It was quicker than he thought. The program would continue to run from his secure server.

He closed the laptop and felt a twinge of something. Power, victory? It was a new feeling for him. It felt good.

The money hidden, he moved to the next step in his plan.

JODY HAD BEEN VISITING HER SISTER IN WASHINGTON, D.C. that week. Lance had talked her into taking the train from the capitol to New York to meet him for an evening tryst. Her sister was in South Carolina on business and would return Saturday afternoon. It all seemed so deliciously romantic and salacious. When Lance insisted she pay cash for her train ticket so it wouldn't show up on her credit card, she was even more excited.

The train pulled into Penn Station and Jody caught a cab to The Surrey Hotel on the Upper East Side. Lance well knew of Jody's fondness of luxury. He reserved a suite, using a credit card from a fictitious corporation and fake identification. The corporation couldn't be traced to him. He was started on his new life.

Lance had checked in, his luggage already upstairs in the suite. He had just seated himself in the lobby and was hoping the monochromatic style he was noticing in hotels would end, when Jody walked in the door. He had to admit, she was a knockout with a beautiful smile and a nice sense of style. She wore a shortish skirt that showed off her great legs. He noticed the doorman turn and follow her with his eyes.

Bringing Jody along was a chance that Lance was willing to take. He had never been happy that Nick and Katherine had a history, whatever that history might be. He wanted to get even, get everything, get Nick's wife. But now, looking at her, he felt different.

Lance stood and walked to meet her, taking her bag and moving her to the elevator. They rode to the room in silence. He noticed that his heart was beating fast. *What's this? What am I feeling here?*

An hour later, they both lay exhausted in bed.

"I don't know about you, but these secret affairs sure have a powerful effect on the libido." Jody stretched languidly. "Is this the first time you've cheated on Katherine?" she asked, "I mean, am I your first affair?"

"Huh? Uh, yeah. You are."

"Me too with Nick."

"How about that." Lance reached over, picked up the telephone and dialed room service.

"Are you as hungry as I am?"

"I'm hungry, that's for sure."

"Hello, room service? Could you send up a bottle of Bollinger Champagne?"

"And some caviar," Jody added.

"And some caviar with all the fixings, please."

"And some oysters."

"And some oysters. And you might as well make that two bottles of champagne."

"Bollinger?" Jody asked. "That's Nick's favorite Champagne."

"I know it is."

They dined in the room, sitting across from each other at the room service table in the robes provided by the hotel, making small talk. Lance had to admit he was enjoying himself, celebrating his new fortune. Jody became caught up in his expansive mood. She figured it was the setting, the secret rendezvous in a distant city, the deal she knew Lance and Nick were completing.

Looking at her across the table, Lance wanted to tell her now, tell her what he had done. But the moment was light and he didn't want to ruin it. He also wanted to wait until the last moment to disappear if she didn't go along with his plans.

After the meal they took a bath together, which led to another enthusiastic romp between the sheets. Lying in bed, panting once again, Jody reached for the television remote control and flicked it on. *Casablanca* was about to start.

"I love this movie. It's been years since I've seen it. Do you mind?"

"That sounds nice," Lance said. He got out of bed and opened the second bottle of champagne. Jody looked at Lance standing there, naked with a bottle of champagne in his hands. She flashed back to a similar time with Nick. She felt a twinge of sadness and guilt, then she remembered that Nick made this happen with his inattention to her and the affair she was sure he was having.

"Bring that bottle and yourself back to bed. The movie is about to begin."

LANCE COULD FEEL JODY STIR. SHE WAS CURLED UP ON his chest, her hair fanned out around his neck. He looked around the bedroom and out at the sitting room. It appeared well lived-in for the short time they had been there. There were clothes on the furniture, robes on the floor, two empty champagne bottles and flutes on the bedside tables, oyster shells on the room service cart. All the signs of a fine evening, Lance thought.

"Coffee," came a murmur from his chest.

"Good morning. Coffee sounds like a fine idea."

Lance picked up the bedside phone and called room service.

Fifteen minutes later they sat at the table sipping coffee and munching croissants and fruit. Lance decided it was time to tell Jody.

"I'm leaving today."

"Back to California, eh? Well, I'll be at my sister's until Sunday, if I survive that long. We make an effort, but we don't see eye-to-eye. Never have."

Lance took another sip. "I took it all. I'm going to disappear."

Jody set down her coffee cup. "What are you talking about?"

"Last night I took all of the money from the company. It's gone. Untraceable. I'm going to follow it."

"The money? All of it? Gone? That means Nick, Nick is ..."

"Broke."

"But why?"

"Well, because I could. You don't want to be with him, or you wouldn't be here with me."

"What about Katherine?"

"I don't want to be with her, or I wouldn't be here with you."

Jody sat back in her chair, let out a breath. Lance let her think about it, took a bite of croissant, a sip of coffee, watched her, waiting for a response.

"So what now?" Jody asked, collecting herself.

"Now you need to decide."

"I do?"

"Yes. Will you come with me? Leave it all behind? Start a

new life, become a new person? You can be anyone you like, do anything you'd like."

"Now? Leave now?"

"No. You go home, play it out and act surprised. Meet me later, in a month or so. I'll send for you, but like me, you will have to disappear."

"How will I do that? How do I disappear?"

"I have it all set. Before I leave I'll give you an untraceable mobile phone. I'll use that to send you instructions. You follow them. We meet up, live the life we always wanted."

It was a lot to take in and Jody sat back again in the chair. She pondered her life. She had no close friends. Her parents were in their own world in L.A., living a life she was happy to have escaped from. She and her sister didn't get along. She's sure Nick would not have married her if she hadn't become pregnant. Now he was broke.

"How broke? How broke have you made Nick?"

"Oh I suspect he will lose the houses, the cars, the plane, the boat."

"The boat? He loves that boat."

"He may get away with bankruptcy, but it will be bad. He will be starting from scratch, I suppose."

"Can I think about it?"

"Think all you want. I have it all set up if you want to join me."

"What if I go to the police? Turn you in?"

"Well, the money will still be gone, your life with Nick will change drastically. And, well, you're kind of implicated. You're an accessory."

"Accessory? I didn't do anything."

"No one will believe you. We have been having an affair." Lance poured more coffee into his cup. "Would you believe you?"

Jody thought about it, then shrugged. "No, I guess not."

"You can stay in a loveless and poor marriage with Nick, or you can reinvent yourself and be wealthy with me."

Jody looked across the table at Lance, seeing him for the first time.

"What are you going to do now?"

"I'm going to disappear. I'll contact you in a while when things settle down."

"Where are you going?"

"If I told you I wouldn't disappear, would I?"

They finished their breakfast and Lance took a shower and dressed. Jody crawled back into bed and stared at the blank television screen, lost in thought.

Lance came out of the bathroom, dressed and all business.

"The room is paid for another night if you want to stay."

"Okay." She felt alone and lost.

"I hope to see you again," he said.

He looked down at her. She seemed diffident and vulnerable.

He gave her a long kiss to reassure her and turned to leave.

"Lance?"

"You are going to be there, aren't you?"

He looked at her and smiled. "I'll be there."

Chapter Thirteen

Lance had put his plan into action a year before. It took seven months to find him, but Arthur Brown was who he was searching for. He watched him and took notes. He needed to know if the guy was approachable, someone willing to do the job he had to offer.

One night Lance saw him coming out of a card room, head held low, looking around the parking lot as if fearful of attack. He walked to his rusty beige Chevrolet Chevette. The door made a metallic shriek when he opened it. He started it up with a puff of blue smoke and drove off grinding the gears. The thing belonged in a wrecking yard. Lance followed him, made easier by one taillight not working.

Lance tailed him to a cheap diner and then to his home. Arthur Brown lived in a crappy little walk-up studio apartment in the Tenderloin District, arguably the worst area in San Francisco. He worked the graveyard shift at a twenty-four-hour donut shop called *The Hole* near his apartment where he cleaned the equipment between serving the few customers. He was a loner—Lance never saw him with friends. A guy his age, making close to minimum wage and living in a dump; he was ripe for the picking.

The next night Lance was sitting in a café across the street looking out the window at the donut shop. He could see Arthur Brown going about his chores, cleaning the display cases, scrubbing the counters, sweeping the floor. He worked well and seemed to take the job seriously.

A man came in while he was sweeping—six-three, shaved head, dressed in black trousers, black shirt and a black leather jacket. He walked up to Arthur Brown and leaned down into his face. Lance leaned forward to get a better look.

The man in black talked to Arthur Brown pointedly. Brown nodded as the man spoke. The man stood up straight and glared down at him. He walked to the counter and took a coffee pot off the burner and brought it to Arthur Brown. Brown braced himself. The man threw the pot against the wall. The pot shattered and the brown liquid poured down the wall and onto the floor. The man in black bent down into Arthur Brown's face again and shook his finger at him. He turned his back and walked out the door. Lance knew then that he had him, had found a weakness he could exploit. It always comes down to money, he thought.

Lance saw the opportunity and waited a few minutes, dropped bills on the table, left the restaurant and walked across the street. The door chimed as he entered.

"I'll be with you in a minute," Arthur Brown said. He was on the floor picking up glass from the coffee pot, blood trailing down his arm. At the counter Lance grabbed a roll of paper towels.

"Here, you're bleeding," he said, giving him a towel.

Arthur Brown looked at his hands. "Oh, thanks."

"Why don't you take a break," Lance said, pulling out a chair.

"Probably a good idea." He climbed up into the chair and let out a sigh.

Lance took a direct approach. "How would you like to make enough money to get out of this dump, pay off your debts and never have to sell another donut? Or for that matter, never have to work again?"

"It sounds too good to be true."

"Well, you'd have to quit this job and leave San Francisco and never return."

Arthur Brown looked around the donut shop. "Oh, I'd hate that."

He regarded Lance, cocked his head to the right and then left, then looked him up and down. "You look like me," he said.

"Yes, we do look alike," Lance examined Arthur Brown. They stood there looking at each other for a good ten seconds.

"I suppose you need an alibi," Arthur Brown said.

"Something like that."

LANCE LEFT JODY AT THE HOTEL, CAUGHT A CAB TO THE southern tip of Manhattan and went to a hotel where he had registered under the same name as he did at The Surrey. He was standing on the balcony of his room gazing out onto the harbor at the Statue of Liberty when he heard a knock. He opened the door and did a double take; it was like looking in a mirror. Lance motioned him into the suite. He closed the door and looked him up and down. It's amazing what a new set of clothes and a first class plane trip will do. The guy probably had never been treated so well. The scruffiness gone, the hair trimmed, the beard shaved. Even the aura of worn-out desperation had been replaced with a slight swagger. A swagger not unlike his own, Lance had to admit.

He walked to the bar and poured two glasses of scotch, handed one to Arthur Brown then walked to the window and looked out across the bay. Lance gave Arthur time to take in the view of Ellis Island and the Statue of Liberty. Arthur sipped the scotch and felt the burn go right down to his stomach. Lance looked at him and then back to the view. It was spectacular on a clear day.

Arthur motioned to the telescope in the corner. "Does that come with the room?"

"Indeed it does. As it should for the price they charge for this place."

"This room is bigger than my apartment."

They were in the Ritz-Carlton Battery Park. The room was hard to get and like the liquor they were drinking it was expensive. Lance wanted to make a lasting impression on Arthur. He walked to the credenza and pulled out a large manila envelope.

"Now, to business. I paid your debts and now you are going to help me disappear." He reached into the envelope, "Here's a mobile phone," Lance said, handing it to him. "Do not lose it. Do not try to call me. You won't be able to. I'll call you occasionally to check in."

Arthur took the phone. It was a cheap prepaid one like the one he was accustomed to.

He reached into the envelope and pulled out a credit card, a debit card, cash, a California Drivers License, and a US Passport. They were all Lance's own cards and documents.

"You are to use what's in this package. Do not use your own identification or credit cards."

"I don't have a credit card," Arthur said.

"Good. You will become me for a while. Put your own ID

away. Slide it into the lining of that suitcase." Lance indicated a wheeled case in the corner. "It's filled with all you need for the next couple of weeks—clothes, toiletries, things to leave behind in hotel rooms."

Arthur shuffled through the cards and IDs.

Lance reached into the envelope and pulled out another smaller, bulging, envelope.

"You're going to start traveling a lot. Most of the places you will be staying will be upscale. None as nice as this, but nice nonetheless. At each place you stay there will be another set of instructions waiting for you. You will know where to go next, where to stay, and how long to be there. Here's an outline of where you will be going.

"You can order room service as much as you like. At some hotels you will check in, perhaps have a meal, then leave an hour later and get on a plane or train. Sometimes I will have left you a car. If the car doesn't start, follow the directions I gave you. If a credit card is declined, follow the directions I gave you.

"If you follow these directions, I'll give you fifty thousand dollars, and you can go back to being you, or whoever you'd like to be, just not me.

"You will use my identification and credit cards until I tell you to send them to me. I will give you the address at that time. When I get them, and I mean all of them, you will get your money. I will give you a prepaid envelope.

"I'll be keeping an eye on how you're progressing, and as I said, checking in on your phone."

Arthur looked at the pile of papers and documents and was a little overwhelmed. He felt out of his league. He had never been arrested or cited.

Lance took off his gold wedding band and handed it to Arthur.

"Here, you might as well play the part all the way," Lance said. Arthur took the ring and slid it on his finger. It was a good fit. He held his hand back and looked at it.

"One more thing," Lance said. He reached into his pocket and put a pin on Lance's lapel. It was a chess piece, a king.

Arthur examined the pin. "Are you in a lot of trouble?" he asked.

"Let's just say I'd rather not be found for a while." Even if Arthur gave him only a week, it would be a good chance to disappear and get far enough away from the authorities. He checked his watch. He had just enough time to get to Penn Station to catch his train.

NOW ALONE IN THE HOTEL ROOM, ARTHUR REALIZED IT was all real. His life had taken a drastic turn; he was out of debt, had a new set of clothes, and cash in his pocket. He looked out the window at the Statue of Liberty, and then down at the stack of identification, credit cards, cash and the itinerary defined by Lance. New York to Boston, Boston to Washington D.C., D.C. to Chicago, and so on. It was obvious Lance had put a lot of work into the plans.

I'm not an idiot, Arthur thought to himself. Lance is on the run. It may be the police or it could be worse than that. Whoever it is will catch up with me soon enough. I'm just giving him time to get away. How long did Lance think it would take for me to be found? I'm not dumb enough to think Lance will hand me fifty grand. He sat down and tapped his finger on the desk. The ring clanked against the wood, and he slid it off his finger and into his coat pocket. It felt creepy to him to be wearing another man's ring.

He got up and opened the suitcase and emptied the

contents onto the bed. The clothes were well made and expensive. Lance had not overlooked or skimped on the details. Arthur checked the mirror and straightened himself, shot his cuffs. He looked good, very good. He never wanted to go back to his old self.

He opened the envelope Lance had left for him. There was $5000 in cash.

Arthur decided he would not leave his own trail. He would not leave his fingerprints behind. He had started on a new life and it would not be dictated by someone else. He looked around the hotel room and retraced his steps. He had touched little since Lance left, the whisky glass, the arm of the chair. He would be careful from now on.

He sat down at the desk, spread out the itinerary, took a sheet of stationery out of the drawer and made notes.

THERE WAS A REASON LANCE AND ARTHUR LOOKED alike.

After World War II a man named Art Brown returned home to San Francisco from Europe. It was 1945 and because of his position during the war as a Finance Officer he attended the *San Francisco Conference* where the charter for the United Nations was created. Art walked out of the Fairmont Hotel and onto California Street when the hat on the woman walking in front of him blew off. He caught it as it sailed toward him. She turned to retrieve it and he handed it to her and smiled.

"Hello, Margaret."

"Art!" She leaned forward and gave him a hug, "I'm so glad to see you."

"It's good to see you, too. Look, I'm attending the meeting here. Can we meet for dinner tonight?"

Margaret considered it. She had missed him terribly; she thought he had died in the war.

"Can we make it tomorrow for lunch?"

"I'll meet you here at noon?"

"Noon it is."

"I must run," he said, turning and hurrying away.

She stood there and watched him disappear into the crowd. He had a trace of an accent, she thought. He must have spent time in England during the war.

The next morning Margaret took extra time getting dressed and applying her makeup. Her roommate Mary took notice.

"You look rather nice today." She said it with a question in her tone.

"I'm meeting an old friend for lunch," Margaret replied. She tried to keep her voice even. She was excited to see Art again; they had had an intense affair before the war.

"Does your fiancé know about your lunch date?" Mary teased. "When is the wedding again?"

Margaret's face turned red. "You know very well when it is. Really, Mary, it's just lunch with an old friend."

Mary took another long look at Margaret. "Uh huh," she mumbled to herself.

A little before noon Margaret closed her dress shop off Union Square and made the ten-minute walk up Powell Street to the Fairmont Hotel on California Street. Art showed up on time. He hailed a cab that took them down the street to Tadisch Grill. The place has been around since the gold rush and they maintain a strict policy of no reservations, so Art and Margaret stood in line with the rest of the patrons.

"Hi, Tom," Art said greeting one of the owners at the door.

"Hello, Art. How are you today?"

"Fine, and you? This is my old friend Margaret. You may remember her."

"Of course. Hello, Margaret. It's been a long time—before the war."

"It's good to see you again, Tom."

"Say, you wouldn't have seats available at the bar would you?" Art asked.

"You're in luck. It looks like something is just opening up."

Tom took their coats and Art's fedora then showed them to their seats at the counter. Art and Margaret sat down at the bar where they were greeted by a bartender.

"The lady will have one of your excellent manhattans and I'll have a martini."

"Right away, sir."

The Tadisch Grill is a San Francisco landmark. Since 1849 it has survived fire, earthquakes, the Great Depression, and more earthquakes. Through the years the restaurant has changed little. There's a long bar that runs down the right side of the room from the front door to the kitchen. A twelve-foot portion of the bar is reserved for drinkers and separated by a brass rail. The rest of the bar is for diners. On the left side of the room there are tables with starched white tablecloths. Deeper into the restaurant there are alcoves and booths for larger groups of diners.

The drinks came and they were excellent. Margaret took a sip, looking at Art over the rim of the glass.

"It's nice of you to remember what I like to drink."

"Well of course I remember, Margaret. We put a dent in this town, didn't we?"

Margaret looked around the restaurant, gathering her thoughts.

Art watched her survey the room, thinking of the times they had had together.

She turned back to him.

"So tell me, how is the conference going? It certainly has the city abuzz."

She was surprised by how they took up where they left off before the war. She was comfortable with Art, always had been. She felt a warmth flow over her as he began to talk.

"Well as you probably know, the conference is at the Opera House and the Veterans Building. The Americans have requisitioned the Fairmont and the Chinese and the Brits are across the street at the Mark Hopkins. The Russians are at the St. Francis, and the rest of the delegations are scattered around the city. But the real action is happening behind the scenes on Nob Hill—that's not public information, by the way. I've been keeping fit running between the places."

"What's your role in all of this?"

"This and that. I'm not at liberty to say."

"Ah, same old Art."

"Well yes, I suppose."

He turned to her and took her hand, looked her in her eyes. "It's wonderful to see you again, Margaret."

She didn't know what it was, but he could always get to her. Had she been standing she knew her knees would be weak. She blushed, she knew it—and could not do a thing about it.

"I see you missed me as well," Art said.

The waiter was watching the couple out of the corner of

his eye, waiting for a chance to take their lunch order. He saw the woman blush and thought it was a good time to interrupt. He figured she could use a diversion.

"May I take your order?"

"Yes. The lady will have the petrale sole and I will have the cioppino," Art said.

"Very good, sir."

After the waiter left Margaret turned to Art and asked, "How do you know I still like sole?"

"Well you do, don't you?"

"Yes, but that is beside the point."

"I don't see why."

"Aghh. I guess I don't like being a foregone conclusion."

"I'd never take you for granted, Margaret."

His self-assurance was the one thing about Art that infuriated her and attracted her in equal measure.

Lunch passed nicely after that. Art tucked his tie into his shirt before starting on his cioppino. Margaret nibbled on her fish and they caught up on each other's lives, avoiding the horrors of the war. It wasn't easy. When they talked of their circle of friends, it became clear that they had lost many of them in the conflict.

"I have something for you."

"What is it?"

"I'd rather surprise you. Why don't we make a stop on the way out." It wasn't a question.

Margaret was curious, curious about what it was Art had to give her, and curious to see his apartment again. They had had some wonderful times there.

When they left the restaurant, Art hailed a cab

to take them up California Street to the Fairmont Hotel.

Leaving the cab, Art ushered her through the and to the terrace level.

"Oh, I've heard about this place. They converted the swimming pool to a bar. I didn't know it had opened," Margaret said. She looked around. There was a floating bandstand in the middle of the room. The place looked like a ship with lots of Polynesian decor.

"They brought a set designer in from MGM to put it together. They call it The Tonga Room and Hurricane Bar," Art said.

"I see where all the negotiations are going on for the conference," Margaret said.

"The Chinese, French, Russians, Americans, Brits–they're all here." Art gave a wave to a table of four in the corner. They all hoisted their glasses in reply.

"Seen enough? We can come back another time if you wish," Art said, taking Margaret by the elbow. He waved and they left the bar.

"Sorry about that. We risked spending the afternoon talking about the war and the conference."

The weather was nice and they walked the remaining two blocks to Art's apartment. The place was much as it was when Margaret had seen it last. It was neat and tidy. He told her during lunch that he had the same housekeeper, May, from before the war. There wasn't much of a view even from the fourth floor, but Art furnished the place in a masculine comfortable style with a leather chesterfield and matching chair. There were framed Maxfield Parrish prints on the walls and a drinks trolley in one corner.

Art took Margaret's coat. She walked around the room looking at artifacts and souvenirs from Art's travels: African masks, a cuckoo clock and a few more things from his time in

Europe during the war. It was an eclectic mix that suited him well and it all seemed to fit together. While she surveyed the room, Art was busy at the drinks trolley, shaking bitters into a mixing glass. She noticed that the ice bucket had been filled before they arrived. She also couldn't help but notice a framed photo on an end table. She picked it up and looked at it. It was from a New Years Eve party before the war. Art was in black tie, she in a strapless pink number. Art had surprised her with the gift of the dress. She peered at the photo. She looked good that night, she thought.

Margaret accepted the drink from Art and they clinked glasses. She sat down on the sofa and kicked off her shoes, slid her feet beneath her, took a sip. "Another perfect manhattan."

"It's the rye. I always use Old Overholt."

Art looked at her, curled up, drink in her hand. He took a seat at the other end of the sofa, also kicking off his shoes. It was as if nothing had changed between them.

"It feels good to unwind," Margaret said. She slid her feet out from underneath her and rested them in his lap. Art set his drink on the end table and massaged her feet. Margaret let out a sigh and took another sip.

"I'm not used to drinking like we used to. I must say I am feeling lightheaded."

"Well, just relax," Art said, massaging her toes.

"Oh, I'm relaxed all right."

They sat quietly. It was another thing Margaret liked about Art. They could spend time together in a comfortable silence, without feeling the need to talk.

After a few minutes Art looked at her and asked "Are you very drunk?"

"Why do you ask?"

"Because I don't want to take advantage of you."

"Art, always the gentleman." She pulled her legs off him

and stood up, a bit wobbly.

"It is I who will take advantage of you." She pulled him up off the sofa, grabbed him by the tie and pulled him into the bedroom.

"It's just like I remember it," she said, looking around the room. She spun toward him.

A bouquet of long stemmed pink roses was in a vase on the bedside table. He always made sure her favorite flowers were in the apartment when she came to visit.

"Damn it, Art. What did I say about being a foregone conclusion?"

"Well, I did say I have something for you."

LATER THAT AFTERNOON, LYING IN BED WITH ART BESIDE her, Margaret had a twinge of guilt thinking about Johan Carlsen, the man she was to marry in a week.

She cleared her throat.

"You always clear your throat before you ask a serious question," Art said.

He does know me well, she thought.

"So what am I going to ask?"

"Well, I couldn't help but notice the rather dazzling engagement ring you are sporting. I suppose you want to know if you should call it off and marry me instead."

"Why you arrogant...." She stopped. He was right, that was exactly what she was going to ask, but not so bluntly, and not with such assurance. She reached for the ring and felt it under the sheet, spun it around on her finger.

"So when is the date?"

"Next week."

"Look, Margaret. We're terrific together. But let me get to

the point. You want to have children, right?"

"Well, yes, I do."

"I don't. I have seen the horrors this world has to offer. I don't want to bring children into it. I just can't."

She sat thinking for a while.

"I thought you had a desk job in London."

"That was later. In the beginning, the war and I were up close and personal." He turned on the bedside light. He reached for her hand and put it on his chest. She examined the scar.

"Bayonet. Missed my heart by a quarter of an inch. It's a strange sensation looking someone in the face as he is trying to kill you."

Margaret was married to Johan Carlsen the following week and nine months later gave birth to her daughter. She knew the instant she saw the baby that the girl was Art's child. Years passed and Margaret's daughter married a Polish immigrant she met in college and had a son. She named him Lance after her father.

Art, Lance's biological grandfather, founded a bank in San Francisco. Margaret had been right about Art. He was a gentleman. When he got his girlfriend pregnant, he stepped up and married her. Despite his earlier feelings, Art found being a father enjoyable and raised a family of his own. He had five children and between them they had five grandchildren. Arthur, named for his grandfather, was the only child of Art's oldest son.

The families had never come face-to-face, but Margaret knew where they lived. She would occasionally read an article in the newspaper about Art's bank and its success, and the winner-take-all attitude he had. It was something that Margaret had not known about him. The newspapers described his ruthless attitude toward his competitors and business in general.

One day, twenty-two years after that night with Art, Margaret was going through some old papers and came across a letter from him, written during the height of the war in Europe. She read the letter twice before curiosity got the best of her. She drove to the other side of town and parked across the street from Art's home. Sitting in the car, she looked at the house, feeling no regrets but wondering how her life might have been. Only Margaret knew she had a daughter from Art, or that Lance was his grandson.

SITTING AT THE RITZ-CARLTON AFTER LANCE LEFT, Arthur decided he needed a computer. He ventured into a huge electronics store on 42nd Street feeling overwhelmed.

"What's the cheapest one you have?"

"You want the cheapest or the least expensive?" the salesman asked, "because the cheapest one's gonna fall apart." He picked up a small laptop. "This one's pretty good. It will get you on the internet for web browsing or e-mail. It has a built-in camera for video conferencing. It doesn't have much memory, battery life, or a big hard drive and the screen is small, but it's reliable."

"Wow. A lot has changed since I was last on-line." Arthur looked at the laptop with awe. For the last five years Arthur had been living an almost technology-free life and only getting on-line at the local library. He hadn't been able to afford a computer and didn't even have an e-mail address. He had been making a point of staying as anonymous as possible.

The salesman, a native New Yorker, held back the multitude of sarcastic remarks and took pity on the guy. "Yeah, a lot has changed." It was a slow day and he worked on commission.

"That sounds good. How much is it?"

"It's last year's model and we are closing them out, so I can give you a good price."

THAT EVENING, ARTHUR SAT AT THE DESK IN HIS HOTEL room. Placing the laptop on the desk, Arthur connected to the hotel's internet and acquired a free e-mail account. Arthur pondered his options. He considered getting cash from this credit card, but realized he didn't have the code to access the account. He ruled out trying to use the card at a bank; he didn't want to take the risk of being caught. He decided the computer purchase would be the last time he used the credit card. He sat back, looked out the window and sighed.

His growling stomach made him realize he hadn't eaten since he was on the plane. He thumbed through the room service menu. They seemed to have anything he could imagine. Lobster. He hadn't had lobster in years. He picked up the phone and called room service.

He walked to the telescope and scanned around until he found Ellis Island across the harbor in New Jersey. His great-grandfather had arrived in the country through Ellis Island from Scotland. Arthur thought his ancestor would have been a wealthy man had he arrived with $5000 cash and a new set of clothes.

Arthur panned around the hotel room and then back out the window at Ellis Island. Yes, he liked what he saw. He didn't want or need this much. He felt relief he was out of San Francisco, out of debt, and even had money.

A knock at the door jolted him out of his thoughts.

"Room service."

He had the waiter put the table in front of the window. He looked across the bay as he ate the lobster and sipped champagne. The room was dead quiet. He watched the birds fly past the window. He was a loner, and he was lonely. He finished the lobster, the tiramisu he had ordered for dessert, and half of the bottle of champagne. The meal cost a week's rent at his apartment in San Francisco. It disgusted him; he decided he had had enough.

He let out a burp into the empty room.

ARTHUR WANTED TO BE AROUND PEOPLE, OR AT LEAST felt he had to get out of the hotel again. He put the *Do Not Disturb* hangtag on the door, grabbed his laptop, and set out in search of an internet café. He asked at the front desk and was told the lobby had internet, but he could find a café open late in TriBeCa. A little tipsy, he took a taxi to Kaffe 1688, ordered a latte, and sat down at a table to log onto his laptop. There was an old black and white movie projected on the wall; the waiter served his coffee drink with a palm tree design in the foam.

He lost himself on the computer searching for a place to go, seeing what the world had to offer. He had been clicking away for an hour before a voice took him away from the screen.

"Do you mind if I sit here too?"

Arthur looked up to see a woman standing above him.

The champagne had worn off somewhat and he stood up and pulled out the chair for her.

"Of course."

"Oh. A gentleman. How refreshing." She smiled at him. Arthur turned red in the face. The last time a woman smiled so nicely at him he was stuffing a five-dollar bill into her g-string. He shook the image from his mind.

She noticed his red-faced reaction and found it sweet.

"I'm not in the habit of introducing myself to strange men, but my name is Fiona," she said, extending her hand.

Arthur nearly replied with "Lance."

"Arthur. My name is Arthur," he said with as much dignity as he could muster.

Fiona dropped her things at the table and set off to order a drink. Arthur watched her as she stood at the counter. She was pretty, but not too pretty for Arthur, and she was well dressed.

He felt like someone real, not like the loser he usually considered himself to be.

Fiona returned with her cup. "So, Arthur. What are you working at so diligently on your computer?"

"I just bought it and I'm getting used to using it."

"You're not from New York City, are you?"

"No, is it obvious?"

"Well, you don't have that edge. West Coast?"

"As a matter of fact, yes."

The conversation continued with mild-mannered chitchat. Arthur had not had such a nice talk with a woman since he dated his ex-wife.

"So what do you do, Arthur?"

"I'm looking for the next thing, sort of starting over. I'm thinking of leaving the city tomorrow."

"It appears you have been successful."

"Why do you say that?"

"Your clothes are excellent–look new–and your shoes are expensive."

Arthur looked down at his shoes. He had not considered them before. They sure were comfortable. He wiggled his toes.

Fiona watched him and almost laughed out loud. Arthur looked up at her and her smile. He smiled back.

He took in a breath. "I want to be honest with you. I don't have much. I have a suitcase of nice clothes and some cash. That's it. Oh, and this laptop."

"Why are you telling me? I just met you."

"I don't want anyone to think that I am something I am not."

Fiona sat back and took him in. "How very refreshing," she said.

AN HOUR LATER ARTHUR AND FIONA WERE SITTING SIDE-by-side. She was teaching him the finer points of surfing the web. They were looking at the weather around the world. It intrigued her that someone his age didn't know much of the current state of the internet, but she was too polite to bring it up.

Arthur looked up from the computer and out at the winter New York night. "It sure would be nice to go somewhere warm."

"You said you are thinking of leaving tomorrow. Where are you going?"

"Well, I bought this computer to figure that out. Where does one go when one is starting over?"

"Well, that depends, I guess."

"On what?" Arthur asked, taking a sip of cold latte.

"Well... are you a wanted man?"

Arthur laughed. "If you mean do I have any legal entanglements, the answer is no," *and I intend to keep it that way*, Arthur added to himself. "No, I am not a wanted man."

Fiona made a snap decision, one she hoped she would not regret.

"I'm driving south tomorrow. Why don't you join me?"

Her offer surprised Arthur. It solved his problem of how to get away and leave no trail of buses, trains, or planes. He didn't even have to rent a car. That he had come to like Fiona in the last three hours was an added plus.

"Yes. I'd very much like to ride south with you. I'll be happy to chip in for gas and do some driving."

That night, back in his hotel room, Arthur had a hard time sleeping. He stared at the ceiling thinking about the trip and Fiona. He wasn't convinced she would show up at his hotel in the morning. He decided if she didn't show he would head south on his own. It was as good a direction as any. He fell asleep around 3:00 a.m. and woke before his alarm rang at six. He ordered room service for breakfast and spent the next couple of hours wiping off anything he had touched. He checked the bed and bath for his hair. Satisfied that the place was spotless and DNA free, he sat down in a chair and waited. At ten minutes to eight, he left his room and rolled his suitcase out of the lobby to wait in the small plaza outside the hotel.

Chapter Fourteen

After Lance left Arthur at the Ritz Carlton he caught a taxi to Penn Station. His two years of planning had paid off. He was now named Merek Faron, a citizen of Poland. The surname was his grandmother's maiden name. His parents died in a car crash when he was nineteen. Lance's father, proud of his heritage, had insisted that he learn and speak Polish at home, making Lance fluent in the language. The language and the accent, the voice and some mannerisms he used were his father's. His hair was cut to make his face appear longer. His contact lenses were tinted blue and custom-made shoes made him two inches taller. Lance would be Merek Faron for the train ride and two other different names for the rest of the trip.

He looked different, even to himself in the mirror. He felt different. He felt alive, free. He could go anywhere, do anything, and he had the resources to do so.

At Penn Station he boarded an Amtrak train to Orlando. It would be a long ride of 22 hours. He bought himself a private room that included a bed, meals, and newspaper. He kept to his room during the daylight hours, sitting in the chair, working on his laptop, making more plans, going over the details, and looking out the window, watching the world flash by. His only interaction was with the porter who, after Lance offered a nice tip and requested it, delivered dinner to his room. By eight o'clock he was exhausted from how much he had done since Friday afternoon. After the sun set, he dropped the bed into position, crawled between the sheets and slept.

At two in the morning he awoke and felt a bout of cabin fever. He had been in the little room for fourteen hours. He opened the door and peeked out. The corridor was empty as he walked down the aisle to the dining car. He had never taken a long trip on a real train, only lots of short trips in various cities around the world. He wanted to take in the smells (a slight bit of diesel, cleaning products, and something metallic), the sounds (the muted noise of the wheels on the tracks), and the swaying motion of the train. The dining car had stopped serving hours earlier, but it felt good to get out and move through the other cars. A few people were awake reading, others squirmed, trying to get comfortable enough in their seats to sleep. One man was snoring. People were leaning up against one another. One family of four all slept wearing Mickey Mouse ears in anticipation of going to that hallowed land of Disney World.

Lance made his way back to his cabin and crawled back into the bunk. He slept a dreamless sleep for the next seven hours, waking up in time to take a shower in the cramped little bath, straddling the toilet, doing yoga to get clean. Before he left the train he took his mobile phone, wrapped it in aluminum foil, put it in a mylar bag, and wedged it out of sight into one of the fold-down beds. He hoped that when it was discovered and unwrapped, he would be far away. If someone found it and turned it on and kept it, all the better. The police would track the phone and not him.

After Penn Station, the Orlando station was a huge letdown. From its original architecture, Lance could tell it had once been a showplace. He took a cab to a hotel near the airport. He wasn't in Orlando to go to Disney World; he was there to obscure his travels, take a non-direct route to his destination. He booked an eight o'clock flight to Edinburgh. He was glad he had slept well, for the next couple of days would be busy.

LATER THAT WEEK, LANCE WAS SITTING IN FRONT OF THE fireplace in a third-floor flat on the Royal Mile in the heart of Edinburgh, sipping a twenty-year-old Glen Grant Whisky in a heavy glass tumbler. He glanced around the room. It was a bachelor's flat with polished pine floors, dark brown leather furniture, and burgundy curtains. There was an expensive stereo in the corner above a large flat screen television. It was a big place with a single bedroom and bath, a spacious living room and a small office. He needed nothing more; it was comfortable and met his needs.

The first thing he did upon arriving was observe the locals, studying the men his age, how they moved, what they wore. He walked to Marks and Spencer and bought clothes. He wanted to blend in, lose his American style—and he needed something warm to wear. He could pick the Americans out of a crowd by just looking at what they were wearing.

He had thought of parking himself on some small Caribbean island, but he figured it would be easier to fade away in a crowded city of a half a million than an island of a few hundred. It seemed every movie he had seen where someone had gotten away with a big heist had ended with them sitting on a beach in some tropical spot. Who would think of looking for someone in Scotland in February?

Months before, Lance had gone on-line, scoured rental listings, searching for a quiet place where he could be for a month or two, a hideout. He had narrowed his options by studying satellite images on the internet and mapping walking distances. He did the entire transaction on-line by e-mail and money transfers, paid the month in advance and gave a sizable security deposit. The leasing agent had been accommodating. He came by to make sure all was fine with the flat. From behind the door Lance told him everything was fine, but he had picked up the flu on his flight and didn't want to expose him to it. He threw in a raspy cough for authenticity. The agent was happy to avoid him and thanked Lance for his consideration.

In Edinburgh, Lance kept a low profile. He had a satellite telephone and portable satellite internet connection, both in the name of an untraceable corporation based in Malaysia. He set up shop in the little office in the flat. He got into a groove: a simple breakfast, move money around, plan his next move, and monitor news feeds of anyone talking about him and his disappearance. After a year of planning, it was all falling into place. He figured the best way to get caught was to move around. So he stayed put, let his trail get cold. He had made it to Edinburgh before Nick discovered his actions, so he had a three-day head start. In a month Jody would join him and life would be more interesting. She had started out as just a way to take everything from Nick, but it had grown to more than that. He and Jody were more alike than he had realized.

There was only one thing that had not gone as planned. What happened to Arthur Brown? It had been a week and he wasn't answering calls. There was no activity on his credit cards except for a purchase at an electronics store the day Lance left New York. Lance could only assume he had been caught, or had taken the $5000 and run. He decided to give up on Arthur. He removed the SIM card from the phone he had reserved to call him, took the card to the gas range and with a pair of tweezers held it to the flame of the burner. It melted with a small flame and a foul smell. He took the mobile with him, wiped it clean and headed out the door. After a while he came to a rubbish bin. He looked around and saw no one paying attention to him. He slipped the mobile phone out of his coat pocket. He wore gloves to protect it from fingerprints, but also because it was Scotland in February. From his inside pocket he pulled out a handkerchief. Lance turned his back to the road and again wiped the phone clean. He then opened the phone and with both hands snapped the phone in two, separating the screen from the keyboard. He dropped the front of the phone into the bin and continued on down the street.

A few minutes later Lance came to another bin in front of a pub. He stopped at it and made sure no one was watching. He thought of all the work and money he had put into his plans for Arthur to take his place in the states. Lance knew it was a temporary fix, but he had expected it to last at least a week. That Arthur had not responded to his calls after the first day was unsettling.

He dropped the rest of the phone into the bin and walked into the pub to order a whisky.

Chapter Fifteen

Arthur didn't bother to check out of the hotel; he was supposed to be playing the part of Lance, and according to Lance's itinerary, he was to be there another day before departing for Boston, the next place on his list. As he was waiting for Fiona to pick him up, the mobile phone Lance had given him rang. He pulled it out of his pocket. He let it finish ringing and turned it off.

Arthur stood in front of the hotel for a few minutes before Fiona pulled up to the curb. His heart skipped a beat when he saw her and he felt a wave of relief. The doorman helped him put his bag in the trunk of the car. Arthur tipped him and climbed into the passenger seat.

Once they had cleared the traffic of the city, they stuck to the coast. It would take them longer to get south, but neither of them was in a hurry. They were just passing Atlantic City when signs on the road beckoned them to try their luck at the tables.

"So have you traveled much?"

Fiona tapped the brakes and changed lanes to avoid a

moving van that cut her off. Arthur looked at her and waited until she settled back into a driving groove before answering.

"When I graduated from college I worked for a Chinese company. After two years an overseas position opened up. They needed someone to write a product manual in English. It seemed like a good opportunity, and I had just gone through a divorce and felt I needed a change, so I took the position and moved to Hong Kong."

"How did it work out?"

"Not so well." Arthur squirmed in his seat. "How about you? Have you traveled much?"

"Mexico, Canada, most of the US, Europe. I've never been to Asia. More than some people, not as much as others. So why didn't it work out for you in Hong Kong?"

"I've never told anyone about it." I didn't have anyone to talk to, Arthur thought.

Fiona stole a glance at him. His eyes were straight ahead. His cheek was red.

"If you don't want to talk, it's okay."

Arthur was silent for a moment. I guess she'll find out eventually, he thought, except the part about Lance. No one would ever know about that. "No, it would be good to talk about it. That part of my life is over." He took a breath. He intrigued Fiona. She could tell it would be an interesting trip.

"I arrived in Hong Kong to work on the manual for a software program. They put me up in a nice furnished apartment in Kowloon. The factory was in the New Territories, also on the mainland. They gave me an office and I set to work. The engineers spoke English well enough to tell me what I needed to know for the manual, but not enough to write it themselves. I wanted to make a good impression, so I worked later than most people. On weekends I explored the area and soon met the people in my apartment building. One girl and I hit if off and started seeing each other.

"What was her name?"

"May Ling. She also worked at the company. A lot of people in my apartment building did."

On the trip south, Arthur had time to reflect on the events that had led to his current situation.

Arthur had been working late the night his life took a turn. His third-floor office was small, square and austere, but it was one of the few offices with a window. The window overlooked the loading dock, but it had natural light and it afforded him a glance of the outside world. He had been at the company four months, but his office was still unadorned with personal items. There were notes taped to the celadon green walls. He was sitting at his desk working between his computer and pages pinned to a bulletin board. He had been walking back and forth, visualizing the flow of the manual he was writing.

Movement outside caught his eye. An anonymous white van had appeared below at the loading dock. He could see the exhaust in the dusk-blue light as it idled. Arthur checked his watch and realized he was late. He was to meet May Ling at the local watering hole in less than half an hour and would have to get moving to get there on time. Arthur gathered his laptop and his notes and tucked them into his beat-up leather messenger bag, grabbed his mobile phone and turned to walk out the door. He glanced out the window and down to the van. It was still there, but now the back doors were open and a man was standing at the back of the van smoking a cigarette. Two men came out a side door, another man in a trench coat between them. They stopped at the back of the vehicle, the man in the trench coat shook his head. The man on the left, dressed entirely in black, gestured for him to get in, and again he resisted. The man in black pulled a gun from beneath his coat. He didn't point it at the man in the trench coat, he just showed it to him. The man looked at the gun, looked back at the man in black, turned and climbed in the van. The doors were closed behind him.

The man in black turned and looked around, lifted his head and looked at Arthur standing in front of his office window. Arthur froze in place mesmerized by what he had seen. Even from that distance he could see the dark scar on the man's right cheek that ran from the edge of his right eye to the corner of his mouth.

Arthur became aware of the ticking clock on the wall of his office. He had not noticed how loud it was until then. Arthur shook his head to clear his thoughts and backed up into the room. He saw the man below him point out his window to the other man. They both ran toward the building. Arthur ran out the door and down the hall, past rows of offices with glass doors, walls covered with framed art on rice paper. All the offices he ran past were dark. He was alone in the building.

He knew the place well. Should he hide or make his way out? There were lots of nooks and crannies to crawl into in the ultra modern building. He ran and pushed the button for the elevator and then kept running toward the front doors. He came to the next set of elevators and pushed the button and turned and took the stairs to the second floor. He stood and listened and heard noises from the direction of his office. He came to an open staircase and looked down into the lobby. He saw a small spot behind the reception desk. It looked like a tall square place for a plant. It had walls about seven feet tall.

From above it was wasted space, an architectural mistake. Unless someone hoisted themselves up and peered down inside, he wouldn't be seen there. Hearing nothing, he descended the stairs to the lobby, moved behind the desk and climbed into the empty space. He leaned against the wall and tried to control his breathing. He felt the mobile phone in his pocket vibrate and took it out and turned it off.

About a minute later he heard footsteps and then voices arguing in Chinese. He couldn't understand most of it, but the English cursing was clear. The voices moved past him and he could hear the lobby doors open and close. He let out the breath he was holding. Arthur felt the need to move, but resisted, wanting to make sure he was alone. Arthur thought he heard something, but it was more like a soft shuffle. He froze as he realized there was someone close to him. He could hear the breathing. Without moving he glanced up and saw a reflection of the man in the high window above him. Arthur could have reached out and touched him through the wall. He breathed deep and took time to study the man. Arthur recognized him from the neighborhood bar and café near his apartment. He was the scar-faced man in black who occupied a table in the back of the café. He was usually with other men and seemed to always be talking on his mobile phone.

Arthur closed his eyes and tried to keep his breathing shallow. The man made a grunting sound, turned, and walked out the lobby doors.

"Wow. That's crazy," Fiona said. "That really happened?"

"All that and more," Arthur said. It all seemed like such a long time ago, five long years of hell.

"I stood in that cramped spot for another half hour, listening for the slightest sound. When I didn't hear anything, I climbed out of the planter or whatever it was, and made my way to a side door. Then I ran as fast and as far from the building as I could. I found a spot near my apartment and called May Ling."

THE TEMPERATURE HAD DROPPED AND ARTHUR SAT shivering against the wall of a car park. There was a strong smell of gasoline and the sound of buzzing fluorescent lights.

"Arthur, where are you? I've been waiting more than an hour for you," May Ling said when she answered the phone.

"I'm in trouble, May Ling. I need your help."

"Are you hurt?"

"No, it's something else." Arthur described to her what had happened at the office.

"It was the guy from the café, the guy with the scar who sits at the table in the back," Arthur told her.

"The guy that always dresses in black? That guy is bad news. He's some gang leader or something."

"What should I do? Go to the police?"

"You don't need to go to the police, you need to go away."

"What do you mean go away?"

"You need to leave Hong Kong. Are you someplace safe?"

"I think I'm safe," he said.

"I'll go to your apartment and grab some things. Don't move. I'll call you in a while."

It was an hour and a half before Arthur heard from May Ling. He'd been shivering in the car park as he waited.

The phone vibrated in Arthur's hand, startling him so much he nearly dropped it. He answered the call and heard

May Ling say, "I went to your apartment. The door was open. I didn't want to go in."

"I'm glad you didn't."

"Do you have your passport with you?"

"Always."

"I'll grab a taxi and come get you. Where are you?"

Arthur told her and said he would meet her at the back of the building.

FIONA AND ARTHUR TIMED THEIR TRIP TO CATCH THE Cape May-Lewes Ferry that crossed the seventeen miles between New Jersey and Delaware.

They had driven the car onto the deck and were sitting on a bench with a view of the Atlantic.

Arthur continued the story. "So May Ling came to get me in a taxi," he said, thinking back to the night that changed his life. One's life really can change in the blink of an eye.

ARTHUR HAD MOVED TO THE BACK OF THE BUILDING AND waited shivering in the shadows.

A taxi pulled up and turned off its engine. May Ling got out of the front passenger seat. "Arthur," she whispered.

"I'm here, May Ling."

"Get in the back and lie down. This is my friend Kang, a good guy. We can trust him."

"Hi, Kang, and thank you," Arthur said.

Kang turned to him and gave him a big smile. In fact his

entire face lit up. He leaned back and took Lance's hand and shook it repeatedly, still smiling.

"Hello, Arthur," he said.

Arthur smiled back at Kang's infectious good nature.

"I was at the café when you called. The big guy came in right after we talked. He went to his table in the back and shouted orders to his men. He was pretty upset," May Ling said.

"The guy with the scar?" Fiona asked. Her voice brought him back to the present.

"Yes, the guy with the scar." Arthur looked at Fiona. She had her arms folded and was shivering. Arthur took off his coat and put it around her shoulders.

"Thanks. Will you be warm enough?"

"I'm fine."

"Please continue," Fiona said. When she'd started on this trip, she had no idea it would be so interesting.

"I was lying down in the back of Kang's taxi and May Ling filled me in."

"We stopped by your apartment on the way to pick you up. I sneaked in the back and walked by your door. I saw it was still open so I didn't stop. There were two men in there ripping the place apart. I kept walking and came right here to get you."

"Well, that's not good," Arthur said.

"Not at all."

"So, now we go to the police?" Arthur asked.

"No, we don't go to the police. We go to the airport, and we go now."

"What do you mean?"

"These are bad people, Arthur. The police won't protect you. You need to get out of Hong Kong while you can."

"You mean go now?"

"Yes. May I have your mobile phone please?"

Arthur handed it to her and May Ling rolled down the window and dropped it out onto the road.

He looked at her confused.

"Arthur, these guys are connected at all levels. They can track your phone. Your apartment will be watched. My uncle was in the police force; he told me all about them. They are very good at making people disappear."

"Wonderful," Arthur said.

"You have your passport. Do you have a credit card with you?"

"Yes, of course."

They were at a stoplight. Kang was looking straight ahead. Arthur looked at May Ling, she was facing Kang, but talking to Arthur.

"We can go to my apartment and find a flight," Kang said. "These bad men do not know who I am."

"That's a good idea. Let's go," May Ling said.

Fifteen minutes later they were sitting in Kang's tiny studio apartment in a high rise on Hong Kong Island. The three of them crowded around Kang's laptop computer.

"So we want a seat on any available flight out. Kang, how long does it take to get to the airport from here?"

"You had better give yourself two-and-a-half hours before the flight to get to the airport and through security."

"Okay, let's find a flight that leaves in three hours that has an open seat," May Ling said.

Kang typed away. "Taiwan, no. Osaka, no. Hanoi, no. Wow, what gives? The flights are full."

"Keep looking. Try anywhere," May Ling said.

"I found one."

"Where?"

"Guam. It leaves in," Kang checked his watch, "three and

a half hours."

"Guam?" Arthur asked.

"Sure. It's an American territory so you don't need a visa and it will get you out of Hong Kong the soonest. You can decide where you go from there."

"Kang, what did you do before you were a taxi driver?" Arthur asked.

"I received my degree in travel industry management and I worked at the front desk of a hotel. There is more money in driving a taxi."

"How about that." Arthur said.

Arthur looked down at his dress slacks and dress shirt. "I'll probably need some clothes if I'm not going to be spotted at the airport."

"No problem. I have lots of things to wear." He walked to a cupboard and opened it. It was stacked with colorful clothes.

"I go to a lot of nightclubs," Kang said.

By the time May Ling and Kang dropped Arthur at the airport, he was dressed for a night on the town and had a back-pack full of garish shorts and t-shirts.

"I have a friend at the airport. They will meet us at the curb, get you a boarding pass and escort you to the front of the security line. No one should bother you."

"Wow. I can't thank you enough, Kang." Arthur leaned forward to shake his hand when they came to a stoplight. May Ling was sitting in the back seat with him, holding his hand on the way to the airport.

"I'm not sure we will see each other again," May Ling said.

"I'm not sure if we will either. Thank you, May Ling. I wouldn't have survived without you." He gave her a long kiss goodbye.

"We're here. There is my friend Bruce," Kang said.

A man in a uniform reached down and opened the door. "You must be Arthur. We have to hurry if you're going to make your flight. Hi, Kang."

Arthur turned to May Ling.

"Go now," she said, pushing him toward the door.

Arthur turned and exited the taxi.

Bruce looked Arthur up and down, took in his silver shirt and shiny black slacks. "Did Kang dress you?"

"As a matter of fact he did, but I resisted the big gold medallion necklace."

"Good call. Let's go."

Twenty feet away from the taxi Arthur turned to wave goodbye. May Ling was back in the front seat. She and Kang waved back.

"Sorry about your friend," Kang said, "he seemed like a good guy."

"Yeah, I'm sorry too."

WHEN THEY EXITED THE FERRY ARTHUR TOOK THE wheel. They were on the Delmarva Peninsula—the eastern shore of Virginia.

Fiona was still sipping her coffee, now cold. "So I guess you got out of Hong Kong," she asked.

"I did. Kang's friend took me to the head of all the lines at the airport and rushed me through. I spent a day in Guam, two days in Honolulu and then on to San Francisco.

"I've been to Hawaii. How was Guam?"

"Hot. Hot and humid."

"Ugh."

"Yeah."

"When I returned to San Francisco, all hell broke loose. My company was trying to track me down. I'd been missing for more than a week. I couldn't tell them what happened in Hong Kong because I didn't know if what I saw was connected to the company in the U.S., so I was fired. I couldn't get a letter of recommendation and the dot-com boom was ebbing."

"Ugh. That sounds like a nightmare."

"It was. My divorce had cleaned me out and I spent the rest of my money getting back to the states. I left Hong Kong with the clothes on my back—Kang's clothes. I ended up with the first job I could find and a little apartment in a bad part of San Francisco."

Arthur glanced at Fiona in the seat beside him. "Suffice it to say I bottomed out."

"How long did that go on?"

Arthur was in no rush to tell Fiona about his last five years of nothingness. "Too long."

"Well, you look fine now."

ARTHUR HAD NO IDEA THAT LANCE HAD ALSO HEADED south, and Lance assumed that Arthur was following the itinerary he had given him and was heading north from New York City to Boston and then west to Chicago. By the time Arthur and Fiona had arrived in Virginia, Lance had been in Orlando for a few hours and was getting ready to board a plane to Edinburgh. The next morning Arthur looked at Fiona in the next bed. She was breathing gently and rhythmically. He eased out of bed and quietly dressed, then made his way out of the hotel in search of coffee and something to eat to take back to the room. He noticed a fishing pier across the way that he hadn't seen when they had arrived the previous evening. As he walked toward the end of the pier, he pulled the mobile phone Lance had given him out of his jacket pocket, wiped it clean of fingerprints, and dropped it in the first trashcan he came to. When he arrived at the end of the pier, he stood and looked out at the ocean and off to the horizon. The morning was cool and there was a wind at his back. He saw that the tide was running out. He looked around; there were a half a dozen fishermen busy with their lines. No one was paying attention to anyone else. Arthur reached into his breast pocket and pulled out Lance's California driver's license, credit card, debit card, and US passport and gave them a wipe on his jacket. He took one more look around and then flicked the lot into the Atlantic. He watched them land, float briefly, and slowly sink. He could see them in the water floating below the surface. The tide had grabbed them and they moved offshore and out to sea. He turned to walk back to the hotel and stopped, remembering one more thing. Arthur reached into his jacket pocket and took out Lance's gold wedding band. He turned back and flicked it over the railing, watching it splash and sink, the morning light reflecting on it through the water until it was out of view.

Chapter Sixteen

The Firth of Forth. Lance liked the sound of it. It sounded better than "The Estuary fed by the Forth River." During his forty-five-day stay, he had grown fond of the Firth and the city of Edinburgh. The people were friendly and the town was interesting and steeped in history. Choosing to stay in Old Town Edinburgh had turned out to be a good choice. He was within walking distance to anything he could want. Rose Street with an astounding number of pubs was just around the corner. He was trying a different whisky most nights, finding some he had never seen in the states. To top if off, there was a castle on the hill in the middle of town. Even with the horrible winter weather, he wished he could stay.

He kept his head down for more than a month, lying low. He walked the town, rarely going to the same place twice, whether it be a restaurant, pub, or store. That wasn't a problem, there was plenty to see and do. He shopped for groceries at different stores. If he went to the same store twice, he would go at a different time of day than he had previously, hoping to not be recognized by any of the staff. He enjoyed the game of hiding out and even tried to vary his look when he visited the same part of town. One day while gazing up at Edinburgh Castle he noticed a vintage Scottish fisherman's sweater in the window of a secondhand shop on Grassmarket Street and bought it. When he wore it the locals assumed he was one of them. It became his favorite piece of clothing.

He continued to move the money through a labyrinth of secure computer servers. He was certain that the money could not be traced. He spent hours on his laptop and enjoyed seeing the dollar signs circling around the globe.

The news feeds on the internet showed nothing about his disappearance and there was no odd activity on his accounts. It seemed as if his plan had worked. He made arrangements to meet Jody.

Jody had no idea where Lance was. He had told her he was somewhere in Asia, keeping it vague. She seemed to accept that. They had been communicating through a complex system he had developed of rotating encrypted e-mail accounts. By the increasing anger, depression, and desperation clear in her messages, Jody, it seemed, was ready to leave San Francisco. Lance painted a rosy picture for their future together, dispelling Jody's thoughts of doing something rash. When she assured him she was ready to leave, Lance set his plans in motion to rendezvous with her.

Chapter Seventeen

Back on *Icarus* in the San Francisco Bay, Nick stood at the helm on a rhumb line for Yerba Buena Island. He felt a knot in his stomach. It would be his last sail on the boat before he turned it over to the creditors, the last asset they would seize. It was a reflective last cruise with Jim.

His friends had rallied when they heard Nick would lose the boat. Katherine knew how much *Icarus* meant to him. Nick had taught her how to sail on that boat. She offered to buy *Icarus* and keep it until he was back on his feet. Jim had made the same offer. Nick declined both. He knew the boat would be a burden. It required constant maintenance and attention.

"Don't be attached to things," his father had once told him. "Nothing is permanent. *Icarus* could hit a reef and break up, propelled by a storm or too much rum."

Too much rum was his father's way of saying "poor judgment."

Deciding to stay inside the San Francisco Bay, they cast off, motored out of the marina, turned right and headed south. They passed Alcatraz then Yerba Buena Island and sailed under the Bay Bridge. Continuing south, Nick was determined to take one last tour of the bay. It was a clear morning and when they sailed past San Francisco International Airport, they watched the planes drop their landing gear at the San Mateo Bridge, a waypoint for inbound planes called the outer marker. They sailed as far south as the channel to Pete's Harbor in Redwood City before they turned around and sailed north under both bridges and along the east side of the bay. They timed their trip to arrive in Tiburon for lunch at Sam's Anchor Café. *Icarus* was too long to fit at the dock at Sam's, so they tied up to a mooring buoy and hailed a passing boat to pick them up. Sam's has been around since the 1920s, and Nick had been going there all of his life. It seemed like a fitting place to say goodbye to *Icarus*. Nick and Jim tried to make light of it, but the event weighed heavily on both of them.

DURING LUNCH THEY TOLD STORIES ABOUT ADVENTURES on the boat. Nick told of the time he and his parents had sailed to Los Angeles and joined the other boats in the Transpacific Yacht Race to Hawaii. *Icarus* was too heavy and slow to be a true competitor in the Transpac, but they had a fine downwind sail with the rest of the boats in her class. All the same, it was a relief to see the outline of Diamond Head Crater on Oahu, which signified the end of the race.

Once in Hawaii they spent the rest of the summer sailing around the islands. They sailed across the Molokai Channel on a smooth day and pulled up to the pier at Kaunakakai Harbor on the island of Molokai to meet with other Transpac boats also cruising the islands.

Nick noticed a stanchion on the starboard side was loose

and he set about repairing it. He was squatting down examining the mounting plate when his father walked by and bumped him. When Nick teetered, his father reached out to steady him and doing so, lost his balance as well. Nick fell over the side with his father close behind. They both came up laughing.

Nick's mother, hearing the splash, came up from below to investigate.

"What are you two doing in the water?"

"I'm helping Nick secure the stanchion," Nick's father replied.

"From there? Here, let me give you a hand up," she said, reaching her hand to him.

Nick's father reached up to grab her hand and then hoisted his leg up to the rail. The movement and the shift in weight caused her to lose her balance. From the water Nick could see the inevitable and his mother joined them in the harbor.

The crew from a nearby boat shook their heads at the laughing family in the water. One of them took a picture and sent it to them later.

THE STORIES NICK AND JIM TOLD TOOK THEM AWAY FROM the thoughts of losing *Icarus*, but that reprieve was short-lived. They sat on the deck of Sam's eating lunch and looking at the boat while they talked. They spent hours at the table, both wanting to delay their departure. A seagull squawked from a nearby piling as the waiter approached and informed them that there were others waiting for the table. Jim insisted on paying the bill. At the dock they waited for a boat to leave so they could catch a ride back to *Icarus*.

Nick pulled the boat into the slip for the last time. Then Nick and Jim did what they always did after a sail; they stowed the gear away. Nick had taken all of his personal belongings off the boat the previous day and it was ready to sail and show to potential buyers. On the way to Jim's car, Nick stopped by the harbormaster's office to drop off the keys to the boat. He held the keys for a moment, looking at the sculptured figure on the fob. He considered taking the fob off the chain, keeping it as a memento. No, he thought, it belongs with the boat; it is part of its history. With a sorrow deeper than he had ever felt, he handed the keys for *Icarus* to Cliff.

"Thanks for letting me stay on board, it helped me out of a jam."

"Well, let's not talk about that," Cliff said, taking the keys from Nick. "It's a real shame you can't keep her. It's been a real honor to have known you, your father and mother, and your grandfather. I hope the new owner shows the respect for the old girl that your family did," Cliff said reaching out his hand to Nick's.

"I hope so too," Nick said, shaking his hand.

THE NEXT MORNING NICK GRABBED HIS DAY PACK AND IN Lance's car drove north across the Golden Gate Bridge past Sausalito and Mill Valley. His destination was Muir Woods at the base of Mount Tamalpais. The forest air was clean and should have been revitalizing, but he remained unaware of the trees, the clear streams, and the crayfish in the shallows. He breathed deeply, taking no notice of the fresh, earthy scent of the forest. The day was clear and bright, but a deep fog had settled within him. He sat down on a rock under a huge Coastal Redwood and pulled a sketchbook and pen from his day pack. He sketched a fern growing out of a rock, but he had a hard time focusing on the drawing. His cash reserves were gone; he had no idea what to do next. He had three dollars and twenty-three cents in his pocket.

That afternoon, Nick walked into the office of his attorney and accountant and was escorted to an empty conference room by a secretary who offered him coffee or water and then closed the heavy wood doors. The doors blocked the sounds of the outer office and the room was silent. He stood looking out the window at the Bay Bridge and Alcatraz. He could see a grouping of sailboats racing in "The Slot" between Alcatraz and Angel Island, where the winds slam through the Golden Gate Bridge all the way to Berkeley. They were heading for a race mark to the north. He turned back to the room to face an enormous walnut table with high leather chairs. He thought about the decisions that were made there. They were probably big money decisions, he thought; whether they were important was something entirely different.

The door opened and Nick's accountant and his attorney walked in, the attorney wearing a three-piece pinstripe suit, a French cuffed shirt with initials on the sleeves, and a $200 silk tie. His wingtips were polished to a high shine. His cufflinks sported the crest of the Boalt School of Law. The accountant was dressed like a college professor: jeans, corduroy jacket with leather patches at the elbows, plaid shirt. He was, in fact, a retired college professor, tired of being told he spent too much time teaching and not enough publishing. He had finally sold out of academia for double the salary.

They gathered at the huge walnut table.

Nick broke the silence. "Okay, gentlemen. Let's finish this. What's the bottom line?" He paused, "After you both take your fees, of course."

The attorney scoffed. Nick's eyes narrowed. There were

few things he disliked more than a mocking tone, less so from someone whom he had already paid a great deal of money. Nick figured that now he was poor, his attorney could treat him that way. He was learning a lot about the people that surrounded him.

The attorney and accountant exchanged glances.

"Based on the inventory we've taken of your homes and what's left of the rest, we do have a number," the accountant said.

"Okay, how much do I owe?"

"Oh, you won't owe a thing. We've been busy negotiating with your creditors on your behalf. Since you were the victim of an embezzlement situation, they've been understanding. As you know, you did not have to declare bankruptcy. Your willingness to liquidate your holdings, while futile, did not go unnoticed. All of your creditors have been willing to settle," the attorney added.

"So where do I stand?"

"Both of your homes have appreciated, especially the one in Tahoe. The flat in Pacific Heights and the aircraft did well. Because of the appreciation of your holdings, you broke even."

"I broke even?"

"Well, if you walk out of here with just the clothes on your back, and I mean that almost literally, you can leave with $1,275.37," the accountant said, without a glance at his notes.

"Twelve hundred and seventy-five dollars?" Nick asked.

"Twelve hundred and seventy-five dollars and thirty-seven cents," the accountant repeated. "You will be locked out of your house, which is pending sale."

Nick wasn't an idiot. They were throwing him a bone, a small bone, hoping he would just go away. They had bled the rest of his holdings in legal fees. His father, if he were still alive, would be furious and be threatening disbarment.

Nick knew a protest and audit would show the true numbers, but a fight would take money. They had all the control and he had none. He gritted his teeth, took a breath, and pulled a fountain pen from his pocket.

The attorney leaned forward, licking his lips. He slid two pieces of paper toward Nick.

"These will give us the power to liquidate your holdings and retain our fees."

Nick scanned the pages and signed on the X.

"Also initial here, please." He did so.

"We will need your house keys, I'm afraid," the attorney said.

Nick set his keys on the table. "Lance's wife Katherine has offered to let me use her address. You can send any correspondence there," Nick said.

"Okay," the attorney said, handing Nick a thick white envelope with the law firm's name printed on it. Nick slid his finger under the flap; it was full of cash and a few coins. He glanced up at the attorney, meeting his eyes.

"If you wouldn't mind signing the receipt in the envelope...."

Nick signed the receipt and slid it across the table.

"It isn't as bad as it could be. You are not in debt and you didn't have to declare personal bankruptcy," the attorney said.

The accountant winced and turned away.

"That's true, but I lost my wife, my inheritance, my house, cars, and my company," Nick replied.

"What are you going to do now?" the attorney asked. The accountant again looked pained.

"I'll think of something," Nick replied.

When Nick had left the room, the accountant turned to the attorney and asked, "How did you know he would take the deal?"

"It was the only sensible option. Nick Thomas has always struck me as a sensible man," the attorney replied.

"And you gave him no choice," the accountant said.

"There is that."

Nick walked out of the plush law offices and onto busy Market Street. He looked to the right and left, turned and headed up Powell Street toward Union Square. It was a crisp, clear San Francisco afternoon and the sun was shining brightly. He walked a few paces and entered a coffee house, ordering an espresso. Sitting at an outside table, he watched people scurry by. The realization hit him: he had nowhere to go—nothing to do. Nick had dissolved the company and dismissed the staff. He had been so busy trying to save first the company and then himself, he had not considered what he would do. He thought back to Jim asking him if he had made any plans. He had not, and now he had nowhere to be and nowhere to go. He had no reason to rush. He sat there trying to enjoy the warm drink and the bustle of the city, watching the people scurry by, always in a hurry to get somewhere.

He laughed to himself. He was a free man; no job, no wife, no home, and $1,275.37–minus the cost of the coffee.

What I need to do is get out of the city, get far away and regroup, clear my head. A cold breeze shot through a gap in the buildings and he shivered. Someplace warm, he thought. He looked at his empty cup and then up and down the street. He saw a tailor's shop, fast food places, a café, and Discount Travel.

He grabbed his day pack and headed up the street. As he walked he saw a homeless man sitting against the wall of a building ahead of him, filthy and unshaven with an expression of tired acceptance of his position. Nick recognized the guy, had often seen him near his stop on the cable car and had watched his decline from panhandling dressed in coat and tie to the rags he now wore. Nick slowed and reached back into his day pack to pull out the envelope with the cash. He stopped and handed the man a bill. The man's eyes lit up when he saw the $100 note. It was close to 10% of Nick's current net worth.

"Thanks," the man stammered.

"I hope it helps," Nick said.

Nick continued down the street thinking to himself, *if I don't figure out something fast, I could end up like that guy.*

He reached the door for Discount Travel. "Last Minute Travel our Specialty" the sign on the door proclaimed. He checked his watch—5:50 p.m. Another sign on the door said the business hours were 10:00 a.m. to 6:00 p.m. As he entered the bell on the door alerted the woman at a desk.

"I'm about to close," she said.

"I'll be quick."

"Okay."

"What do you have in warm places?"

"We have Hawaii and Mexico."

"Anything more exotic?" Nick asked, looking at a poster on the wall behind her. It was a deserted beach with a boat pulled up on shore, palm trees casting a web-like shadow on the sand.

"How about the South Pacific? Tahiti, Fiji?"

Nick glanced around the office. There was a faded poster of a beautiful Polynesian woman on the wall to his left. It was labeled Miss Tahiti 1997.

"Tahiti sounds good. How soon can I leave?"

She laughed, "Well, I just had a cancellation on a flight

out of SFO at midnight tonight." She mentioned a figure. "It's a great deal. The fare is heavily discounted right now."

Nick thought about it. "Why not?"

"Huh?"

"Sounds great, I'll take it."

"You'll take it?"

"Yes, is cash okay? It's all I have." He reached for the envelope in his day pack.

"Yeah, okay." Shaking her head, she typed into the terminal.

"You do have a passport?" she asked.

"Yes, it's current," he said, pulling it out of his backpack.

"How about a return date?"

"Make it a year from now."

She raised her eyebrows. "A tourist visa to French Polynesia is good for one month, renewable for two more months when you arrive."

"Okay, one month then."

She typed away and the printer next to her spat out papers by her right knee.

"Any hotel or car?"

"No, I guess I'll figure that out when I get there."

"O-kaaaay," she said, drawing it out. "Is there anything else I can do for you?"

"That should do it."

He walked outside and pulled out his pre-paid mobile phone. Before he dialed, he noticed he was almost out of minutes. Jim answered and Nick told him his plans.

"Tahiti?" was Jim's response.

"I need a break; I need to clear my head."

"Well that ought to do it. When are you coming back? You are planning to come back, right?" Jim was surprised at

Nick's announcement, but had to admit, the idea appealed to him.

"I'm not sure of any of that."

"Well, I've got to run. I'm meeting Maggie's parents for dinner. Send me a post card."

"I will."

They hung up and Nick dialed one more number with the few minutes he had left on his phone.

"TAHITI?"

"That's just how Jim reacted when I told him. Why shouldn't I go? I need a vacation."

"Okay, you need a break. But Tahiti?"

"Option C," Nick said.

Nick and Katherine were sitting in a bar at San Francisco International Airport later that night and the terminal was bustling with travelers. The airport lounge could have been a nice bar anywhere in San Francisco with brass and wood and subdued lighting. From their booth Nick and Katherine looked at the tarmac through tinted windows.

"This is your 'Option C?' But you're broke." Katherine said, grabbing the check for the drinks.

"Just about." Nick thought about the envelope in his day pack.

Katherine reached into her purse and pulled out her wallet. Nick put his hand on hers. A quiver and a memory coursed through her.

"Absolutely not. Katherine, you're letting me use your address. That's enough."

"But what are you going to do? Do you have a place to stay?"

"I'll sleep on the beach or something. I don't know, I'll figure that out when I get there."

"Really, Nick."

"I'll make you a deal. If I get into trouble and need money, I'll let you know."

Katherine pouted. "I feel partly responsible. He was my husband after all. I feel bad about the whole situation."

"It wasn't your fault. I sincerely believe that, and you should, too. You need to move on as well."

Katherine looked around the bar. A woman walked by wearing a well-cut black business suit with a silver blouse. She had on a bowler hat and five-inch black and white platform shoes. Stainless steel spikes shot out of each nostril. Her eyes were hidden behind large white sunglasses with leopard-spotted frames. Katherine wondered how she would get through security.

"Well, you always did like islands. I suppose you're right. Perhaps I should go on a vacation as well."

"Maybe one of us will run into Lance," Nick said.

Katherine rolled her eyes. They broke out laughing.

"What about the FBI?" Katherine asked. "Detective Mitchell has been to see me. Quite often, in fact."

"As far as I'm concerned, this is over. They can chase Lance all across the planet if they wish."

"Won't it seem suspicious, leaving the country?"

"They can chase me all across the planet as well—at least to Tahiti."

Chapter Eighteen

After delivering the divorce papers to Nick, Jody took a cab to the airport where she dropped her suitcases in the baggage storage. Then she took BART under the bay to Berkeley, exited the train, walked up Shattuck Avenue and turned down a side street. She was snaking around behind a hair salon that fronted the avenue. Jody found the alley she was searching for and walked to the door at the back. She pushed the intercom button and waited, tapping her foot and peering around the dingy space, noticing a camera on the wall pointing down at her.

The intercom buzzed and a disembodied voice came across the small speaker.

"Yes?"

"I'm Jody. I have an appointment."

"No names, dear. Please come in."

The door opened and a face poked out.

Once inside, Jody scrutinized the woman. She looked like Jody's grandmother—gray hair, eyeglasses, conservative clothes. The woman bolted the door behind them and gestured for Jody to follow her.

"You can call me Lana."

In the cavernous basement there was a hair cutting area and a lighted make-up station. Racks of clothes of every color, size, and style imaginable hung along the wall. The salon fronted for an underground railroad for women wanting to escape their lives. The basement was a factory to change the appearance of a woman, the first step in disappearing. They asked no questions and only asked for whatever the person could afford. The clothes were donated and picked up from local charities.

"Now dear, why don't you sit down and tell me a little about who you would like to be."

Lana listened, asked questions about Jody's abilities, where she thought she would end up in her relocation.

"Europe? Do you speak any languages?" Lana asked.

"My French is still fluent. My Spanish is not as good."

To Jody's amusement, Lana continued their conversation in French.

Jody walked into the alley dressed like an upper-class brunette San Francisco woman of leisure. She walked out a hip, chic European-dressed blonde.

From there she walked further up Shattuck Avenue and turned down a street. She checked the numbers, found the apartment building, and pushed the button for apartment "E".

"Yes?" came a disembodied voice.

"Uh, Merek sent me?"

"Okay, come on up." The door buzzed. Jody entered and climbed to the fourth floor. She was greeted by a twenty-year-old computer science major from UC Berkeley. "The Changer" was an expert in graphic design and computer hacking. He belonged to a tightly controlled and secret network. He could, through the network, get a passport for almost any country in the world, the European Union, even the biometric passports with electronic chips. He could build an identity with an address, credit and family history, and health records, and even sprinkle the internet with the person's information if needed. The apartment was spartan, containing a desk, a chair, a laptop, printer and few other tools for assembling a passport. A suitcase stood off to one side. It was clear to Jody that the Changer would disappear as soon as he finished with her.

Jody Thomas walked out of Apartment E with a prepaid mobile phone, credit card, laptop computer loaded with e-mail, a European Union passport, and a first class airline ticket to London, all in the name of Antoinette Duval of Lyon, France.

A BEARDED LANCE SAT IN A RENTED SLING-BACK CHAIR on a knoll overlooking a field of tulips. A wide-brimmed black hat and tinted glasses obscured his identity. He had read that London had nearly two million cameras observing the city. After a month of lying low in Scotland, he wanted to complete his final goal of meeting Jody. He also had to admit to himself, he enjoyed being with her and wanted to see her again.

He had made his way to London on the train, having checked out of his flat in Edinburgh. It was a gray winter day in London's Hyde Park, but the English made their gardens look good in the winter. He watched a couple walking their dog. The man looked a lot like Nick. Lance considered what he had done to Nick, who probably didn't deserve it, but someone had to lose. Lance wasn't going to live the rest of his life taking handouts and he didn't want to live off his wife's money, even if he could. It was doled out like a teenager's allowance from the trust fund. He knew he could have had it all himself if he had just waited for the company to mature, but he wanted more. He wanted to be the admired one, the one who could share his toys and houses and yachts and planes with others. He wanted to be the hero, the good guy, the guy with it all. The thought of it made him excited. There was one final piece to be moved before the game would be finished.

An audience began to gather at Speakers' Corner. A man was standing atop a wooden crate expounding on the virtues of honest living and the sin of greed. Lance listened for a while and shook his head. This guy has obviously never had anything worthwhile, he thought.

His mobile phone vibrated in his pocket. It was an automated text message; Jody's plane would arrive soon at Heathrow. He would watch her from a distance for a few days and determine if she was being followed. He knew the risks involved and he had thought long and hard whether he should connect with her, or just walk away, leave all of his old life behind. He was torn between leaving and completing what he started, having everything Nick had. That, of course, included his wife. Lance realized that Nick might never know of their affair. To Lance it didn't matter; he had satisfaction in knowing he had won.

He walked up and put a hundred pound note on top of the crate the man was standing on. The man looked down and his eyes lit up at the amount of the bill then glanced around at the people listening. He put his foot on the note to keep if from blowing away in the winter breeze. He smiled down at Lance from his perch. Lance smiled back, turned, gave a small bow to the crowd, and left.

Several days later, Lance was sitting in the American Bar off the lobby of The Savoy Hotel on The Strand in London. His drink was on the little black and chrome table in front of him. He was drinking the "Cocktail of the Month," a sweet concoction of fruit juice and a South American liqueur. The £11 drink was nauseating. Eleven pounds for a cocktail! It's good to be a millionaire, he thought.

It was going on seven in the evening and the jazz musicians were assembling in the art déco bar. He looked around at the sports paraphernalia and realized that he had gravitated toward the familiar, an expatriate bar in a foreign city. Or was it that American culture was all prevailing? He chose The Savoy because he had heard of it all his life and always wanted to stay there. The American Bar just happened to be in the hotel, at least that's what he told himself. He checked his wristwatch, stood and walked out to the lobby and onto the street. A black London taxi pulled up in front of him. The door opened and the occupant handed shopping bags out of the taxi to the doorman. They were bags from designers, seven all together, and high-end designers at that.

A shapely leg appeared from the taxi and Lance leaned forward and offered his hand.

Jody popped out of the taxi and did a double take. "Oh hi, Lance. I didn't recognize you with a beard and sunglasses and a hat. I did some shopping," she said, giving him a kiss on the cheek.

He glanced at the doorman holding the pile of packages. He leaned forward and whispered, "Kyle. It's Kyle, Jody. And that's the last time I call you Jody, Antoinette."

"Oh right, Kyle. I forgot. I love the beard." She gave it a tug, put her arm through his and walked into the hotel. "I just love London. Nick and I met here, you know."

Chapter Nineteen

One Thursday night when Nick was in France during his junior year in college, he decided that he needed a break from the bustle of Paris, so he boarded the train and rode under the English Channel and into the bustle of London. It was Easter weekend and he had four full days to explore the city. He dropped his bags at a hotel in Knightsbridge and set out on a rainy walk around the town. He found himself in front of Harrods. To his mother, Harrods was a shopping Mecca. Nick ducked into the store and out of the rain to see if he could find her a gift. To him, the place had always been overwhelming. He wasn't much of a shopper. With directions he made his way to the women's accessories department. With the help of a friendly sales clerk he found a simple hair clip with pearls, a present he knew his mother would enjoy. He had it gift-wrapped and looked for a place for dinner.

"Do you still have restaurants in the store?" he asked a uniformed security guard standing at the edge of the department.

"Of course, Sir. We have many places to dine. What are you hungry for?"

"Oh, something not too fussy. I arrived from France this afternoon. Something not French would be nice."

The man smiled at Nick. "I'm sure you will find something here at Harrods." He reached into his pocket and pulled out a brochure and handed it to Nick. "Here is a list of the restaurants we have and their descriptions."

"Thank you."

The guard touched his cap and walked away.

Nick leaned against the wall and perused the brochure.

"They are so darn polite here, don't you think?" said an American voice to his left.

Nick turned to the woman. She was pretty and had a feisty little smirk.

"You're American," he said.

"Well so are you. I heard you just got in from France. Me, too. Were you touring or on business?"

"I'm going to school in Paris for the year."

"You are? I'm spending the year in Lyon. Want to grab a bite?"

"I do. My name is Nick."

She grabbed his hand. "I'm Jody. Come on, I know a place down the road that makes a great curry." She pulled him toward the door. Nick waved as Jody dragged him past the guard.

"*Au revoir*," called the guard as they headed out into the rainy London night.

An hour later they were sitting in Haandi, a North Indian restaurant close to Harrods. Nick was sipping a glass of Kingfisher beer.

"I have to say, that was one of the finest meals I have ever had, Indian or otherwise. You made a great choice."

Jody beamed at the compliment. "I love Indian food. It's nice to share my find with someone."

THE NEXT DAY NICK MET JODY AT HER HOTEL IN Victoria. Nick took one glance at the room and offered the other bed in his own hotel. She cocked her head and looked at him. It was an expensive trip for her and the place was a dump, but she didn't want to appear easy.

"Are you going to be good?"

"Scout's honor," he said, holding up three fingers.

"You were a Boy Scout?"

"Well, yes."

"Were you an Eagle Scout?" Jody asked with a twinkle in her eye.

"No. I just earned the merit badges my father wanted me to. You know, I learned how to tie a knot, cook, not get lost, read the night sky, amputate a leg. Things like that. It was good, but I didn't want to make a career of it."

"Well I suppose I can trust a Boy Scout," she said. "Just go easy on the knots."

Nick and Jody spent the rest of the weekend showing each other what they knew about London and learning about each other. Jody grew up in Los Angeles, her parents both in some form of the entertainment business. She was studying communications at UCLA.

By Sunday night they were sharing the same bed. Monday afternoon they were sitting in rented sling-back chairs in Hyde Park. The sun was struggling to come out, but they were bundled up and keeping warm, holding hands.

"It's about 500 kilometers from Lyon to Paris," Jody said.

"That sounds about right, a two-hour train ride."

"You checked?"

"Of course. I want to see you again, too." I like this girl, Nick thought. She has a strong spirit.

THAT FOLLOWING SUNDAY THEY TOOK THE EARLY afternoon train to Paris where Nick showed Jody his apartment. Jody's eyes got big when she saw how nice it was.

"This must cost a fortune." Jody walked around, poking her head into each of the rooms. "You have two bedrooms?"

"My parents insisted," Nick said. "They need somewhere to stay when they visit, so they rented this place for a year."

"They must be loaded," she said. "You don't have a problem having your parents stay with you?"

"We get along well. When you can get my dad out of his office, he's a lot of fun. My mom has a great sense of humor. No, we all get along well, with the occasional lapse into the parent/child thing. They had me later in life; maybe that mellowed them."

"You're lucky. I'd jump in the Seine if my parents came to stay with me."

Jody spent that night and took the early morning train to Lyon, just getting to her class on time. They saw each other on weekends and e-mailing or calling during the week. One of them would leave on the train on Friday afternoon and return early Monday morning for classes.

A month later Nick's parents arrived for a visit. By then they had realized Nick and Kathy were no longer an item and Nick had prepared them to meet Jody.

Jody was a nervous wreck. She fretted about what to wear, her makeup, and even her diction.

"You don't need to worry. They won't bite."

"What if they don't like me? You said they practically had you married-off before you left for France."

"They'll like you fine. Just be yourself."

"Where will I sleep?" Jody asked.

"Sleep in my bed as you have been. My parents aren't stupid. It will just make it awkward if I sleep on the couch and give you my room. And we won't be fooling anyone," Nick said.

"I can be incredibly sarcastic, you know."

"My mom will love it. She likes a sparring partner."

His parents arrived the following afternoon and his mother realized Jody's discomfort. Nick's father, as usual, was oblivious but cordial.

"I think we girls need to have a day in the city to ourselves," Nick's mom announced at the breakfast table the morning after they arrived. "You boys talk boy talk. I've hired a car and driver for Jody and me. Come Jody, let's see what Paris has to offer."

The women left after breakfast leaving Nick and his father sitting on the balcony with a view of Paris and the Eiffel Tower in the distance. At his feet his father had a stack of Wall Street Journals he'd carried across the Atlantic to catch up on his reading. Nick was working on a school assignment on his laptop. They shared a comfortable silence between them with not much more than pages turning and keyboard clicks and the sounds of Paris below them.

"Jody seems nice," his father said.

"I like her."

"She's not at all like Kathy."

"True. They come from different worlds."

"Did we push too hard?" Nick's father set down his paper and turned to Nick.

"A bit."

"Your mother was excited about you and Kathy. I think it was Kathy's mother who started her off. The situation kind of took on a life of its own. Your mother and I just want you to be happy. We trust your judgment."

It was a rare exchange with his father.

"Thanks, Dad. That means a lot to me."

His father patted him on the knee and reached down to pick up a newspaper. Nick looked at him for a moment and returned to his laptop.

Later that evening Nick had finished his schoolwork and his father was waking up from a nap when the women returned. They came into the apartment, their arms full of shopping bags. Jody looked like a different person. Not only were her clothes new and different, she was smiling and animated.

"We had such a great time," she announced to the room. "I have to show you what your mother bought me. Your mom is great." She ran off into the bedroom with her bags.

Nick walked to his mother and planted a kiss on her cheek. "Thanks, mom."

"You have a real live wire there. I like her. She's bright and funny, and she's nearly as sarcastic as I am."

NICK AND JODY DATED FOR THE NEXT FEW YEARS. HE went to school at Berkeley and she at UCLA. There was a lot of driving on Highway 5. It was a six-hour trip, with the hardest part getting through LA traffic. Once Jody saw Nick's family's home, she was happy to make the drive North, and she always wanted to stay with Nick's parents in San Francisco. Nick tried to introduce her to all that was strange and wonderful about Berkeley: the food, the shops, Telegraph Avenue still stuck in the 1960s. It didn't thrill her. Nick would take BART across the Bay and meet her at his parents' home on Friday afternoon. His parents loved the company, but Nick felt that Jody was more into the lifestyle than being with him. She was excited about the parties, the charity events, and the clubs. They were things that Nick had endured for his parents, but nothing he wanted to spend his life doing. By the beginning of their senior year, Jody seemed to spend more time with Nick's mother than with him. Nick's mother enjoyed the company; Nick was having second thoughts about Jody.

It was near the end of their senior year that Jody dropped the bomb.

"I'm pregnant," she said. She had wanted to meet Nick at his apartment in Berkeley and now he knew why.

"I assume you're sure about that," Nick said trying to control his breathing.

"I took a couple of drugstore pregnancy tests and then went to the clinic at school. I'm about two months along."

A car horn blasted outside the apartment. It continued for almost ten seconds.

"I want to have the baby, Nick," Jody said.

Nick thought about how fast life can change. He closed his eyes for a moment. When he opened them again he looked at Jody and said, "Will you marry me?"

"Of course I will," she said jumping up and giving him a hug and a kiss. "Now let's go tell your parents."

The couple returned to school the next Monday and finished college that semester. In June, Jody and Nick moved in to Nick's parents' house. She and Nick's mother handled all the arrangements. Nick was sharing a room with Jody but seeing less and less of her. Their plan was to find a place to live when they returned from their honeymoon.

Nick stayed out of the way of the wedding plans. He was still in a daze and feeling out of control. Willie, Nick's closest friend had moved to Japan and couldn't make it back for the wedding, so Nick asked Lance to be his best man. Lance rented a car and driver for the night and they hit the hot spots of the city for Nick's bachelor party. When Lance and Nick's other college friends showed up to collect Nick, Nick's father came out to the car and handed Lance an envelope.

"You men go out and have a good time. It's on me."

Lance peeked inside the envelope, and when he saw a stack of one hundred dollar bills, he exhaled in relief. He was, after all, still a college student.

"Thanks, Mr. Thomas," he said.

They avoided the raunchiness of North Beach and had a spectacular Italian meal at SPQR followed by a tour of the finer bars in the city. They drank at Rye, Sip Bar and Lounge, and Bourbon and Branch, and finished the evening by closing down Smugglers Cove, known for having more than 400 rums, many of them rare.

Lance enjoyed showing off to Nick his knowledge of the finer spots in San Francisco. It turned out to be a fine night, not forced like many bachelor parties tend to be. The mood was a good one and there were no strippers and no shouting drunks being ejected from bars. Still, the next day Nick was feeling raw from the previous night. He, Jody, and his parents were sitting at home in the parlor having evening cocktails. Jody and Nick were sipping water.

Nick's father cleared his throat. "Margaret and I have an offer for you."

"What is it, Dad?"

"Well, this house is too big for us. You will be having a

family soon, and we would like you to have it. We found a smaller place a few blocks away that we will be moving to."

"Wow," Jody said, surveying the room.

"That's incredibly generous, Dad." Nick turned to his mother, "You too, Mom."

"It was your father's idea. We talked about it and it seemed the right thing for all of us."

"There are certain tax advantages if we give you the house this year," Nick's father said.

Nick's mother rolled her eyes. "We would like you two to have it," she said.

It was a July wedding on a mid-week evening at the Palace of the Legion of Honor at Lands End, on the northwestern tip of San Francisco. Nick's mother was on the board of directors and pulled strings to make it happen. She even scared up 300 people for the event. A judge, a friend of the family, married them.

The couple spent their honeymoon in Santorini where they chartered a sailboat to explore the nearby islands. It was a nice trip and the wedding had gone off without a hitch. Despite his misgivings, Nick became caught up in the festivities. Now standing at the helm of a sailboat in the clear blue Aegean, he was even getting used to the idea of being a father at twenty-one years old.

They were off the coast of Santorini when Jody appeared in the companionway.

"Nick, I don't feel well."

"I'll have you take the wheel. It's the best way to get over seasickness."

Jody grabbed her abdomen and moaned.

Nick studied her ashen face. “You’re in pain.”

“A lot of pain. I’m nauseated and I’m bleeding, Nick.”

“Bleeding? Oh. Okay, sit down here.” He gestured to the bench beside him. When she was settled, he started the engine and set the wheel toward the mainland. In the cabin he put on headphones and using the radio, was patched through to the hospital in nearby Fira. He told the physician on duty about Jody’s symptoms and that she was pregnant.

“What is your location?” the doctor asked in perfect English.

Nick gave him his coordinates.

“Please hold for a moment.” Nick could hear talking in the background.

“You can get to us faster than we can get to you. Can you make for the harbor at Fira?”

“Nick checked the GPS and dialed in the port. “Yes, we can make Fira.”

“Good,” said the doctor. “Call us back when you get close. There will be attendants with an ambulance waiting for you when you dock.”

“I will,” Nick said.

“This is a common occurrence and your wife is probably not in any danger. Keep her comfortable. We will see you soon.”

Nick kept the RPMs on the diesel engine high as they made their way back to the island. He held Jody’s hand while he drove.

“I’m having a miscarriage, aren’t I?”

“It seems like it. The doctor says you’ll be okay. Just try to stay comfortable. Let me know what I can do to help.”

“I’m sorry, Nick.”

“Me too.”

The port was hard to miss with the whitewashed homes

clinging to the side of Caldera Cliffs. Nick pulled into the little port about two hours after calling the hospital. The waiting ambulance took them up the winding hill, dodging the tourists on donkeys. It was slow going and the driver hung out the window pleading with people to get out of the way. With Nick beside her, Jody looked out at the people passing by in the cable railway that climbed the mountain.

Back in San Francisco Nick's mother greeted them at the door. She gave Jody a hug. "You can try again later, dear."

Jody never became pregnant again.

Chapter Twenty

Lance and Jody were "shacked up at the Savoy," as she called it, and had been ordering room service. There was a stack of unread newspapers in a pile by the hotel room door. The condition of the room was much like the one in New York: clothes on the furniture, empty champagne bottles and room service plates on trays.

"I feel like John and Yoko at the Amsterdam Hilton," Lance said. "Maybe we should invite the press in, give an interview."

"Aren't you a little young for that reference? I know I am."

"I had a roommate in college who was a Beatles fanatic. One of his favorite songs was 'The Ballad of John and Yoko'. Why do you know it?"

"My parents, also Beatles fans."

It had only been two days they had been encamped at the hotel and he had to admit, it was much better than he had any idea it would be. It was a lot more enjoyable living in the lap of luxury with someone than going it alone, and Jody was a lot of fun to be with.

"The main difference is John and Yoko were famous and

not on the run from the law," Lance mused.

Jody sat up and threw off the covers, walked naked to the window, pulled open a curtain and peered out. "Well, I'm ready to properly see London." The spell of the Savoy had been broken and the light of the outside world flooded in.

They toured London and had a good time, although Lance soon grew tired of Jody's favorite pastime of shopping. The hotel room filled with bags, and Jody had housekeeping bring in a wheeled rack to hold all of her new clothes. Then there were the shoes; there were boxes of shoes spread across the room.

After a week at the Savoy Lance was getting antsy and needed to move. He knew the hotel was a crazy spot to be staying and that having Jody with him was a bad idea. He knew it could not last with her; it increased the chances of him being found.

Later that week, Jody and Lance were sitting at a table at a restaurant in the Earl's Court district of London.

Jody took a mobile phone out of her purse and set it on the table beside her plate.

"That's your old phone, what are you still doing with that?" Lance asked.

"I love this phone and it works great here."

"You made calls with it?"

"Sure. I called you, I called the hotel, I called you on your mobile."

"Damn."

"What's the matter?"

"The authorities are looking for me, and because you have disappeared, they are probably looking for you. Now they know you are in London. They will connect me to you and us to the hotel, if they haven't already."

"Oh." Jody looked at her phone. "So what do we do now?"

"We can't take any chances. We move, and we move now." He stood up. "I'm going to get my things and check out; you do the same. Tell the front desk you are going to Hamburg to the Kempinski Hotel Atlantic."

"Hamburg? I don't want to go to Hamburg."

"We're not going to Hamburg, we're saying we're going to Hamburg. We'll even buy tickets to Hamburg. We are going to Milan."

"Milan? There's great shopping there."

"And give me your phone. You can buy another one later." She pouted and handed him the phone.

"You can finish your shopping. Meet me back at the hotel..." Lance looked at his watch, "at two. We are leaving London on the first flight we can get."

"Can't we stay longer? I just got here."

"That's not going to happen. I told you the rules. You ignored them and left a trail a blind man could follow. Meet me in the lobby in two hours. I have arrangements to make."

When she was gone, he walked to a pay phone and dialed a London number. Then he got into a cab and headed to the Savoy. He hurried through the lobby and up to the room. The hotel room still looked like a dressing room in an expensive boutique, but he had kept his things organized. He filled his leather carry-on, scanned the room and left. He didn't worry about fingerprints; there was nothing he could do about that.

Lance had his hat down low and sunglasses on as he passed through the lobby. At the main desk he heard a man say, "I'm looking for two Americans, have you seen either of these two?" He handed two photographs to the man behind the desk.

The man peered at the photos. "No. No one looking like that."

Lance continued out the door of the lobby and into a

black London cab. He exhaled as the driver pulled away from the curb.

“BACK SO SOON?”

Lance was in the Mayfair district of London, having his appearance changed yet again. “It’s good you left your hair a little long.”

“I just need to change enough to get on and off a plane. I need two looks, one for travel and one for living. I’ll also need two more sets of papers, for both looks,” Lance said.

“That will be expensive.”

Lance had planned for multiple identification changes, but he didn’t expect the need for a new one so soon.

I’m running out of accents, he thought. He sat in the chair, having his hair cut. Jody will take me down if I let her. She was fun, but he didn’t so much want to be with her as he liked the idea of stealing all of his best friend’s money and his wife. When Jody’s flirting with Lance became serious, he had decided he could risk taking her in on his plans—to a point. He had arranged it all for her, the new look, the new ID, her plans to disappear, and her new history and credit cards. He put $50,000 in an offshore account she could access. He was not fooling himself. Sooner or later they would part and he hoped the money would keep her happy for a while, and hopefully, silent.

Sooner or later was now; it was time to jettison the cargo.

He had bought them both tickets to Hamburg and train tickets to Milan where they were supposed to meet again.

He wouldn’t be going to Hamburg or Milan. He looked at his suitcase and travel bag leaning against the wall.

He was going somewhere else.

Part Two

BEGINNINGS

Chapter Twenty-One

As Lance was finalizing his plans to ditch Jody and get out of the UK, Nick's plane landed in Papeete. It was just after noon when he took a bus to the waterfront and sat on a bench. The day was cooler than he had expected. A breeze rustled through the palms; he thought the temperature was perfect. To his right the *Club Med II*—some eighty-plus meters of cruise liner sailing ship—was docked. Behind him cars sped by on the four lanes of Boulevard Pomare. In front of him yachts were tied stern-to, some with boards lashed from the transom to the shore as gangplanks. A slight oil slick gave off a rainbow of colors on the water.

Nick looked at the yacht crowd. There was a young family with two children on a wooden ketch named *Marley* from Johannesburg. The children, a boy and a girl, had long hair in dreadlocks. The entire family was tanned a deep brown and dressed in well-worn handmade clothes. The father was busy repairing the netting attached to the lifelines; the mother turned fish on a barbecue attached to the stern. Next to his mother, the boy sat eating a papaya, his hands and face covered in juice; the girl was playing with a headless doll.

The entire family laughed and talked back and forth, occasionally singing a lyric to the reggae music coming from the cabin.

Alongside, on *401k* hailing from Monterey, a well-preserved older couple sat sipping martinis under an awning in the cockpit. The sailboat was a clean, sleek, white fiberglass sloop; the minimal woodwork was polished, the lines neatly coiled. The couple chatted with the crew of *Marley*, all of them speaking French.

Further out in the harbor the crew of a long black yawl hoisted what appeared to be most of a Harley-Davidson motorcycle out of the aft lazarette. Moored behind them was a long Monte Carlo thing, helicopter and two tenders on the deck. Above him a three-engine business jet with HB in the tail number was on a steep climb out of Fa'a'ā Airport. It made a small turn to the northeast, heading, Nick assumed, for somewhere in North America, maybe to San Francisco.

Nick let out a deep sigh and scratched his stubbly chin. His stomach growled. He glanced over his shoulder and across the street to *L'Auvent Rouge*. It was inviting with its red awnings, red directors chairs, and red velour booths. Gaudy, but inviting. He rose and moved toward the bar. Rumpled chino trousers, faded light blue chambray shirt, a web belt, well-worn boat shoes—sans socks—he looked like any other sailor on the waterfront. The day pack on his shoulder was of tan leather and held a sketchbook and pencils, khaki short trousers, a navy blue cotton anorak, a spare pair of boxers and some toiletries, his passport, and the rest of his US dollars he had exchanged for French Polynesian francs at the airport.

DODGING TRAFFIC, NICK CROSSED BOULEVARD POMARE,

entered the restaurant and slid into one of the red velvet booths in *L'Auvent Rouge*. A white tablecloth and a frangipani blossom floating in a bowl decorated the table. With a mixture of exhaustion and excitement, he thought about what he would do next. He took what was left of the stack of bills out of the white law firm envelope and spread them on the table. The waiter approached.

"Oui, monsieur?"

"Excusez-moi. Parlez-vous Anglais, Espagnol, Allemand?"

"*Oui monsieur,* I speak English, Spanish, and German."

"Thank you. English then. My French is rusty and will be hard on your ears."

"Your pronunciation is quite passable. How may I help you?" he said, eyeing the money on the table.

"I am hungry. I am hungry and thirsty. What's the best champagne you have?"

"Many like Dom Pérignon, but I find that it tastes like dust. I believe many people buy it because it is among the most expensive of champagnes. I would recommend the Bollinger."

"I like Bollinger. Do I have enough for a bottle of that, and an excellent meal?"

The waiter scanned the notes. "*Oui, monsieur.* I believe you will not leave here hungry."

"I am in your hands then. What's your name?"

"François Pardee, *monsieur*. I am the proprietor of *L'Auvent Rouge*."

Nick stood and put out his hand. "Nicholas Thomas," he said.

"Welcome to Tahiti, Monsieur Thomas," François said, shaking his hand.

"Please call me Nick. And François—make sure you leave enough for your tip."

"We do not tip in Tahiti."

"Right. First the champagne, if you will then, François."

"*Oui*, Nick," François said with a smile and a nod. He returned with a bottle, glass, and a bucket full of ice. François placed a towel over the cork and twisted. Muffling the pop, he poured the wine into a crystal champagne glass. He crunched the bottle back into the ice bucket.

"Please take what you need," Nick said indicating the money. "I would like to pay as I go."

François raised an eyebrow and reached forward, delicately pulling a pile of bills toward him. He felt he had now seen it all in his waterfront café.

"As you wish, Nick."

"Will you join me, François?"

"I would be delighted, Nick. Perhaps later. Now, what can I get for your hunger?"

"Anything you would like to bring me would be fine. Once again, I am in your hands."

"Okay," François said, heading for the kitchen.

Nick surveyed the scene, taking a deep breath of scented Polynesian air. Papeete was like most small towns. Katherine had told him the place was a pit, but it must have come up a lot since she had been through on her honeymoon with Lance. To Nick, it seemed to be like many other coastal towns. It was bustling in the late afternoon, but *L'Auvent Rouge* was not yet busy. A couple sat eating ice cream at a sidewalk table under the red awning. The man at the panini counter attended the takeout crowd with grilled sandwiches; the bartender was polishing glasses. Nick looked at the glass in front of him and then at what was left of the pile of notes. He reached for the glass and brought it to his lips.

"To destitution," he said to himself aloud, and took a sip.

"Destitution?" François asked, appearing at his elbow. "What do you mean?"

"Poverty."

"Yes, I understand the meaning of destitution and poverty," François said. "But why toast to this? You are not a poor man." He gestured at the Rolex watch on Nick's wrist. Nick regarded the watch.

"That, too, will go, I suppose."

"And this," François said, spreading his hand above the notes on the table. "This is all you have?"

"This is it."

"Ah. *C'est magnifique.* You are at the bottom and you toast your failure with the best champagne and food. I will join you after all. Irony is not unknown to the French—or the Polynesians."

François retrieved a champagne flute from the bar, pulled up a chair and sat. Nick filled his glass.

"We have fresh shrimp I can have the chef put in a coconut curry sauce, or perhaps fresh mahi-mahi au gratin."

"Whatever you like, François, will be fine."

"To destitution," François said, lifting his glass.

"To destitution," Nick said, clinking François's glass with a perfect single chime.

THE FOOD CAME, AND NICK'S MONEY FLOWED LIKE THE champagne. It was a meal to remember: coconut shrimp; chicken curry with *fei*—the local bananas; sweet potato; fresh fish and raw vegetables marinated in lime juice and coconut cream; and braised swordfish. François joined Nick at the table whenever he wasn't going back and forth to the kitchen. The café filled with those having drinks and a bite to eat.

Nick and François laughed and drank and told stories in English and French, Nick's college French returning to him as the evening continued.

"So, tell me how you came to be spending all of your money at *L'Auvent Rouge* here in Tahiti," François asked, placing a vanilla bean *crème brûlée* in front of Nick.

Nick began his tale. He realized it would not be the last time he would do this. He got into a rhythm with the story—adding little bits of charm and humor—drawing it out. He shook his head in disgust at the best friend's treachery and applauded Nick's impulse when he bought a plane ticket to Papeete.

"So here I am, François, flat broke in paradise and determined to enjoy it," he said, concluding.

"There was no sign of Monsieur Lance?"

"No. He sent a gloating letter and disappeared."

"This is an indelicate question, but how much did he take, if I may ask?"

"A little more than thirty-two million."

"Dollars?"

"Oui."

"Thirty-two million," François whistled. He sat back and took a long reassessing look at Nick.

Nick shrugged.

François leaned forward. *"C'est fantastique!* I have heard many stories about people who have run off to Tahiti. You will be the toast of Papeete," François said, lifting his glass. Nick lost count of the number of times he and François toasted. They clinked glasses once again and finished the rest. He took the bottle and poured the last drops into François's glass, then put the bottle, neck down, into the champagne bucket.

Nick looked at the small pile of notes left on the table. He and François had been sipping the champagne, savoring each expensive drop until it was gone.

They were sitting back, Nick in the booth, François in a chair, both bloated and happy. François stifled a burp.

"François?"

"Yes, Nick?"

"I'm a bit thirsty. Do I have enough for one more drink? I still have money left."

"And I am here to help you spend it." François stood up. "I shall return, as one of your great Americans once said."

When François returned, he slid into his chair with a bottle and a smile. He lifted another bottle of Bollinger bottle onto the table.

"I don't have money for that," Nick said.

"No. No. You use what is left of your money and I'll take care of the rest."

"No, really."

"It would be an honor to buy you a drink."

"A drink, yes, but an entire bottle?"

"Do not argue, Nick. I have taken all of your money. In fact, I took the last of your thirty-two million dollars."

"Since you put it that way, François. All right. Thank you for the bottle. You will join me, of course."

"Of course," François said, pulling off the foil and popping the cork. He poured and they drank, getting mellower as the sun set.

"I like your little town of Papeete."

"You should have seen it twenty years ago."

Nick thought about that. "You always hear that, don't you? 'You should have been here twenty years ago?'"

"Think about it. Do you recall San Francisco twenty years ago? Didn't you like it more then?"

Nick sipped the champagne. "Well, there were fewer

people, less traffic. Some of the more interesting things have been torn down and replaced with others. Yes, I suppose time takes its toll."

"You see Papeete with new eyes, so this is normal for you. Twenty years ago it was a run-down port, but not without a certain charm. Now it's becoming like every other place. Cleaner, safer, but... different. Look at this place. We're sitting in a red velvet booth in the South Seas."

"I have to admit, it's not what I expected to see here."

"I hope you get out to the other islands. You will see what it was like twenty, even fifty years ago."

"I'd like that."

They talked on, the second bottle now only half-full. They were sitting a little lower in their chairs.

"So, Nick, how long will you stay in Tahiti?"

"I have a visa for a month."

"Then you will go back home?"

"Home? Oh, I don't know where I'll go." He looked out across the boulevard to the waterfront and the sailboats. The older couple were casting off, waving goodbye to the boy and girl on *Marley*. The wind had picked up and fluttered the awning outside of *L'Auvent Rouge*.

François noticed his restaurant was full. "This has been enjoyable. I must work before the dinner crowd arrives."

"I have been keeping you from your work."

"It has been a great pleasure. Please come by again," he said, shaking Nick's hand.

"I will, François."

François headed to the kitchen. At the door he stopped and looked back. He wondered what Nick would do next.

For what felt like the hundredth time, Nick looked out at the passers-by. There seemed to be no let up in the traffic.

For the first time in his life, Nick was at a loss. There was nothing left to put back in his wallet, he had no place to go, no place to be. Maybe it was the champagne, but he wasn't concerned. He didn't understand it, but he felt the need to cast off his previous life. He knew it was irrational, but there he was, broke and in a foreign country. He wanted to start fresh and on his own terms. How many people get that chance?

He grabbed his pack and the bottle, stood up, squared his shoulders, picked a champagne cork off the table, put it in his pocket, and headed out into the throng. He looked left and right and turned right onto Boulevard Pomare.

From the door to the kitchen, François watched him go. He looked forward to spending more time with his new friend.

KEEPING THE BOTTLE OUT OF SIGHT UNDER HIS JACKET, Nick walked down the Boulevard Pomare. A group of French sailors stormed by shouting with shore-leave fever. He walked until music coming from a doorway drew him to a television monitor on the wall showing a jazz band playing inside the club. It seemed the perfect place to be. Straightening himself, he strode past the bouncer at the door.

He found a chair and table off to the side of the stage and set down the half-full bottle of champagne as a waitress approached.

"Gobelet, s'il vous pla"t," Nick said, showing the bottle. It confused the waitress. How did he have a bottle without a glass? She shrugged her shoulders and left him. When she returned, she had a champagne flute and an ice bucket. She slid the bottle into the bucket with a spin, gave him a conspiratorial eyebrow raise, and left.

"Merci."

It's a good thing they don't tip in Tahiti; I would be out of luck.

He turned his attention to the band. They were rather good, he thought. A little Miles, a little Dizzy; they were playing the classics. There was a sax, a guitar, drums, and a string bass. He surveyed the club, taking in the shiny chrome ambiance of *Le Paradise*. The tables were black and stainless steel. There was a definite lack of color in the room. An image of the band was projected through the smoky haze onto the wall behind them, beaming the band into a fourth dimension. I'm in Tahiti? Nick asked himself. It was all too high tech for a tropical paradise; it was not his idea of escaping to the South Seas.

The music continued, and an hour later he felt himself grow sober. He didn't much like it; with a clear head he would think about the future. He had no money and no place to sleep. He reached forward and poured champagne into his glass. He sat through an entire set by the band which, although fine, lacked the enthusiasm suggested by their choice of music. They were fine musicians, just not inspired. He checked his watch; it was 10:30 p.m. The bottle was empty; he was nursing the final sips in the glass, surveying the crowd of nicely dressed but bored looking patrons.

THE DRUMMER TOOK UP THE FIRST BARS OF TAKE FIVE, A piece by Paul Desmond and made famous by Dave Brubeck. The song was one of Nick's favorites, but one that called for a piano. It was a difficult piece of music with a 5/4 meter. The bass player was doing his best playing the piano part, but it wasn't the same. Nick eyed the piano, sitting alone, neglected

—and the perfect instrument for the song. He did not wait until the band got to the second bar; he grabbed his bag, stood, and walked the ten feet to the stage. He stepped up to the piano, sat down on the bench and joined in. He had his back to the band and couldn't see the players' reactions, but buoyed by the strength of his playing, the saxophone playing increased in intensity. He brought up the tempo and the volume, forcing the rest of the band to follow. The drummer joined him and they played together in a duet. The patrons took notice; the rest of the band looked on. Nick and the drummer encouraged each other. The sax joined in and brought the band up a notch; Nick's influence was taking hold. When the song was over, the crowd was on its feet, applauding. This is what they had come to hear. Nick started with another Brubeck number, "Blue Rondo a la Turk", a piece with an upbeat beginning. The bass and drummer came in next, followed by the saxophone.

Noting the expanding audience, Alain Marchand, the club owner, told the waitress to give the piano player whatever he was drinking. When she reached for a bottle of Bollinger, he looked at the full house, shrugged and nodded. She took the bottle to the stage, set down a towel on the piano bench beside Nick and put a bucket and bottle beside him. She set a filled glass on the piano. He glanced up at her and she gestured to the manager who nodded and bowed.

By 2:00 a.m. the band had worked their way through Brubeck, Miles, Armstrong, Desmond, and even "Europa" by Carlos Santana. The crowd was on its feet, shouting for an encore. The band played two more songs before quitting for the evening.

The patrons trickled out of the bar and the band packed up. Pierre, the saxophone player, approached Nick first, *"Formidable, merveilleux."*

Guy, Maurice, and Xavier introduced themselves and joined in the accolades. Nick had played with the band for many hours but had met none of them. He had, however, formed opinions of each of them by their playing.

Pierre, the saxophone player, was the most outgoing and playful. Nick could see it in his eyes and hear it in his playing. Guy, the guitarist, was moody and intense. He seemed focused on his guitar. He smiled rarely and was a fantastic musician. Maurice was the wild man drummer and liked to break loose whenever he could. He had tattoos of flames on the backs of his fingers. Xavier was detached and shy, hiding behind his string bass and dark glasses, the essence of cool.

Soon they were all sitting at a table talking animatedly about the night. True to form, Guy focused on the arrangement and technique. Maurice and Pierre were wound-up. Xavier sat and listened.

"So, Nick, you are visiting Tahiti? How long will you stay? Where are you staying? Can you play with us again tomorrow night?" Guy blurted. Maurice barked a laugh; Pierre rolled his eyes.

"Well," Nick said, turning to address them all, "I arrived this afternoon from San Francisco and I have a visa for one month. I do not know where I am staying. I haven't figured that out but I would very much enjoy playing with you again."

"Good. You will stay with me," Pierre said.

There were enthusiastic nods all around.

"Who are you bringing home now, Pierre?" Arrested by the voice, Nick looked up to see the most striking woman he had ever beheld. With hints of Polynesian, European, and Chinese, she stunned him. His expression betrayed him, and the rest of the band, accustomed to such responses, laughed and smiled. Even Xavier's face wore a grin.

"I am Maire," she said, extending a hand.

Nick rose to greet her. "*Enchanté*. Nicholas Thomas," he squeaked. There was a pause and then a roar of laughter from the band, Guy leading the crowd in volume. Maire smiled; she knew her effect on men. It had been happening her entire life. It was the men that squeaked with whom she had no problems. They were like puppies. She turned to Pierre and shot off a torrent of French.

In a lull, Nick said, "I have no wish to intrude."

"No, no. You are welcome to stay with us, Nicholas. Occasionally I find it necessary to keep Pierre in line."

Another gust of laughter issued from the crowd, this time at Pierre's expense.

Pierre shrugged, "What can I do?"

"You play beautifully, Nicholas. You are a great asset to the band," Maire said.

"Thank you," Nick squeaked once again.

There was another blast from the band and Maurice said, "My God, he's got it bad."

"It is late; let's go," Pierre said, wanting to spare Nick more embarrassment. "Where are your bags?"

"This is it," Nick said, indicating his day pack. This is all I have, he added to himself. His new friends would learn that soon enough.

Chapter Twenty-Two

Jody spent two hours walking around London's Earl's Court district. She poked her head into The Troubadour, the famous coffee house and music club where in the 1960s the likes of Bob Dylan, Jimi Hendrix, Paul Simon and others once played.

Earls Court was picturesque, but the shopping not to her taste. She looked at her watch and made her way to the tube station, departing at the Charring Cross station and walking the short distance to the Savoy. There she packed and made her way to the lobby. She told the front desk she was checking out and going to Hamburg. She moved to the lobby, sat down, and waited for Lance.

A half an hour later she had read the magazines on the table and had walked around and inspected the lobby in detail. She reached into her purse for her mobile phone to call Lance before she realized Lance had taken it from her.

The man at the front desk smiled at her. His name tag stated "Simon".

"Simon, could you ring room 209, *s'il vous plaît?* I'm waiting for the gentleman to come down." She had stayed in her French character, not wanting to irritate Lance more than she had. He could be such a pain.

"Certainly, Madam."

He picked up the phone and dialed the room. When there was no answer, he turned to the computer at the desk.

"I'm sorry, but the gentleman has checked out, however, the room is paid through Friday morning."

"He checked out? Are you sure?"

He clicked away some more. "Yes. He checked out about an hour ago."

"An hour?"

"Yes, madam."

She pulled a piece of paper from her pocket and handed it to Simon. "S'*il vous plaît* could you call this number for me?'

"Certainly." He took the paper and dialed the number and handed her the telephone.

The phone rang and was answered with "I'm sorry, this number is not in service at this time."

She handed the phone back to him. "*Merci, Simon.*"

Jody felt a twinge of panic.

"Would you please have my bags taken to my room?"

"Of course. I will have a bellman assist you."

Chapter Twenty-Three

Lance, sans beard, was exploring Hong Kong, a city he had always wanted to visit, and now could do so in style. After the long flight he walked past the hotel's fleet of green Rolls Royce cars and into the Peninsula Hotel, a place he had heard about from Nick. He dropped his bags with the bellboy, entered The Bar off the lobby, plopped into a rattan chair, and ordered a negroni.

He looked down at his cocktail and then up at his reflection in the mirror. He looked awful and felt worse. The flight from Heathrow to Hong Kong was brutal, even in first class.

Thanks to Jody, he was getting used to spending money. He had needed to get out of the UK right away and without leaving a trail. The next morning his new identity was ready–adding a €5000 premium to the already outrageous cost of the documents. He bought a last-minute ticket to Bangkok. That was more than €7600. Then he bought another ticket in Bangkok for Hong Kong. That was another €1100. He did a quick calculation–-Jody had cost him $25,000 to get himself out of the UK.

He grunted and reached down for his travel case, pulled

out his laptop computer, set it on the bar, and logged on to the hotel internet and then to a secure private server and virtual private network he had set up months ago. His internet traffic was being channeled across the globe. He logged into the site for Jody's debit credit card and reviewed the account. She had been on a spending spree in London, shopping at high-end boutiques. It appeared as if she had been wearing out her credit card in the Mayfair district. She spent €3200 at a shoe store.

He thought about the high-end stores attached to the Hotel: Tiffany, Louis Vuitton, Winston Jewelers, Cartier, Chanel. Jody could drop a bundle there, and that was crawling distance from his suite.

Lance scowled and made changes to her account.

JODY WALKED OUT OF THE SAVOY, TURNED LEFT ON THE Strand, walked past a clothing store and into the first pub she saw. The Coal Hole was a traditional English pub with lots of wood paneling and beer and ale taps.

It was late in the afternoon and the place was packed with people. As Jody walked up to the bar, the bartender leaned forward and asked, "What'll you 'ave, love?"

She thought of her situation. When things turned bad, Nick had always ordered champagne to celebrate. What an idiot. "I'll have a Hendrick's and tonic with a slice of cucumber, love."

The bartender let out a laugh. The man beside Jody turned to look at her, did a double take at her beauty, then stood and offered her his stool.

"*Merci*. I really need a break today."

"Bad day?" the man standing next to her asked.

She turned to look at him. He was a good-looking fellow in a fine black suit, French-cuffed shirt, expensive watch on his wrist. She sneaked a peek at his shoes. They were expensive, too. He was drinking whisky neat.

"A Hendrick's and tonic for the beautiful French bird. Here you are, love." The bartender put the drink in front of her on the bar.

She smiled a thank you and took a sip. Despite her troubles, she was rather enjoying the role she was playing. Since she had become Antoinette Duval, she had undergone a personality change. She was aware of the change and embraced it. She enjoyed the effect her beauty had on men and acting French seemed to have amplified her power.

"*Oui*, it was *un jour terrible*. But one must carry on."

"Yes, that is what we British say."

She took another look at him to see if he was serious. She saw a slight smile on his lips. He was flirting. Perhaps this man could be of some help, Jody thought.

"I'm looking for a good hotel. I am next door at the Savoy and I would like something different. Do you know of one?"

A woman's left hand with a large diamond on the ring finger appeared on the man's shoulder.

"I'd recommend 41," said the person attached to the hand.

The man turned and said, "Hello, love." He leaned forward to give her a kiss on the proffered cheek.

"Hello, love? I rather like that greeting."

"Yes, 41 is a good choice," he said.

Jody took in the couple. There was something between them, some level of comfort. She could tell a strange woman talking to her husband didn't threaten the woman. They were secure in what they had. She and Nick had that once. She knew he had been good to her. For the first time since she left, she felt a pang of regret. And Lance? She could not believe he had ditched her.

Oh well, his loss.

"41?" Jody asked.

"41 Hotel," the bartender said, asking with a gesture if the others would like a drink.

"Yes, 41 Hotel. It's a stone's throw from Buckingham Palace and perhaps the best hotel in London. The service is fantastic. It feels like a private club," the wife said.

"That sounds like the place I should be," Jody said.

WHILE JODY WAS PONDERING HER FUTURE ON HER OWN, Lance was enjoying the best of the orient. Opened in 1928, the Peninsula Hotel was called "The finest hotel east of Suez." The hotel is in Kowloon on the Hong Kong mainland, the last stop on the Trans-Siberian Railway. The British returned Hong Kong to China in 1999 with much fanfare but it kept its British Colony flavor.

That night Lance had a great room-service dinner of madras curry with prawns, crispy pistachio puffs, and a bottle of Bollinger champagne. He had come to like the champagne, and the symbol it represented. He stood at the window overlooking Victoria Harbour. "Thanks, Nick," he said, lifting his glass in a toast.

The hotel is spectacular, Lance thought, but it's time to get out and see the town. He was not above playing tourist. He decided the next day he would explore Hong Kong.

After a good night's sleep he stood at the front door of the hotel and looked past the cars across the street to the big silver dome of the Hong Kong Space Museum. Beyond the Museum was Victoria Harbour and Hong Kong Island.

Across the harbor was the steep Victoria Peak. He started at the top. At the concierge desk he booked himself on a tour of Kowloon and Hong Kong Island.

An hour later he was sitting in the tram, lying on his back from the steep assent up The Peak. The view from the top was magnificent; the day was clear and he could see all the way to Macau, another place on his list to visit.

He spent the rest of the day touring the island, taking in the beach at Repulse Bay. He looked at the "dragon windows," the large holes built into the skyscrapers throughout Hong Kong. Legend has it that dragons reside in the peaks of the island and they possess a positive and potent energy. As the dragons make their daily journey away from the mountains to the sea to drink and bathe, their energy wafts though the island. As more huge buildings were constructed, they formed barriers for the passage of the dragons to the sea and impended the normal air flow through the city. When the problem became noticeable, architects added *gates* or *windows,* enabling the dragons and the wind to make their way through the metropolis to the sea.

After the homes on The Peak, Repulse Bay was the next most expensive place to live in Hong Kong. In Aberdeen Harbour there were the Jumbo and Tai Pak floating restaurants, huge ornate boats with many decks. The island was more interesting to Lance than the mainland, and even more densely populated. The price for an apartment in an area where he would like to live was astronomical. He was trying to decide how long he would stay, and whether he wanted to.

The tour guide had been talking about Macau with its Portuguese flavor and new and old casinos. Lance decided he would go there next. But first he wanted a new suit.

Chapter Twenty-Four

Across the harbor in Kowloon, on the street side of Nathan Road, Lance searched for a tailor recommended by the concierge of the hotel. The street was filled with grocers and shops of all types. The concierge told him the tailor was between a grocery and an apothecary and up a flight of stairs. Lance had passed four sets of stairs, none between a grocery and apothecary. He came to the next set of stairs. There, a hand-painted sign read:

Fortunes Told.
2nd FLR, H. Wu.

An arrow pointed up.

Lance stopped and pondered the sign. He turned and looked up the stairs. The staircase was wooden and worn, the paint chipped and peeling. The walls appeared to hold their original light green paint.

Despite his analytical mind, Lance had always been superstitious. He put it down to the beliefs of his old-world Polish father. He looked up and down the crowded sidewalk then turned and climbed the stairs. Lance came to a landing and knocked on the door. It opened instantly.

"Good afternoon."

"Are you H. Wu?"

The man looked him up and down. "Yes. You are here to have your fortune told?"

"I am."

"Please come in."

It was Lance's turn to look him up and down. Mr. Wu was tall, wearing black Chinese pajamas and a black and red skull-cap. His braid fell down his back. Lance wasn't sure what to make of this relic. Was he in costume for his customers, or was he the real thing?

"Please sit down," Wu said, gesturing to a chair in front of an ancient desk.

"Okay," Lance said, feeling timid.

Wu walked to a sideboard and turned a knob on a small old hot plate. He kept his back to Lance observing him in a mirror. The water came to a boil. Wu took two scoops of tea from a metal tin and poured it into a teapot. The teapot was as old as the rest of the things in the place. It was red and yellow and blue with a dragon motif, the handle and spout covered with wicker. He took two cups and the teapot, returned to the desk and sat down.

"We wait," he said.

"Okay." Lance turned away from Wu's intense eyes and looked around the room. It seemed to him the place had been frozen in time. There were no modern touches except a tele-phone; even that was an ancient rotary. There was the smell of sandalwood, cloves, and cinnamon in the room. Wu opened the lid of the teapot, peered in, replaced the lid, and poured tea into the cups. He handed one to Lance who took a sip. It was good, fragrant, and sweet. They regarded each other as they drank. Wu leaned forward and looked into Lance's cup. He gestured to Lance to hand it to him and studied the tea leaves in the bottom. He shifted his head from side to side. Wu reached in a drawer by his right elbow and extracted a pen and a thick book bound in black leather. He turned to an empty page and filled it with Chinese characters while Lance watched. Wu stopped writing and reached behind him to pull a bamboo tube full of sticks from the shelf. He covered the tube with his hand and shook. Holding the tube toward Lance, he said "Please take a stick." Lance reached forward and drew a stick from the tube. Wu took it and read the characters printed on the end. He again glanced up at Lance and returned to writing in his black book.

Wu finished his work and sat for a moment, assessing Lance.

"May I see your hands please?" It was more of a command than a request. Wu's performance overwhelmed Lance. He leaned forward with his hands palm up. Wu adjusted his spectacles and leaned forward to examine each hand. He reached into the open drawer of his desk, pulled out a magnifying glass, and returned to Lance's right palm. He leaned forward and looked harder. Lance also leaned forward and looked as well. Wu looked up at Lance and then back down at the palm. He set the glass down, turned over Lance's hands, checked the backs of the hands, and then set Lance's hands on the desk. He took up the old book and wrote. Lance was transfixed. Wu set down his pen and reviewed his writing and then sat back in his chair and studied Lance.

"You travel," Wu said.

Lance cocked his head and let out a bark of a laugh, his timidity gone. "I am a foreigner in Hong Kong. Tell me something less obvious."

Wu smiled at Lance's reaction. "You have been traveling a great deal with short stops at each location."

Lance gave him a bored look and shrugged.

Wu referred back to his notes. He tilted his head back and looked Lance in the eyes.

"You travel under many names."

That got his attention. "Go on."

Wu returned to his notes in the old black book. "You have come into a great deal of money."

Lance swallowed hard. Again, Wu looked him in the eyes and then back at the book.

"What about my future? Your sign says 'Fortunes Told.'"

"You will have a run of good fortune.... No, you will have success in some form. It is not clear."

"And then?"

"Let me see your palm again, the right one, please." Lance held out his palm and Wu studied it. His eyes narrowed.

"Water. Something to do with water."

"Water?"

"Yes. You will take a trip over water."

"Then what?"

"Then you will stop traveling."

"We are done here," Wu said, setting Lance's hand down on the table.

Lance sat back.

"I travel a lot and then I will stop traveling? That's not much of a fortune."

"That may be so, but it is your past and your future."

"What do you think that kind of fortune is worth?"

"Pay what you like, or nothing at all. It is up to you. It will change nothing," Wu said standing up.

Lance pulled out his wallet, took out two hundred Hong Kong dollars and placed them on the desk. It was about twenty-five US dollars. "Well, it was an interesting show, I'll give you that."

Wu nodded and moved to the door. He held it open. Lance walked past him and down the stairs. When he reached the bottom he turned. Wu was standing in the doorway gazing down at him. He held Lance's stare, turned, walked back inside and closed the door.

Lance stood at the bottom of the stairs leading up to the fortuneteller. He shrugged his shoulders, turned left and walked down Nathan Road, back toward the harbor and the hotel. He came to a grocery and then an apothecary. Lance stopped, backed up and looked down an alley between the businesses. He saw the sign for the tailor he had been seeking. He headed down the alley, up the stairs, and into the little shop where he picked out material for a black suit, had his measurements taken, and was told to return the next afternoon for a fitting.

He returned to the Peninsula and spent the day at the hotel. Macau could wait. He enjoyed the time he had worked so hard to get. The Peninsula had several places to relax and after a tour of the hotel, he decided that the pool terrace was the place to be. It was reserved for hotel guests only, so it wasn't crowded. The pool, a beautiful blue, was long enough to get in some laps. He could see the peak on Hong Kong Island from the water. The hotel served food near the pool and on the terrace, and the service was exceptional. It seemed all he had to do was think about another drink or something to eat and someone was by his side asking to do his bidding.

He swam for an hour and then lolled away the day doing

not much of anything. He used his laptop to explore the next place to go and how to get there. Lance kept an eye on non-extradition countries, but other than the islands in the Pacific and maybe South Korea, he had no interest in being that remote or stuck in one place. He would just have to be careful and not draw attention to himself. He closed his laptop and reached for the book, *The Complete Upsmanship* by Steven Potter, which he had found in a book shop in Edinburgh.

The inside cover held the plate:

Monmouthshire County Council
County Library

He turned to the first page:

The Theory and Practice of Gamesmanship
OR
The Art of Winning Games
Without Actually Cheating

The concept of cheating at games hadn't occurred to Lance, but he always liked increasing his odds of winning. Perhaps he could learn something before his gambling trip to Macau. He turned the page and began to read. The fact that the book is satire, and good satire at that, was completely lost on him.

THE NEXT AFTERNOON LANCE BOARDED A JETFOIL FERRY in Hong Kong for the trip to Macau. Macau was a Portuguese colony from 1887 until they returned it to China in 1999. It's a mixture of old Chinese, colonial Europe, and modern

China. There are floating casinos, modern museums, and ruins of a Catholic Cathedral. In recent years Macau has surpassed Las Vegas for gambling revenue, and the Venetian in Macau has become the largest casino in the world. Macau is not a big place, only eleven square miles.

Lance departed the ferry in Macau and walked. Many blocks later he found himself at the front of the Grand Emperor Hotel and Casino. Flanking the entrance were two large Chinese men in Beefeater uniforms holding machine guns. Lance decided it was worth a look, so he walked into the lobby and stopped. People were spread about studying the floor. Lance glanced down and saw that he was standing on a glass panel with a gold bar encased in it. He glanced around the lobby. The gold bars were placed every couple of feet. He would later learn that there were 78 of them and they were real. Lance walked back out past the guards, noticing the machine guns looked a little too much like plastic. He walked a couple of blocks, taking in the glitter and polish of the other new Macau casinos, and then came upon the Grand Lisboa. The casino was trying to keep up with the Venetian and the Wynn. The Lisboa was one of the most bizarre examples of architecture he had ever seen. The base resembles a squashed dome or sea anemone shell made of diamond-shaped glass panels of different colors. It is topped with a huge torch-like spire of hotel rooms that must have been an afterthought because it is a different style of architecture. Add lancet gothic arches at the base and you end up with one strange structure. Lance studied it in awe. What were the designers thinking? He laughed out loud and decided he needed to see the interior.

He turned and walked up the street past a dozen licensed prostitutes. They call it the "the fishbowl", and many of the girls wore short pink or lavender dresses. They were walking from one end of the corridor to the other, then turning and walking back. Lance made his way past the many invitations for a drink and entered the casino. He was disappointed there were no *pai gow* poker tables. It was something he learned to play in high school and was quite good at.

James Bond may have had baccarat and its parent *chemin de fer*, but they were based on *pai gow*. Lance had looked forward to the more complicated *pai gow* with its seven cards made into two poker hands. *Baccarat* was a much simpler game played with two cards. The object for all the games, *pai gow*, *baccarat*, and *chemin de fer*, is to get a score closest to nine. Only the first digit of the total counts in the score. If the cards count to thirteen the score would be three, fifteen would be five. Face cards count as ten.

Lance made his way to the high-stakes area and slid into a seat at a *Baccarat* table. Sitting to his right was a heavy-set Chinese man with a large gold ring, a heavy gold bracelet, and a heavy gold chain around his neck. He was wearing a black suit, black shirt, black tie. On his right cheek he had a scar starting just below his eye, traveling down his cheek in an arc and stopping just above his lip. Another man in a black suit with a gold necktie stood behind him, arms at his sides, his eyes darting about the table and the room.

Beside the Chinese was the quintessential Brit, a holdover from the Royal Crown Colony days of Hong Kong. He was in tweed and wore a thick mustache and looked to Lance like a walrus. Beside the Brit was a German couple. They were both silver-haired and appeared fit. Both were clothed in black and wore rectangular glasses. Beside the Chinese man in black was a Chinese woman of unparalleled beauty poured into a black cheongsam. He noticed her chiseled features and high cheekbones when she turned to him as he sat down in the empty seat next to her. To Lance's amazement, she had green eyes. He peered closer at her and he could not see the edges of contact lenses.

Hours later, Lance was still sitting at the table. There's a great deal of luck involved with baccarat, and the chess player in Lance found it boring. But he was doing well and as the pile of chips at his elbow grew, he found it hard to leave.

The Chinese man looked at Lance, meeting his eyes.

"Where are you from?" Scarface asked Lance. His eyes were piercing and made Lance uncomfortable. Lance had noticed him glancing at him throughout the evening.

"Oh, here and there. I travel a great deal," Lance said using his Polish accent, leaning forward to peek at the cards just dealt him.

"You look familiar. Have you been in China long?"

Lance kept his voice steady and his eyes on the cards. "I just arrived. This is my first visit."

"You look familiar."

"I hear that often," Lance said, setting down his winning hand of a natural nine. The dealer placed a stack of blue $50 chips in front of him.

Scarface took the cards from Lance and dealt them. "I have a very good memory for faces."

"I was once mistaken for Winston Churchill," the walrus-mustached Brit said. "Churchill had already been dead for more than ten years. The man had been drinking." He took a sip of sherry.

"Ya. Everyone says I look like David Hasselhoff," said the German in black. Lance, Scarface, and Walrus all looked at him. Scarface shrugged and they all returned to their cards.

"Everyone says I look like Marlene Dietrich," the German woman said with a bored expression.

"Ya, you do. You do look like Frau Dietrich."

Scarface surveyed the table and stopped at Lance. "I

never forget a face." He leaned back and whispered to the man standing behind him. The man nodded and left.

Lance felt a chill run through him. Something was happening and he could not get a handle on it. Scarface thought he was someone else, that was obvious. He didn't seem like law enforcement, more like a thug. Was there a price on his head? It rattled him and he took another card. His hand totaled seven. What was he doing? He lost the hand, got up from the table, and excused himself.

It was a little after midnight when Lance boarded the jet foil back to Hong Kong. In his pockets were 160,000 Hong Kong dollars. He had doubled his stake, not that he needed the money.

He wondered who Scarface thought he was. He didn't notice the man in the gold necktie standing in the corner behind him.

THIRTY-TWO MILLION DOLLARS IS A GREAT DEAL OF money to hide, even if you split it into lots of pieces. Lance had opened an account in Hong Kong six months previously. But when he tried to move money, he ran into many new regulations imposed by the Bank of China. Fortunately, he had the foresight to open multiple accounts with different banks.

Across from Victoria Harbour on Hong Kong Island, Lance walked by a gold dealer. He wasn't fond of gold. He didn't like paying to buy it, paying to keep it, and paying to sell it. Precious metals were also too volatile for his taste, but as an investment held for the long run, it could hold its value and one could sell it on the open and black markets. He wasn't planning to make money from it; he needed a place to park cash. So he spent the week collecting gold, going from dealer to dealer first on Hong Kong Island and then on the Chinese mainland. Once he started, his gold collecting fervor took hold. Within ten days he had amassed forty pounds of the shiny stuff, all packed into his room safe at the Peninsula. It totaled a million dollars. As the days passed by it became harder to find gold. He noticed that his actions were affecting the local prices, so Lance searched for other places to put money.

Lance's buying spree did not go unnoticed. "So what has he been doing?" A big black vintage 1960s Mercedes-Benz 600 limousine with tinted windows was parked on Peking Road, a small side street around the corner from the Peninsula Hotel.

Scarface and his henchman were in the back. A driver in full livery was sitting behind the wheel.

"Well, he bought a new suit at a place on Nathan Road. And he's been buying gold," the henchman said, gesturing to his gold tie.

"Gold?"

"A lot of gold. He's been hitting every shop on the island and Kowloon side. That was most of last week."

"Where is he keeping it?"

"The gold? Hard to tell. Perhaps at the hotel. He seems to be staying away from banks."

"Do we have anyone there?"

"At the hotel? I'll check but I don't think so."

"Keep on top of him, Midas."

"I will." The henchman got out of the car and walked to the hotel.

"Hmmm," Scarface grunted. The driver knew better than to ask him where he wanted to go.

"He has to be the same guy," Scarface said to himself.

"Let's go back to the office, Ignatius," he told the driver. He never understood the desire of Hong Kongers to give their children odd names. All the same, he thought his men lucky to be branded Midas and Ignatius. The names are better than "Bobsled" or "Porpoise" or some of the other names people were using in Hong Kong.

LANCE WAS ON A ROLL. HE ENJOYED HITTING THE ODD spots in Hong Kong, far off the tourist path, bartering with the gold merchants, going from shop to shop. The locales were exotic and the people interesting. He asked the concierge at the hotel if there was another way to get around Hong Kong, perhaps something more "local." The concierge suggested the Red Top Minibus would take him about anywhere. The hotel manager overheard, and glaring at the concierge suggested Lance take one of the hotel's green Rolls Royces, or perhaps a taxi. But when a minibus pulled up near the front of the hotel, Lance asked the driver if he could take him to the Lin Heung Tea House for what he heard was the best dim sum he would ever find.

"Sure. I'll take you to Lin Heung. Good choice. Get in. Sit down," the driver shouted at Lance.

"Okay," Lance shouted back, boarded the empty bus, and sat down near the front. The moment he was seated, the driver sped off, his foot to the floor. He slowed for some intersections and shot through the rest at what seemed to Lance like suicidal speed. Lance was holding on to the seat in front of him. He understood why the hotel manager was irritated at the concierge for suggesting the minibus, and why he wanted Lance to take a taxi. As they rocketed down the ramp and into the harbor tunnel, he decided if he lived through the ride, he would take the Star Ferry back to his hotel. He was through with wheeled transport for a while. As they shot out of the Cross-Harbour Tunnel onto Hong Kong Island he heard an explosion. It was a canon being fired.

"Noon Day Gun!" yelled the driver, "Fired every day for tourists!"

Three kilometers later the driver slammed to a stop and declared, "Lin Heung Tea House." Lance sat dazed, not able to move or speak. "What do I owe you?" he croaked. He pulled himself out of the seat, paid the driver, and exited the bus. As he stood at the curb, he felt as if the ground were moving under his feet as though he had been at sea on a boat for a month. As he gathered his senses, an ancient little Chinese lady climbed the stairs of the minibus. Lance wanted to grab her, pull her out of the abyss, save her from certain doom. But before he could react, she moved to the second row and sat down. With both hands she gripped the bar on the seat in front of her. Lance saw her throw her head back and heard her let out a cry of joyous laughter as the bus shot off down Wellington Street.

Lance shook his head in wonder, turned and walked up the stairs past the pastry shop to the restaurant. He surveyed the place, frozen in some age before he was born. They had updated nothing. There were round steel tables scattered about and the place was packed with people. There were women pushing dim sum trolleys loaded with bamboo steamer baskets. He stood at the entrance, waiting for a place to sit. Lance felt a gentle tug at his sleeve and a man took him to a table of diners. He slid into a seat and smiled hello to the others. They nodded and returned to their food. A trolley appeared at his elbow, with a woman opening the lids and showing the contents to the table. A spirited Cantonese discussion ensued amongst the diners. They pointed to various dishes, gesturing at Lance. The man next to him nudged him with his elbow and pointed to a dish. Lance smiled at him and nodded and gestured to the woman by the cart. She put the dish in front of Lance. A man came by and poured tea. A fork appeared at the side of his plate. He reached for the chopsticks and received nods of approval from the table. He picked up a dumpling and took a bite. Lin Heung was all he had heard. He had had good Dim Sum in San Francisco, but this was amazing. He tilted his head back in ecstasy and let out a pleasant noise. The diners all laughed. One patted Lance on the shoulder and nodded. They all competed in introducing Lance to the best the restaurant offered. He was so full by the time they had finished he could barely move. All the food was amazing and the desserts rich and in perfect flaky pastry. He gestured for no more as the cart passed again. He sat back, drinking his tea, looking around the table at the other men. They all had the contented expressions of having just finished a fine meal.

Lance excused himself and proceeded to the counter to explain that he wanted to pay for the entire table. There was a lot of confusion until a woman standing behind him translated. The cashier asked him to wait while he collected the tabs for the men. More confusion and commotion ensued as the cashier approached the table and took the check, said something to the men and pointed to Lance. The men at the table looked at Lance, who bowed to the men. They turned to each other, exchanged comments and turned back to Lance, smiling and nodding to him.

It was after two in the afternoon when Lance paid the bill and walked out of the restaurant and down the steps. He decided he needed a long walk after such a large meal; the thought of getting into any vehicle made his stomach jumpy.

Chapter Twenty-Five

A week after arriving in Tahiti, Nick woke up in the hamlet of Paea, south of Papeete on the West Coast of Tahiti Nui. He had been living with Pierre and Maire since his first night in Tahiti. The band had by then heard a brief version of his story and François Pardee had filled them in on the details. His new friends and their families had adopted him. Each of the band had invited Nick to dine with his family. By the end of his first week in Tahiti, he could walk anywhere on the island and someone would recognize him with a greeting.

He had become accustomed to the roosters crowing throughout the night, the rats scampering across the tin roof in search of fruit, and the sound of the waves. But the night before there had been a torrential rain. He dreamt he was trapped below deck in a capsized boat. He awoke in a deep sweat, feeling lost and wondering why roosters in Tahiti don't sleep at night like they do in the rest of the world.

Nick's bedroom was located at the back of the house. The double bed faced glass doors overlooking the garden. Across the tile floor was the door to the studio, the only way into the main part of the house without going outside. Nick made his way to the bath, a large cinder-block room with an open curtain separating the shower from the rest of the room. Nick stood at the sink and lathered his face with his grandfather's shaving brush, one object of his past life he carried with him. He turned on the shower and walked under the spray. Nick stood there staring at the cinder block wall for a few minutes, letting the water wash away the late night of champagne, smoke, and the intensity of playing for an audience. He finished his shower and dried himself. He reached down and pinched his stomach. Thanks to the excellent food and too much champagne, it wasn't as flat as it used to be. Making a mental note to get running shoes and do some sit-ups, he tied a pareo around his waist and walked to the kitchen.

"Oh, Nicholas, in your pareo you are a Tahitian now," Maire said, as he poured himself coffee. He turned away from her and smiled. He was crazy in love with her; he couldn't help it. Pierre knew, the band knew, and she knew. He would have to live with it. They were all nice enough to let him work through it on his own, although Maurice took pleasure in ribbing him. It was a Saturday morning and they were all home. Maire was standing barefoot at the stove making crêpes and toast.

"*Allez a manger,*" Maire said, heading to the patio with a brunch platter piled high. They settled in and ate.

"So, Nick, what do you say we take a tour of Tahiti today?" Pierre asked, reaching for another crêpe.

"That would be fine," Nick said.

"You men go. I will clean the house today," Maire said.

Pierre was recovering from a motorcycle accident and didn't work during the day. The rest of the band had jobs, but with Nick's arrival they had been playing music in the evenings. Pierre had converted a room in his home to a rehearsal studio, and had covered the inside walls with sound-board and old carpet. He and Nick spent hours in the room trying out new sounds and arrangements, each gaining respect for the other's talent.

After breakfast the two men piled into Pierre's little white Peugeot and headed south around the island. Soon they were at Port Phaeton with its botanical garden and Gauguin Museum. The museum had printed copies of the artist's work and little else. The original paintings were in museums and on the walls of private collectors' homes. The only thing touched by Gauguin was a spoon they encased in a plexiglass box. To Nick, that didn't seem like much of a tribute.

"*The Moon and Sixpence*," Nick said, examining the spoon.

"Pardon?"

"A novel by Somerset Maugham. It was fiction, but he based it on the life of Gauguin."

"Yes, Gauguin lived and painted here. He had two Tahitian wives and some children. He moved to the Marquesas Islands and died there. That was in the early 1900's. He still has grandchildren and great-grandchildren here."

They walked through the garden and came upon a pair of tortoises encircled with a half-meter high rock wall. The wooden sign indicated that someone brought them from the Galapagos Islands in 1920. Nick stepped up to them. They were ancient, their faces wise and knowing. There was no telling how old they were or how old they had been when they arrived. Nick thought of what they must have seen since their arrival in Tahiti. Throughout the years, a parade of faces had observed them in their rock pen. Pierre approached a tortoise and bent down to scratch its neck. The tortoise stretched its neck out full length, enjoying the attention. Nick reached down and felt its velvety skin. The tortoise gazed at him with deep black eyes. The three stayed that way, Pierre and Nick scratching its neck, Nick and the tortoise locked in an unblinking gaze, until the tortoise, perched on the rock wall, slipped, startling them all.

"*Au revoir,* Monsieur Tortoise," he said. Then he turned to Pierre. "How do you say Tortoise in French?"

"*Tortu.*"

"*Au revoir, Monsieur Tortu.*"

They moved on through the garden, heading to an isthmus. There was a slight breeze, the warm air fragrant. They walked through tree ferns, Polynesian vanilla, iron trees, and palm trees. They continued inland through a sandy field potholed with crab burrows. The ground was alive with crabs, huge prehistoric monsters battling and scurrying about. They seemed to ignore Pierre and Nick, content to duke it out with each other.

"What a contrast," Nick said, watching two of the bigger specimens go at it.

"What is?"

"The crabs, the tortoises. Here the crabs are fighting and clawing away at each other. Meanwhile, the tortoises are getting their necks scratched by passing tourists. It seems there is everything in this Tahiti of yours."

"Life is the same everywhere—on the *Champs-Êlyées* or an island in the South Pacific. It is cruel and it is benevolent," Pierre said, watching a big crab defend his cache of guava fruit.

"Maybe," Nick said, "but I've been the crab for too long. I think I'd like to try being a tortoise now, have my neck scratched by the occasional visitor."

Pierre considered Nick's pronouncement. "There is one good thing about being a tortoise."

"Yes?"

"Tortoises live longer than crabs."

THE NEXT DAY NICK WAS SITTING AT HIS FAVORITE TABLE in *L'Auvent Rouge,* outside of the restaurant under an umbrella. The chair he chose had just the right amount of sun, the breeze was just cool enough, bringing with it the smells of coconut oil on the passersby, diesel fumes from the passing traffic, the kitchen at *L'Auvent Rouge,* and the unmistakable smell of tropical decay. With a glass of iced tea sweating at his elbow, he sketched the Papeete waterfront. His book was filling, now that he had time to draw. He had completed portraits of each of the band, François Pardee, Alain Marchand, and the waitresses at *Le Club Paradise.* From across the street he had sketched *L'Auvent Rouge.* When François saw the sketch of his restaurant, he exclaimed "Nick! *Merveilleux! C'est bon!*" Nick tore the sketch from the book and handed it to him.

"Would you like it?" Nick asked.

François's eyes lit up. "Oui. Consider your bill paid in full. But first you must sign your work."

Nick took the drawing and signed it in the corner.

"I have always wanted a picture of *L'Auvent Rouge,*" François said, admiring the drawing.

THE FOLLOWING DAY WHEN NICK CAME TO THE restaurant, he saw his drawing framed and mounted on the wall in the foyer.

His drawings were whimsical—a new style for him—the perspective flattened or skewed, the portraits not caricatures, but exploiting what he knew about the subject. Each of the band members had a portion of his instrument included in the portrait; Alain Marchand was pouring a bottle of champagne; François appeared with a corner of the bistro banner behind him.

The book was crammed with little sketches—the bottom half of a beer bottle, the transom of a sailing yacht claiming to be *Raison d'être* with a home port of Nice, the arm of a chair overlapping the glass table. Only the pages with portraits held single images. They were his views of his journey. One page was a panorama of the yard behind Pierre and Maire's house, a sketch of how Nick perceived the garden would be when he had completed it.

François pulled up a chair, studying Nick's current sketch. He had captured the essence of a bottle of Hinano beside a half-full glass of beer. The glass was sweating, the reflection of the sun on the bottle suggesting a hot, sultry day. It was good enough to be an advertisement for the beer. François licked his lips; it made him thirsty. He gestured at the book and Nick handed it to him to review.

"It is my favorite time of day, seeing your work, viewing Papeete through your eyes. I see things I have never seen before. Now I walk around observing shapes, shadow, and form. You have done that for me, Nick." He was studying a portrait of Maire, wind blowing back her hair, Tahitian black pearls in her ears and on a strand around her neck.

François flipped through the book, calling attention to what he liked. Nick listened, getting pleasure from François's enjoyment.

François flipped to the next page and gasped. He glanced up at Nick who blushed. It was a drawing of Maire, sitting on the beach in a simple dress, waves lapping on the shore in the background.

"*Merveilleux*. This is fabulous. You have captured the essence of Maire. It is like you have stripped away her covering and have exposed her soul to the world. She is a beautiful woman, yes, but you have shown her beauty, intelligence, and passion. How long did she pose for this drawing?"

Nick squirmed in his chair. "She didn't pose for it. I did it from memory."

François looked at Nick. A small smile crept to his lips. He took one last glance and gently closed the book.

"*Tres merveilleux*," he said.

A FEW DAYS LATER GUY CAME RUNNING ONTO THE PATIO during breakfast. "*Regardez*!" he gasped, out of breath, thrusting *La Dépêche de Tahiti* on the table. On the front page of the newspaper was a photograph of the band playing at *Le Paradise*. "Listen to this," Guy said, and read from the paper.

> Le Group Paradise, which has been playing for two weeks at the nightclub Le Paradise, has finally begun to show some talent. The talent has come in the form of an American piano player named Nickolas Thomas. The band has been playing to a full house since the arrival of M. Thomas, who has seemed to inspire the other musicians. The club's owner, Alain Marchand said, "I don't know where he came from, but he has been good for business. The combo is playing very well now. Come in and hear for yourself.

It embarrassed Nick. He knew he was playing well, but

he attributed it more to his need for belonging and focus than to any form of musical brilliance.

NICK HAD THAT AFTERNOON TO HIMSELF, GIVING HIM some time to think. Everything that had been important to him was gone. He had spent the last ten years amassing a fortune beyond the one he inherited, gathering things—yachts and planes, a beautiful wife. Nick's closest friend had been Lance, the man who betrayed his trust and took it all away. They had been best of friends, which, if not making it much worse, made it more confusing.

NICK WATCHED A ROOSTER CHASE A CHICKEN ACROSS THE yard, both birds screaming as they ran. He considered any signs of Lance's impending departure, but he couldn't think of any. They had worked together for the past four years and both had a solid grasp of the business. Each had full signature authority on each aspect of the enterprise. There was an implied trust between them. Nick had never questioned it. Now, with nothing left, Nick felt like a different person. It was an odd mixture of relief and aimlessness. He was on a lonely odyssey with no known destination. Yet he had a full stomach, shelter, and a new group of friends. He was wearing Pierre's shirt and Xavier's trousers. He had a pile of clothes donated to him by the band and their families—more clothes than he owned in San Francisco. Pierre and Maire insisted that he stay in their guest room and make it his own. He did as much cooking and cleaning as they would allow. He had taken on the yard work and reclaimed the vegetable garden from the tropical foliage. The gardening gave him much time to think, perhaps too much time.

THE BAND, SANS GUY, WAS IN ATTENDANCE, SITTING IN A corner booth at *L'Auvent Rouge*. It had become their rendezvous. François was serving drinks. He and Nick acted like old friends. "I helped him spend the last franc he had." He was fond of telling the band.

They were discussing the arrangements and the play list for the week. The band was still enjoying full houses at *Le Paradise.*

As was his custom, Guy came running in, excited, chest puffing. "Can you guess what happened?"

Xavier rolled his eyes.

"Tahiti has seceded from France?" Maurice asked.

"You have finally met a woman?" Pierre suggested.

"Does she have a sister?" Xavier asked.

"No. No. No. Can not you be serious?" Guy pleaded.

"You are serious enough for all of us," Maurice said.

"Well, I want to know," Nick said. "What has happened, Guy?"

"Ah. First I must have a drink. My throat is dry. A Hinano, please, François." He pulled up a chair and sat down at the table.

"Ahhh," Maurice moaned with accompanying groans from the rest of the band.

"He is so dramatic. Why is he not an actor?" Pierre asked his friends.

Now that he had their attention, Guy was making the best of it. François, now curious also, fetched the beer for Guy.

Nick sat back to enjoy the little drama. François placed a frosty glass and bottle in front of Guy. He poured the beer down the side of the glass and took a long sip, letting out a contented sigh. They all leaned toward him. He cleared his throat and used the back of his hand to wipe the beer foam off his lips. Nick couldn't help but admire the brilliance of Guy's performance. He had his audience just where he wanted them.

"Well, my friend works at *La Dépêche*, and she said a judge for the Miss Tahiti contest had to leave the island unexpectedly. It seems he was caught with the wife of a certain government official."

"Pfff," Maurice said. They all leaned back. It was good island gossip, but hardly worth the effort Guy put into his performance. Pierre told him so in rather harsh words. Guy sat there with a smug look, tapping his finger on the table.

Xavier recognized the expression for what it was and said, "There is more to the story. Regard the expression on his face."

"You are correct, my friend; there is more."

"What more is there?" Maurice demanded, now bored with the game. He took a sip of beer.

"The election committee would like our band to take the place of the judge who left." There was silence around the table accompanied with a few dropped jaws.

"So this is a big deal?" Nick asked.

"A big deal? The Miss Tahiti Election is the biggest event of the year in French Polynesia," Maurice said, regarding Guy's news with a new respect.

"Ah," said Nick.

THAT NIGHT THE AUDIENCE AT *LE PARADISE* WAS AN ODD mixture of locals, tourists, and sailors. Next to Nick on the stage was an open bottle of Bollinger in an ice bucket. Alain Marchand had sent one to him as he had each night since Nick's arrival. The band had reached a comfort level and had fallen into a groove. They were playing well and the audience was a good one.

By 2:00 a.m. the house had thinned and the bottle of champagne was empty. Nick knew he was drinking too much —but the champagne was too good to go to waste. He tried to share it with the rest of the band, but they preferred the local beer.

They closed the final set with "Skylark" by Hoagie Carmichael. As they were packing up, a man approached Nick. He was overdressed for the tropics, wearing a European-cut double-breasted suit of dark blue wool, a crisp white shirt and a maroon silk tie. His balding head glistened with perspiration. Nick thought his eyes were a little wild, shifting back and forth as though he thought he would be attacked at any moment.

"Are you Nicholas Thomas?"

"Oui."

"I am Louis Jourdan, Department of Immigration," the man said, flashing his credentials at Nick.

"Louis Jourdan, like the actor?" Nick asked, studying his identification card. The man in the picture had a full head of hair. Nick looked up and eyed him. He was the same man.

"May I see your passport, please?"

Nick reached into his back pocket and withdrew his well-used passport.

"I see you travel often," Jourdan said, pursing his mouth as he thumbed through the pages of visas and entry and exit stamps. You have a thirty-day tourist visa?"

"That is correct. But I was planning to extend it."

"You do not have a *Carte Sejour*, a work visa?" he asked, mopping his brow with a handkerchief.

Nick could see where the conversation was headed. "No. However, I am not paid to play the piano. I do it for pleasure."

"The others are paid, are they not?"

"That may be so, but I am not."

Pierre approached, "Is there a problem?"

The immigration man turned to him, "Louis Jourdan, Department of Immigration. This does not concern you."

He turned back to Nick, "I will research this matter. Where are you staying?"

"I am staying with friends," Nick said.

"I need the address and a way to reach you."

Nick gave him the address and telephone number for Pierre and Maire.

"I will contact you soon," Louis Jourdan said, turning his back and walking away.

"Who was that?" Xavier asked, joining them.

"Louis Jourdan," Pierre said.

"The actor?"

"No, trouble."

THE NEXT DAY NICK WAS SITTING UNDER A RED AND white umbrella at *L'Auvent Rouge* writing postcards to Jim and Katherine. He had just finished when François walked up and sat down. They made small talk and watched the passers-by on the Boulevard Pomare.

"Here I am, destitute, with only a return plane ticket, hand-me-down clothes, and no money to my name. I'm happier than I have been in years. I was, am, a product of my culture, where more is never enough. Now I'm realizing that less can be more."

François looked out at the traffic. "What are you going to do when your visa has expired?" he asked.

Nick followed François's gaze out at the boulevard and the traffic and people rushing by. Even here in the middle of the Pacific, people had things to do. "I don't want to think about it. I want to savor this moment and this happiness. I think I've earned it. It cost me my home, my wife, and all the things that go with them. When I think of the future, I become uneasy. The future will come soon enough."

"It always does."

"Besides, what can I do? Tahiti is treating me well. I'm healthy. I'm going to enjoy life for a change. I had mortgage bills, power bills, cable television bills, bills for credit cards, car payments, boat payments, insurance, trash collection, water, and of course all the bills from my wife's shopping. Life was complicated." He paused and then added, "Not much different from anyone's in America, I suppose."

"Or French Polynesia," Françoise said. "Was she very beautiful?"

"My wife? Yes, very. But she wasn't happy. She had been in an abusive relationship before we got together. I gave her no abuse and it made her uneasy. She told me about it when we first met. She said she tried to destroy the good that happened in her life—her friendships, jobs, school, relationships. She said she would destroy us, too. I should have listened to her. It took her six years, but she did it. She kept looking for things that were wrong, making them up when she couldn't find them in reality. I now realize it had been over long before she finally left; I gave her a good excuse to go. I was broke and had lost all I had. Just at the end, even before Lance disappeared, it seemed she was angry with me about something, hinting at some misdeed. I couldn't think of anything I had done to her, and she wouldn't discuss it. It's odd because I tried hard to make her life easy for her."

"But it was her nature to be unhappy. You can't expect to change a person's nature, it must come from within," François said.

"Yes, I realize that now." Nick looked down at the wedding ring still on his left hand. He twisted it around his finger then slipped it off and put it into his shirt pocket.

"She sounds like my first wife."

"I guess it's universal. That's sad."

"I think that's the way with many beautiful women. I have met few who were happy. They choose the wrong man early and he ruins them. The beautiful, they have things given to them and come to expect it. Few reach their potential. The exquisite ones become models or read the news on television and seldom have to use their brains. They seldom find out if they have any."

"You could be right. My wife is very intelligent but doesn't think she is." He paused. "I should say 'soon-to-be ex wife,'" he said staring out across the harbor.

"My philosophy is to have a plain and happy wife and a beautiful mistress."

"That is one approach, certainly a French one," Nick said. He took a sip of beer. "Now my responsibilities are to the band and to my garden."

"It sounds like a good life you are leading, Nick," François said with a sigh.

"I am very focused."

"I must see your garden. Pierre says it's beautiful."

"A neighbor has given me orchids and bougainvillea. I've learned that gardeners like to share their beauty. Things grow so fast here. I have only been here fifteen days and I must keep on it to clear the weeds. I have recovered the lawn, but I need to find grass seed to fix the holes."

When Nick paused, François said, "You must have been successful in your business in San Francisco."

"I did well."

"Too bad about—Lance, is it?"

"Yes, Lance."

"Too bad about Lance taking all of your money."

"Yes, I suppose," Nick said, pausing. "Well, maybe. Not really. I was never really happy with all the things. I see that now. I was playing a game, collecting things when I had time. I mean besides my boat; I loved that boat. No, I was never really happy. Not like I am now. I suppose I have Lance to thank for that. Funny, I bet he wouldn't like that at all."

Chapter Twenty-Six

Back in San Francisco, John Mitchell sat with Katherine at her kitchen table sipping a cup of coffee. He was reading a postcard Katherine had received from Nick in Tahiti.

The card was a picture of a Tahitian woman, grass skirt, hips caught in mid sway.

> Katherine-
> I made it to Tahiti where I've joined a jazz band,
> made some friends, am drinking too much, and am a
> judge for the Miss Tahiti Contest.
> Why didn't I lose everything before?
> Cheers!
> Nick
> PS No sign of Lance. Will probably be deported soon.
> NJT

"I guess he's bounced back," Mitchell said.
"It does seem that way."
"The Miss Tahiti contest?"

"Nick's always been one to come up smelling like roses. It's another thing about him that Lance resented."

"Insecurity seems like an odd motive. But if anything this profession has taught me, people will do just about anything for any reason, and thirty-two million dollars is a lot of reasons."

"I'd bet you've seen a lot." Katherine said.

"Yes, I've seen quite a lot. I try to keep the idea in my head that people are basically good. Sometimes it takes a lot to do that."

"I'd bet it does. I wonder what Nick means about being deported soon?"

"He is crossing swords with the head of immigration. He's in Tahiti legally, so I'm not sure what's going on."

"How do you know that?"

"I'm keeping tabs on him."

"Is he still a suspect?"

"Everyone is a suspect."

"Even me?"

Mitchell flipped the postcard over and looked at the dancer. He hadn't told Katherine about Lance and Jody. He had warned Nick about telling her as well.

"Are you hungry?" he asked.

Mitchell drove them to *Bobo's*, a steak and crab place on Lombard Street.

"Nice place. I guess FBI agents do well."

"After my divorce I started to dabble in real estate investing. It pays my restaurant bills. Eating out is one of my passions and San Francisco is one of the best places in the world to do it. There are thousands of restaurants in the city, but I'm putting a dent in the list. This is considered one of the top steakhouses in the country."

Katherine often ate at restaurants in the city, but had not

been there before. She made a note to expand her dining repertoire. She glanced around at the stylish decor and clientele, subdued lighting, and the prices on the menu. That's when she realized she was on a date, the first date since she and Lance had got together. She settled into the booth. This isn't so hard, she thought.

"What sort of real estate do you do?"

"I had a couple of lofts South of Market. I got in and out before the boom and bust. It turned out well."

"Why don't you quit the FBI and retire?"

"I like to catch bad guys. I guess that means your Lance. Sorry about that."

"Hey, he's my Lance no longer. But I guess he has what he felt was coming to him. Not that it matters."

"Why doesn't it matter?" he asked, reaching for a bread stick.

"Well, he didn't hurt me. As a couple, we were almost through. I was tired of his insecurity."

"What about Nick?"

"He seems happy enough. He's a survivor. He needed to get away from his spouse just as I did. Lance just made it happen. I don't think either Nick or I would have left our spouses without something serious happening."

"Such as Nick losing everything?"

"Exactly."

"Seems like a high price to pay," Mitchell said.

"Big land baron like you, you know it's just money being moved around. Nick will make it all back if he wants to."

"People lost their jobs."

"That's true and very unfortunate."

"I'd like to find Lance and bring him to justice."

The waiter arriving at the table interrupted Mitchell's thought. They both ordered the specialty of the house.

"It's about the chase, isn't it? You finding Lance? You get a thrill out of the chase, don't you?" Katherine asked, taking a sip of her drink.

"Yes, I suppose I do."

"What about me? Am I all about the chase?"

He set down his glass and held her gaze.

"No, you're about the thrill."

"Do you pick up a lot of women whose husbands have left them?"

It was after another dinner; Katherine and Mitchell were sitting together on the chesterfield in Mitchell's loft condominium, fingers intertwined. It was a masculine room, with leather furniture, dark wood, and a monstrous flat screen television mounted on the wall. The stereo was Danish and expensive.

"Only if they've taken millions of dollars with them."

"Does that happen often?"

"First time."

"Is this a Persian carpet?" Katherine asked, rubbing her bare toes across the silk.

"It was my grandparent's. I always sat on it when I visited them when I was young. I used to trace the pattern with my finger. They left it to me when they passed."

Katherine surveyed the room, picked up a framed photograph on the table in front of her.

"Who's this in the photograph with you?"

"That's my son."

Katherine took another look. They were standing with arms over each others shoulders, looking seriously at the camera.

"He a good kid?" Katherine asked.

"He's okay. He needs to get his act together. He's coasting through Stanford and not living up to his potential. His education is costing me a fortune, but I'm trying to keep my mouth shut and hope he'll grow out of it."

"Is it hard to be a parent?"

"He takes after his mother," Mitchell said. Katherine let the comment stand, not wanting to break the intimacy they were enjoying by bringing an ex-spouse into the conversation.

Mitchell was drinking a dry martini, two olives. He had made Katherine a cosmopolitan martini, a thin slice of lime floating on top of the pink liquid. He had procured the ingredients after she had ordered one on their first date.

She took a delicate sip.

"They're out of fashion," Katherine said.

"What are?"

"Cosmopolitans," she said, taking another sip.

"Martinis come and go, but I still like them. Kind of like old friends," Mitchell said, taking a bite of olive. "What about Lance?" he asked.

"What about Lance?"

"Well, did you see this coming?"

"Nick asked the same question."

"And?"

"No, but obviously he had the potential, so maybe I just didn't want to see it."

Mitchell reached for the remote and lowered the volume on the stereo. He turned to look at Katherine.

"How well do you know Jody Thomas?"

She realized he was in detective mode and wanted him to know that she knew, and then finally saying it.

"Funny, I'm sipping my favorite drink, the ingredients you obviously took the effort to assemble; there's soft jazz on the stereo; and damn if I don't think I'm on a date. But your small talk is lousy."

"It's my new interrogation technique. I ply beautiful women with their favorite alcoholic beverage."

Katherine sighed. "I'd say I know Jody Thomas well. Nick knew her for about a year before they were married. The four of us did a lot together."

"I'd like to interview her again. Have you seen her lately?"

"No, not since she walked out on Nick."

"Do you know where I can reach her?"

"No, Nick said she presented him divorce papers and walked out. I don't think he's seen her since."

Chapter Twenty-Seven

In Tahiti the days passed by and Nick fell into a routine of playing music late into the night—either at *Le Paradise* or in the studio at Pierre and Maire's home. He slept late into the morning and then wandered through the garden to decide what needed to be done next. He worked on the garden until mid-afternoon and then hitchhiked to Papeete and *L'Auvent Rouge*. When he hadn't checked his watch for a week, he sold the Rolex to a jeweler on Boulevard Pomare for a ridiculously low price. It had been a gift from Jody and wearing it had always given him an uneasy feeling of being ostentatious and pretentious. The tan line disappeared in the tropical sun. The first thing he did with the money was stock Pierre and Maire's house with food and wine.

Because François would not let Nick pay for his meals, Nick started going to other restaurants in the area. Before long François spotted him at a competing restaurant.

"Is my food not good enough for you?" he confronted Nick.

"No. No. Your food is fantastic, the best in town. However, I want to pay for my meals. I do not want to take advantage of our friendship. You won't let me pay," Nick explained.

"Nick, Nick. It is rare that I find someone interesting and nice to talk to in my restaurant. Sure, some people are nice—most I've known their entire lives and they are boring, and the tourists come and go. You have a keen intellect; you are fresh and interesting. You have passion not burned out by the tropical sun. I look forward to your visits and our discussions. For this I will feed you. The day I find you dull, I will present you with a bill."

It was a long speech for François.

"Oh, okay. I ran out of money again anyway. Thanks François."

"Nick, when you own a restaurant, feeding a friend costs you nothing. I always have extra food. I give much of it to the poor."

"I'm poor."

François looked him up and down. "With or without your Rolex, you will never be poor, Nick."

Nick paused and reflected. "No, I suppose not."

"You won't."

"I do feel guilty about living off Pierre and Maire. I don't feel the gardening is enough to repay them," Nick said.

"Nick, Pierre told me that since you joined them, the band is now receiving twice the money for each gig."

"Pierre told you that?"

"He did. So you do not have to worry about not earning your keep."

Nick thought about it. "Well, that makes me feel pretty good."

"Well, good."

A FEW DAYS LATER, PIERRE, MAIRE, GUY, AND NICK were standing outside a waterfront club. Pierre knocked on the door and a little door opened within the door. A face stared out. Pierre said some magical words, and with a grunt, the man behind the face opened the main door and allowed them in.

Next in line for the billiard table, they sat with their drinks, watching two fishermen play out their game. Soon the eight ball was sunk and the game completed. Pierre moved forward and racked the balls.

"We'll play teams. Guy and I will play against you two," Pierre said.

"Okay," Nick replied.

They lagged for break and Pierre shot closest to the cushion. He set the cue ball and gave the rack a healthy break. He sank the two ball and called solids.

"Nick, I do not know how to play this game," Maire said.

"Oh, we'll get by," Nick said.

Pierre sank the one ball off the seven.

"We will lose. Pierre is very good," Maire said.

"I see that he is a fine player. Why don't you go stand opposite Pierre?" Nick said.

"Why?" asked Maire.

"Just trust me," Nick said.

Maire moved to the other side of the table.

"Okay, now what?"

"Lean forward," Nick said, joining her.

"Okay."

"Now look up at Pierre as he shoots," Nick whispered in her ear.

Pierre, with a simple straight shot, faced Maire's flirtatious gaze and exposed cleavage.

The effect was severe and immediate. He shot the cue ball

past the seven ball and into a corner pocket.

"I've never done that before," Pierre said.

Nick smiled at Maire. No stranger to pool tables, Nick stepped forward and sank the nine, ten, and twelve balls in rapid succession.

"Oh, Nick. You are also good at this game," Maire said.

"Adequate, but you are catching on fast. With your help we may have a chance," he said, missing a shot at the eleven ball. She had thrown Nick off his game as well.

Guy came forward to take his turn. Maire leaned across the table and gazed into Guy's eyes. Guy missed his shot and the cue ball rolled clear of the other balls on the table.

"It always works. Men are such boys," Maire whispered in Nick's ear. Her breath gave him a shiver.

"We are stupid that way," Nick agreed, shaking his head to clear it. "Just try not to distract me."

Nick made his shot and leaned back to watch Maire play her version of the game. Her unselfconsciousness enchanted him.

IT WAS SATURDAY EVENING AND AGAIN THE ITEM IN THE newspaper had done its work. *Le Club Paradise* was full, and there was a waiting line out the door for seating.

The bartender had replaced Nick's usual bottle of champagne with a glass of ice water. He had cut back his drinking a week before. He felt better and the owner of the club was happy to be saving money.

At a corner table a man waited until the band finished their set. He walked to the stage. A towering man, he stood a foot below the stage but still saw eye to eye with Guy, who was standing on it.

"My name is Rémi Legrande," he said in a melodious tone. Although a bear of a man, his grip was gentle, but not soft. Guy thought the man could crush his hand if he wanted to.

"My employer would like your band to play for him at a private celebration at Bloody Mary's on Bora Bora. Your travel arrangements and accommodations will be provided for and the band will be paid for the performance. Here is my phone number with the dates on the back. Please discuss it and call me with your decision," Legrande said. He then handed the card to Guy, nodded and left.

The band watched him walk out of the club. Guy glanced at the card and handed it to Pierre.

"Decision? What decision? We will go. Bloody Mary's, Bora Bora," Maurice exclaimed.

"Bloody Mary's?" Nick asked.

"A tourist place, a restaurant, an institution. A place worth seeing," Xavier said. "But it is on Bora Bora and that means everything. It is perhaps the most beautiful place on earth."

"I have heard that," Nick said, taking a sip of water.

"Legrande, indeed. Did you see the size of that man?" Guy said. "The man is a giant."

"First Miss Tahiti and now Bloody Mary's. You have brought us great fortune, Nick," said Maurice, twirling a drumstick in his hand.

"Well, I guess it all balances out eventually," Nick said.

"What can I do to stay in Tahiti?" Nick asked, for he knew he had to address the issue before he was escorted to a plane that was aimed at the distant horizon. He and Louis

Jourdan were sitting in Jourdan's office on the Papeete waterfront next to the harbor.

Jourdan looked down at his desk. "My friend, Monsieur de la Chambre, he has a daughter, Moea, in the Miss Tahiti contest."

Nick took a long look at the man and forced himself not to shake his head. It's the same the world over, he thought.

"And?" asked Nick. He paused and waited. He would not make it easy on the corrupt bureaucrat sitting opposite him.

Louis Jourdan kept his eyes averted and squirmed in his chair. He then brought his eyes up and focused them on Nick. The hubris was back, the dust of self-doubt blown away with the trade winds.

"It would be best for you if she won," he said.

"So if I vote for Monsieur de la Chambre's daughter, you will extend my visa for two additional months?"

"I can make no promises," Jourdan said, returning to the paper on his desk and dismissing Nick with a wave of his hand.

NICK WAS SITTING ON THE SEA WALL, OVERLOOKING Papeete harbor and the yachts. The little girl on *Marley* was popping up from inside the companionway, smiling and waving at Nick and then disappearing back inside the boat. Nick played with her from across the water until her mother called her to dry the dishes.

Nick contemplated his situation, or rather, how much his situation had changed. He had become a piano player in a jazz band, he was in the news, he was drawing again and now he was a beauty contest judge. Life is truly strange. Latitudes away, what was left of his past life was stashed in boxes in a storage facility in some little ranching community in the middle of nowhere. He tried to imagine what his life had been like then, such a short while ago. It seemed like ancient history.

Should he talk to the band about Louis Jourdan's ultimatum, or should he keep it to himself? He knew he would do what he thought was right—vote for the best person. If he told the band, they might vote for Moea de la Chambre to keep him in Tahiti. They seemed like loyal friends. But he wouldn't sell out and he wouldn't want his friends to, either.

He had only a little more than two months left in Tahiti, if he could extend his visa. But with Louis Jourdan putting pressure on him, he didn't have much chance of staying if Moea de la Chambre did not become Miss Tahiti. Of that he would not delude himself.

He looked out at the harbor and to the horizon. There's always the horizon, he thought.

"What do you know about Moea de la Chambre?" Nick asked, taking a sip of bottled water. It was a boiling day with little wind, and he and François were trying to catch the breeze to cool off.

"She is the island favorite to win the Miss Tahiti contest," François replied.

"But is she the best for the job?"

François looked sideways at Nick. He turned his gaze back toward the water. "Her father is a powerful man in Tahiti."

"So I've heard," Nick said.

"From whom?"

"I had a visit from a man named Louis Jourdan the other day."

"Louis Jourdan?" François said, leaning forward to polish the table top with a towel.

"Yes."

"The immigration man?"

"Yes. You know him?" Nick asked, taking another sip.

"Sooner or later all of Tahiti passes through *L'Auvent Rouge.*"

"Of course."

"Jourdan told you Monsieur de la Chambre is a powerful man in Tahiti?"

"Yes."

"I see," François said, emptying his bottle and setting it on the table. They were quiet for awhile, staring across the boulevard to the water.

François let out a sigh. "This happens nearly each year," he said.

"What happens?"

"Someone in power has a daughter or a niece they want to be the next Miss Tahiti." François fanned himself with the newspaper. "They start their campaign of pressure to make it happen."

"Monsieur de la Chambre wants his daughter to be the next Miss Tahiti," Nick said, taking another sip.

"Correct. He hears *Le Group Paradise* will be among the judges and he figures a way to manipulate the group. He reads about the band in the paper and sees that an American named Nick Thomas is the piano player."

"And they say all press is good press," Nick mused. François looked at him quizzically.

"Then de la Chambre sits down to lunch with his friend the Governor."

"The Governor then calls Louis Jourdan at immigration," Nick said.

"*Voila*. Pressure is applied," François said, still fanning himself.

Nick drank some water.

"It is worse than you think," François said.

"Why is that?"

"Monsieur Jourdan recently suffered a rather public humiliation."

"How is that?"

"He is a cuckold. His wife ran off with another man."

"Did she run off with another public official? The one was to judge the Miss Tahiti Contest?"

François sat back and appraised Nick. "You are very well informed with the local island gossip."

"It's a small town."

"That's true."

"Once again I seem to be right in the middle of it all."

"It would seem so."

Nick sloshed his bottle of water. "Hey, have you read *The Sailor from Gibraltar*?"

"*Le Marin de Gibraltar* by Duras. Yes, I've read it."

"Jourdan reminds me of the narrator. You remember, the chronically bored civil servant who spent eight years copying birth and death certificates?"

"It's been awhile since I read it, but I get your point. He does resemble that man."

François stood up and glanced out at the boulevard, the tarmac shimmering with heat.

"*Merde,* it's hot. I need another beer. Are you still drinking water?" François asked.

"I'm giving my liver a rest. Alain Marchand brought me a bottle of champagne every night at *Le Paradise* when I started playing with the band. It was getting out of hand and I had to ask him to stop."

"Well, I want another beer." François left the table and went into the restaurant. Nick picked up the newspaper and flipped through it. The Miss Tahiti Contest was featured prominently in an article with photos and a mini interview of all of the contestants. Nick turned to the center spread and found a separate, longer, profile of Moea de la Chambre. Her father was working hard to make her victory a reality.

François arrived with a beer for himself and another cold bottle of water for Nick.

"So tell me about Moea de la Chambre."

He sat down heavily, handed the bottle to Nick, and took a long sip from his beer.

"What that article doesn't say is that she's—how do you say it?—a party girl. She is beautiful and her family has money and therefore power."

"Does she have any brains?" Nick asked as he rubbed the cold bottle across his brow.

"She is not very smart, or at least she doesn't seem to use her intelligence."

"Maybe this will be the thing she needs. Some people just need a push in the right direction." Nick wondered if he was trying to convince himself. Maybe she was the best one for the title. He was trying to keep an open mind. Just because he was getting pressure didn't mean he should vote against her. He sighed. He could feel a storm brewing.

"I doubt she can handle the responsibility of being an ambassador to the world for Tahiti. The title of Miss Tahiti is a public relations job. My friend employs Moea in his shop down the boulevard. He tells me she is never on time."

"That's too bad. So she's not high on your list of contestants?"

"I don't think she is responsible enough.

"It was a nice early spring day by San Francisco standards. Mitchell and Katherine were having coffee at a funky outdoor café on Union Street in the Cow Hollow district. They were bundled up sitting close together under a heater.

"We had a hit on Jody's mobile phone," Mitchell said.

"I didn't realize you were looking for her. Where is she?"

"The phone is in London with a SIM card prepaid with cash. The phone died shortly after it was used. Scotland Yard is checking into it, but it seems the trail has already run cold."

"Interesting," Katherine said. A woman in her sixties wearing a tie-dyed dress skateboarded by. "Do they still call it that?"

"Scotland Yard? It's called New Scotland Yard, but officially it's the Metropolitan Police Service."

They watched a woman walk by balancing five cups of coffee.

"Katherine?"

"Yes."

"Lance and Jody," Mitchell said. He made it a statement, not a question.

"What about them?"

Mitchell dropped his head, looked her in the eyes.

"What? You mean the two of them did this together?" She was too well bred to shout it. Like her mother, she lowered her voice when agitated.

"We think it was mostly Lance's doing. As you recall, Jody stuck around for a month after Lance emptied the account before she disappeared."

Katherine sat back in the chair, shaking her head.

"I take it you had no idea."

"No. I had no idea." Katherine looked at the passers-by. "How long have you known?"

"A couple of weeks."

"Why didn't you tell me?"

"The investigation was still moving, the fewer people who knew the better."

Katherine accepted that. He had to do his job. "Does Nick know?"

"I had an inkling, but he was the one who figured it out and confirmed it. Don't be mad at him for not telling you. I kind of threatened him with obstruction of justice if he mentioned it to anyone."

"Lovely." Katherine sipped her coffee. It tasted bitter to her. "How did he take it?"

"I think he's kind of numb. He's been through a lot."

"I can relate."

They watched the crowd, both intrigued by the people walking by.

"So. You and Nick, huh?"

"Yes. Me and Nick, a long time ago. You're not going to be insecure about that like Lance was, are you?"

"No. It's not that."

"You're working? It wasn't enough to tell me about my husband and Nick's wife?" Her voice became soft again and he realized he crossed a line.

"It's an occupational hazard," Mitchell said, backpedaling. "Look, I'm sorry. I've been alone too long and I need to learn how to be with someone, to be with you."

Katherine considered the man sitting across from her. I do like this man. It's nice that he wants to try to grow.

"Give me another chance?"

"I guess this is new to both of us."

They sat looking at each other.

"My God. Lance and Jody," she said to herself, shaking her head. "As if Nick hasn't gone through enough." Then she thought of Lance cheating on her. She wasn't even upset, which surprised her.

"How long has it been going on?"

"Who knows? Months, years?"

Katherine thought about it. She leaned forward.

"Come here and kiss me," she said.

LATE IN THE MORNING A WEEK LATER, NICK AND PIERRE were standing in the kitchen drinking coffee. Both their faces held smiles. Barefoot and wearing a *pareo*, Maire padded into the kitchen and poured a cup for herself. It was the day of the interviews and pre-judging of the Miss Tahiti contestants at the *Le Meridien* hotel. Maire, once a beauty queen herself, had filled in the band on what to expect as their duties as judges.

"The two of you seem happy—going off to leer at beauty queens in bathing suits."

Nick looked at Pierre, who raised his left eyebrow salaciously. Nick turned to Maire.

"*Oui*," he said.

"Be back in time for the plane to Bora Bora; it leaves at four-thirty and it's the last plane," Maire said.

"Why is the last plane so early?" Nick asked.

"The runway on Bora is not lighted. We must land before it is dark," Pierre said.

They finished their coffee and climbed into Pierre's Peugeot. They were on their way to meet the rest of the band at the hotel.

"Uh, oh," Maurice said, slowing the car after a few minutes. A gendarme was standing beside the road, gesturing Pierre to pull to the side. He complied. As the officer approached the car, Nick could not help but notice the outrageously short and tight blue uniform trousers the officer was wearing.

"You are not wearing your seat belts. They are compulsory in French Polynesia," the officer said.

"Ah," Pierre said.

"And your friend?" He gestured to Nick.

"He is visiting from America. You may recognize us. We are in *Le Group Paradise*," Pierre ventured.

The police officer leaned down and peered in the window. "Nick Thomas, the piano player? I heard you play. You are very good."

"Thank you. You must come again soon," Nick said.

"What about me? I am the saxophone player. Don't you recognize me?"

The officer studied him. "Non," he said. "The citations are fifteen hundred francs each. If you pay me now, they are only one thousand francs."

"But I do not have the money on me," Pierre said.

"How about your friend?"

Pierre turned to Nick who looked back at him blankly.

"Non," he said.

"Ah, then it will cost you more. But I won't charge you for your friend," the gendarme said, completing the citation and handing it to Pierre.

Pierre took the ticket and looked at it. "We are going to Bora tonight. My friend in the police department there will make arrangements about the ticket tomorrow."

"Ahhh," the gendarme said, aware that he lost the round to Pierre.

As they were driving off Nick shook his head, "Hell of a town you have here."

"It is, isn't it?"

"What's with the very short trousers?"

Pierre shrugged.

IN THE BANQUET ROOM AT THE HOTEL THE BAND SAT stiffly at the judges' table. They had suffered through a formal luncheon with the other judges, the captains of industry—the big fish in the small Tahitian pond. Nick sat next to the Pacific manager for an Australian airline—a man named Jack Dewey. They chatted away about international trade, living in the islands, and dealing with the French bureaucracy. Friends by the end of lunch, they were drawn together by a common language and an understanding of business in a less provincial setting.

"I've read about your band. You've made a splash in Tahiti, eh?" Dewey said.

"It seems that way. It has all happened very quickly," Nick replied. "It seems like only last night when I walked in and sat down at the piano."

"I must hear you play."

"Let me know when you're coming. I'll save a good table for you." He reached into his pocket for his wallet and extracted a business card. With his fountain pen he drew an X across the printed side and wrote the number for Pierre and Maire's home. Jack Dewey took the card and reached for one of his own. He glanced at the crossed-off back of Nick's card.

"Early retirement," Nick said, heading off the questions.

It was one o'clock and the judging was about to start. Nick was outside getting air. As he re-entered the room he came face to face with François.

"Are you a judge, too?" Nick asked.

"Every year. I am sort of a fixture in Tahiti," François admitted. "But I dislike the food here, so I always skip the banquet and eat at *L'Auvent Rouge*."

"Hello, Jack," François said, turning to Dewey. "How has Tahiti treated you?"

"I can't complain. I'm almost done here, just tidying things up."

"What's your next port of call?"

"Honolulu. Marlene is already there with the children, getting settled in a house."

"Good. Perhaps we can sit together and have a talk."

"Of course, François. It would be a pleasure."

Ten minutes later Nick and the band were sitting together at a table, beholding the contestants—a parade of beautiful, exotic women who now were standing on a small stage, each wearing a one piece bathing suit with the Hinano beer logo, a silhouette of a sitting Tahitian woman, on the chest. He looked at his fellow band members. They, too, were entranced.

"Look at the hair," Nick whispered to Maurice.

"To Tahitian men, all a woman needs is good hair and to be a great dancer," Maurice said.

The women wore their hair long—to the waist in most cases—the type of hair to flow with the rhythm of an island dance. Nick couldn't wait to see it in motion.

Once all the women were introduced, the judges were given score cards and told how to rate the contestants. The band members sat at their table, each with an idiotic grin on his face, thinking he was very happy at that moment in time. They checked off the names on the score cards, gleefully comparing the women, giving most of them high marks. The female judges were much more critical, eyes focused, examining the women millimeter by millimeter.

The swimsuit competition completed, contestants were brought up one by one, escorted by the pageant organizer and a former Miss Tahiti, who, in small-island fashion, was a friend of Maire and Pierre.

Since the band had replaced a single person, they were to act as a single unit with a single vote for each portion of the contest. Nick, well experienced with working with committees, thought it a disaster in the making. Add a cross-cultural element and men having to agree on a single woman? He winced when he thought of the arguments to come. He wondered if the band would survive the day. That night they would have time on the trip to Bora Bora to decide how to cast their final collective vote on the night of the contest.

The band members took turns asking the contestants a question.

Guy, keeping in character as a dedicated musician, asked, "If you play an instrument, what is it, and if you don't, what would you like to play and why?"

Maurice was next. In his wild man drummer fashion he asked, "If you have a tattoo, where is it and what is it?" He followed the question with a leer and a tongue wag. Xavier blushed and rolled his eyes. A couple of the judges squirmed in their seats.

Xavier's question was much more in keeping with the spirit of the event. "What family member do you admire the most and why?" It was Maurice's turn to roll his eyes.

Then it was Nick's turn. He had been agonizing about it

for some time. He had asked Maire to help him with the phrasing and practiced the question in his mind to get it perfect.

"If you could not be in the Miss Tahiti contest, which of your competitors do you think should win and why?"

The other judges, including the band, sat up and listened for the answer.

Pierre was last, and he didn't much care to be following Nick's question with his own. "If you could travel to any country in the world, where would it be and why?"

QUESTIONING ENDED, THE BAND STOOD AROUND MAKING idle chitchat with the other judges. Nick noticed Pierre checking his watch for the fourth time in as many minutes.

"Are we late?" Nick asked Pierre.

"Very. We still have to pick up Maire and the instruments on the way to the airport."

"Where are you headed?" Dewey asked, walking up to the group.

"Bora Bora. We're on the last flight out at four-thirty this afternoon. I hope we make it."

"Air Tahiti?"

"Yes. The four-thirty flight."

Dewey reached into his pocket for his mobile phone, dialed a number, identified himself, and asked that the plane be held for some dignitaries who were running late.

Pierre turned to Nick. "You make friends quickly."

"Well, that's that," Dewey said. "I'd get moving if I were you. There's nothing to do here until the pageant on Friday. They won't hold the plane forever. Bora Bora is calling."

Chapter Twenty-Eight

They raced to their homes to gather instruments and luggage. There was a digital piano at Bloody Mary's, and the proprietors had borrowed a drum set for Maurice. Pierre, Maire, and Nick arrived at the airport first, followed by the others. Both Xavier and Guy had guitar cases and duffel bags. Pierre had his saxophone.

"I brought my electric bass. I didn't want to bother with a big string bass on such a small plane," Xavier explained.

As they boarded the twin-engine turboprop airplane, their fellow passengers looked back at them, wondering who these dignitaries were. As they made their way to the few empty seats, the aircraft began to roll. Soon they were airborne, leaving the island of Tahiti behind them.

Pierre and Maire were both glued to the windows of the aircraft. They watched as the islands of Tahiti and Mo'orea slid away beneath them, then sat back, each lost in thought. Pierre was thinking about meeting his cousin who lived on the point; Maire was thinking about visiting her family and female friends and dancing with them. Nick's thoughts jumped from the Miss Tahiti contest back in Papeete, a new tune he wanted to try out with the band, the excitement of going to a place he had read about for years, the immigration officer who was taking an uncomfortable interest in him, and what he would do with his life. Plane rides seemed to promote introspection in him.

His thoughts turned to the contest. It was obvious to him, and he suspected any judge who was unbiased would feel the same. There was only one contestant worth considering, and her name was Orama. The others could dance and were beautiful. There was only one who had all that and poise and intelligence. The others paled in comparison.

After Lance and his duplicity, Nick was not willing to compromise with Louis Jourdan. What can he do? All he can do is kick me out of the country. I'm already broke. I've made friends and have a roof over my head. If I get put on a plane back to San Francisco, I can always stay at Jim's house until I get back on my feet. It was a fallback option. He thought about going back to San Francisco, broke and failed, a victim needing a handout. The thought held no appeal. Selling out and casting his vote for Moea would be worse.

The sun was setting. Pierre leaned forward. "You see that island below us, the one to the right? That island belonged to Marlon Brando. He married a Tahitian woman when he was filming *Mutiny on the Bounty* in the 1970s and bought the island."

Nick looked down at the patch of green in the distance and could make out a runway.

"It would be interesting to own your own island. It would be like having your own little country. Or even your own little world," Nick said. He looked out the window through the spinning propeller and watched the sea pass by below. I need to sail more, Nick thought. I need to come back here on

Icarus. He winced and felt a pang of sadness, realizing *Icarus* was gone and he would not sail on her again.

There was a change of pitch in the propeller noise. "Are we already near Bora Bora?" Nick asked Pierre.

"We will land soon."

Coral islets called *motus* surrounded the islands. Bora Bora, to many, is one of the most beautiful places on earth. About five million years ago an underwater volcanic eruption pushed the island of Bora Bora through the surface of the water. Through the millennia the landmass settled, leaving the island with a mountain peak and a circle of *motus*.

The plane banked and leveled and turned on final approach to the short runway on a motu. Nick could see a boat docked near the hut that served as the airport office. A few people milled about, some greeting friends and others waiting to take the plane back to Tahiti.

After the plane landed, the passengers scurried off. By the time they arrived at the shuttle boat, the plane had reloaded for departure before the sun set.

Pierre had called ahead and had his friend Hoanui meet them at the main dock. Maire sat in the front and the men piled into the back of his pickup truck. They headed to Matira Point on the southern end of the island and past Yacht Club Bora Bora and the village of Vitape. The island was enchanting in the faint light of the crescent moon, and the reflection of the moon off the water was breathtaking.

The accommodation provided for them was a hut, a little grass shack with coconut tree walls and a second-story loft. The island was busy with visitors and the hut was the only accommodation available. The band piled into the hut on the beach. It had running cold water, refrigerator, full bar in the corner, television with a satellite dish, and framed Gauguin prints on the walls. The tight thatching was visible inside the hut and the lagoon was thirty feet from the glass front doors. They all explored the structure and staked out their places to sleep. Pierre and Maire took the loft double bed. Nick, Maurice, Guy, and Xavier slept on the couch, the two beds, and the floor.

After settling in, they walked up the road to a snack shop for a quick bite. Later they sat on the beach in front of the hut, looking out at the lagoon. The moon reflected on the water. The surf was flat, the lagoon like glass. There was the slightest breeze moving the palms overhead.

"This is not Papeete," Guy remarked.

They all nodded reverently.

With his thoughts on the pageant contestants, Maurice broke the silence. "I think Moea de la Chambre is a good choice."

"*Elle est une vamp,*" Pierre offered.

"*Elle est une sexy vamp,*" Maurice elaborated. He was drawing a female form in the sand at his feet.

"I think Orama is a good choice," Guy offered.

"She is also beautiful and talented," said Xavier.

"But Moea is hot," said Maurice, drawing the breasts larger.

Nick was silent during the exchange, listening to his friends. When he spoke he focused on Maurice.

"Tell me, who is the best suited for the job of Miss Tahiti? Who would you want to represent Tahiti to the world?"

Maurice looked at Nick and he answered with a shrug.

"Is it only about who is the 'hottest'?"

Guy stepped in "It is about beauty, yes, but also about showing the best side of Tahiti."

"Is it about being intelligent?" asked Nick.

A wind came up and sent ripples across the lagoon.

"Orama is intelligent. Moea de la Chambre is kind of

stupid," Xavier said. He was staring out across the lagoon in a daze.

"Yes, but she is hot," Maurice said.

"Is it about representing the best of Tahiti to the world?" Nick asked.

Pierre looked at Nick. A small smile played on his lips.

"Who cares about the world? We are in Tahiti, in the middle of the ocean. No one will see the winner but us," Maurice said.

"But Mareva Georges won the Miss Tahiti title and went on to become Miss France," Guy said.

"And she was a finalist for Miss World," Pierre added, taking a sip of beer.

"I think the next Miss Tahiti should be Orama," Xavier said.

"I agree," said Guy.

"I think so too," Pierre said.

"But Moea is so hot," Maurice said.

"Have you taken a good look at Orama lately? She is also hot," Pierre said, glancing at Nick.

"She is hot, isn't she?" Maurice thought for a minute before he turned and smiled. "Okay. I, too, vote for Orama," he said, brushing his sand drawing away with his hand.

THE NEXT MORNING XAVIER, MAURICE, AND GUY scattered, visiting various friends and family on the island. They made plans to meet again in the late afternoon before the gig.

"Today we will jet ski around Bora Bora," Pierre said. He held a papaya in one hand and a machete in the other. He sliced the fruit into four slices and scooped out the seeds with the tip of the blade.

"Have some breakfast," Pierre said, handing Nick a wedge. Nick thanked him and together they walked out of the hut and down to the water.

"How far is it around the island?" Nick asked.

"About sixty kilometers. It will take us most of the day. We will stop and visit my cousin along the way."

They stood in the lagoon eating the papaya. When Nick finished the first slice, Pierre handed him another. Nick stacked it on top of the first rind and continued eating, the water lapping at his shins. They finished the papaya and rinsed their hands and faces in the lagoon.

"*Allez*," said Pierre. "The island awaits."

Pierre and Maire rode on one watercraft and Nick on another. The jet skis were the high performance models, and Nick opened his flat-out to keep up with Pierre and Maire. Once off the island, they stayed near the ring of motus surrounding Bora Bora. They stopped and watched the tourists swim in the crystal clear water with sharks and rays, which were penned in together and well fed. They made another stop to watch a photographer shoot pictures of a nude model on a deserted motu. The motu was small with white sand and a single palm tree. The white sand motus, the clear water, and the warm weather with a mild breeze dazed Nick. He wondered who lived in the small houses and huts on the motus. He would have the opportunity to find out as Pierre and Maire were heading straight for one. Nick followed as they pulled up on the sand.

A Polynesian man sauntered to the jet skis. He was barefoot, wearing a pareo and a large black Tahitian pearl on a cord around his neck. A few minutes later, Nick and Maire's cousin Tunui were sitting on the sand talking about his life on a motu and his small pearl farm.

"I have a small breakfast and then take my boat to the hotel to work. I eat a large lunch at the hotel. If the weather is bad I may stay there on a cot in the supply room. On my days off I fish for my meals and work on my pearl farm. It's not bad here and I like the privacy."

"It is nice," Nick said, looking around the island and at the hut. "I see you have a solar panel on the roof."

"I even have mobile phone coverage," Tunui said.

"Do you really need a wind turbine?" Nick gestured to the propeller. "That's a lot of power."

"Ah," Tunui said.

"Uh, oh," Pierre and Maire exclaimed.

Tunui walked to the windmill and released the brake on the blade. The turbine spun and a panel below it lit up. Tunui turned knobs then went into his little hut. Wagner's "The Flight of the Valkyries" exploded from the building. Tunui came out with a remote control in his hand.

"Tunui, please don't," Maire pleaded.

"Two thousand watts!" Tunui yelled, pointing the remote at the hut and increasing the volume. Nick, Pierre, and Maire covered their ears.

"I'm told they can hear me all the way to Bora." Tunui shouted above the music.

Maire grabbed the remote and punched the mute button. Silence fell across the motu.

"The demonstration is over," she declared.

Tunui seemed to take it well. He smiled and then headed into the hut to turn off the stereo.

"He's a lunatic, your cousin," Pierre said.

"Yes, but he's a brilliant lunatic. It's a good thing he lives by himself on a motu," Maire said.

Tunui came back from the hut smiling.

"Come, I'll show you my little pearl farm," Tunui said, gesturing Nick to follow him.

"We've seen it. Take your time. We will visit friends. We'll come back later," Pierre said.

"I like to give my cousin a bad time," Tunui said as they walked down a path.

"Your English is excellent," Nick said.

"UCLA. My mother married a French medical student who was in Tahiti on holiday, he received his degree in the States, but my mother insisted that I be born in French Polynesia. This is my family's motu. We came back for holidays and summers. I got out of L.A. as soon as I graduated from University and moved back here."

Tunui and Nick strolled a short distance behind his hut to a small lagoon. They walked onto the short pier where they came to a desk and chair. A clamp was mounted to the desk at eye level.

"This is where the magic happens," Tunui said. "These surgical tools are for nucleating the oyster." He handed Nick some odd-shaped stainless steel tools.

"I open the oyster and put it in this clamp. Then I take a piece of mantel tissue from another oyster. I make a small slice in the gonad and insert the mantel tissue and then a shell bead. If all goes well, in two years the oyster will coat the bead with nacre, or as you probably know it, mother-of-pearl, and *voila* we have a pearl."

"Where did you learn how to nucleate pearls?"

"I spent a year in Japan learning from a master. It's a lot of science and art. The success rate is usually only 60%, but I'm up to 74%." Nick put the tools back on the desk.

"Some oysters can be nucleated up to three times. The pearls are larger each time."

"Where does the bead come from?" Nick asked, picking one up from a box on the desk. It was heavy and banded from its original shell.

"A muscle from the Mississippi River. Most of the beads used for nucleating pearls come from the U.S."

Beyond the pier were rafts made of large bamboo that was lashed together. They walked down the pier and got into a small rowboat. Tunui took the oars and rowed out into the lagoon. They crawled out of the boat and walked along a raft. Tunui reached down and pulled a rope out of the water. There was a cage full of oysters at the end.

"The oysters are hung from the rafts in cages or bags. I pull them out once a week and clean them and put them back.

"What's that raft out there?" Nick gestured to a raft off by itself.

"Tahiti is known for Tahitian black pearls, from the *Pinctada* Margaritifera oyster. I'm experimenting with the *Pincata Maxima*, the South Seas Oyster. They are also grown here. It produces the largest pearls. That raft is just for those."

Nick looked around the little lagoon. "The water sure is clear."

"Clean water makes for the finest pearls. They have the best luster."

"This is fantastic, Tunui. I'd like to see some of your pearls."

"Let's go back to the hut."

They made their way back to the pier and up the path to Tunui's hut. The hut was much like the one they were staying in on Bora Bora. This one had a high ceiling and tin roof. There was a small laboratory in the corner and a sorting table in front of a window overlooking the beach. Next to that was a jewelry bench and a complete set-up for casting silver and gold jewelry. The kitchen and bath were outside.

Tunui sat down at the sorting table and dropped pearls into Nick's hand.

"This one has green overtones, they call it pistachio in the trade. Look at the luster—the level of sharpness in how it reflects light." Nick held it near the window.

"That's nice."

"Now look at this one." He handed Nick another pearl.

"Wow, this one is so much better."

"Luster is important, as is size, shape, color, nacre quality and surface quality." Tunui gave Nick a lesson in pearl grading. In the next hour, Nick had seen hundreds of pearls from Tunui's farm.

Maire and Pierre appeared in the doorway. "Your cousin is amazing," Nick told them.

Tunui beamed.

"We need to get going soon, while there is still light," Pierre said.

Nick stood up from the table.

"Thank you, Tunui. That was a great experience."

"It's nice to share it with someone who is so interested."

They said their goodbyes and made their way down to the jet skis. As they were about to leave, Tunui called for them to wait. He ran back to his hut and came back to Nick.

"Here, I want you to have this. You will appreciate it." It was a small pearl set in a sterling silver wave on a leather cord. "This is the wave I see out the window from my bench in the hut."

Nick took the piece and examined it, running his fingertip across the crest of the wave, over the pearl mounted on the face. He looked at the silver wave and then at the water.

Turning back, Nick said, "This is excellent. The luster, shape, surface, the color—do I see blue overtones? Tunui, this is too nice."

"Enjoy it."

"Thanks. I will." Nick put it around his neck and tucked it inside his life jacket.

They pushed their jet skis into the water, waved goodbye and sped off. Before dusk they were back at Matira Point and having dinner in front of the little grass shack.

SINCE ITS OPENING IN THE 1970S, BLOODY MARY'S HAD become an institution on Bora Bora and in French Polynesia. The restaurant was a large open-beamed room with a sand floor, reminiscent of a Polynesian canoe house. The tables and stools were made from coconut palms and highly polished. Out front, the names of rich and famous visitors were displayed on a wooden sign.

The party was a birthday celebration for the girlfriend of a wealthy Frenchman, Raphael Sanchez. The couple and their entourage of nine had heard the band in Papeete, and after three days on tranquil Bora Bora, dispatched Legrande to bring the band to the party.

Before the guests arrived, the band set up in a private dining area in the main room of the restaurant. The quintet played subdued jazz during the dinner.

Raphael Sanchez sat at the head of the table, next to his haute couture-wearing girlfriend who was dripping in jewels. Also at the table were Legrande, two other couples, and two solidly built men with watchful eyes. Mild talk and laughter drifted to the band. Sanchez was the center of attention, playing the host to the hilt. Except for the obvious bodyguards, they were tanned, happy, and relaxed.

Nick studied the crowd and saw the over-privileged, a status he had once held. He thought about how Lance and

Jody were coping, having all of his money. He realized he didn't care.

It was boring for Nick to play for the small crowd, not at all like playing in the club in Papeete. The evening droned on until the serving of dessert. The waitress, a Tahitian, lost her balance and dropped a crème brûlée in Sanchez's girlfriend Jacqueline's lap.

"*Connasse*," Sanchez cursed, and backhanded the waitress sending her to the sand-covered floor. The band stopped playing and the restaurant fell silent, all were focused on Sanchez and the woman sprawled on the floor. Sanchez got up; Jacqueline put her hand on his arm to stop him.

"It's okay, Raphael. It's nothing," she said.

He sat back down. Another woman helped the waitress up. The owner was at Sanchez's side. Sanchez took out a billfold and handed the owner some bills. "This is for the waitress," Sanchez said.

"*Oui, Monsieur*," said the owner.

"Tell the band the bar is open, and to pick up the tempo."

The owner nodded, pocketed the money, and headed to the band.

"You may order anything you wish to drink," he said, and Monsieur Sanchez asks for you to bring up the tempo."

Nick looked at Raphael Sanchez and then at the waitress crying in the corner. He looked at the two large men at the table. Bodyguards—or worse, he surmised. He looked back at Sanchez, seeing the coldness in his eyes, Nick thought him a man capable of extreme violence.

"Dom Pérignon," Nick said to the owner.

Pierre cocked his head at Nick. "Dom Pérignon," he told the waiter.

"Dom Pérignon," said Xavier, Guy, and Maurice, in unison.

"*C'est bon*," said the owner with a smirk. "I will bring a bottle for each of you."

When he was gone Maurice said, "I don't even like champagne."

"This champagne you will enjoy," Nick said. Even if François thinks it tastes like dust, he thought to himself.

The evening wore on and the champagne bottles emptied. The band became raucous and the music turned from jazz to blues-rock to rock-and-roll. The host didn't seem to mind and by midnight the rest of the restaurant patrons had joined the private party dancing on the sandy floor.

NICK SAT ON THE BEACH IN FRONT OF THE SHACK. THE moon had long since set, the Southern Cross was setting, and fingers of dawn were piercing the sapphire blue sky and reaching out across the lagoon. A lone palm cast a long morning shadow into the clear lagoon. He thought the scene would make a fine painting. Nick was alone, at least until a dog wandered up, lay down beside him, and rested his chin on his leg. He petted the dog, thinking Xavier was right, this must be the most beautiful place on earth, and he had it all to himself. After awhile he went for a walk. The dog followed him. In the distance Nick noticed a solitary figure walking toward him along the beach. As he grew near, Nick saw a stern-looking Tahitian man.

Their eyes met in the dim morning light.

"*Ia orana oe*," Nick called the Tahitian greeting.

The man's expression changed; now he had a smile and a twinkle in his eye. He plopped down on the beach and continued eating the mango he carried.

"You are not French," he said.

"*Je suis Américain.*"

"Ah. Then I will speak English. My name is Arenui," he said, extending his hand to shake. He paused. Mango juice covered his hand. He extended his elbow instead.

Nick shook his elbow and said, "Nicholas Thomas."

"Your name sounds familiar," Arenui said.

"Oh?"

"You are dressed like a French resident of Papeete."

Nick looked at his clothes: A French-cut shirt and short trousers. "I am staying with friends in Papeete. They gave me the clothes."

"Ah. I see. How do you like Papeete?"

"I like it here better."

They were silent for a while, staring out across the lagoon, waiting for the sun to fully rise. It was, Nick noted, the start of what would be another perfect day.

"I am stunned by the beauty of this place," Nick said, feeling the sun on his face. "It wells up inside of me like—I don't know what it's like. It's hard to describe."

"The emotions in the islands are extreme. When you are happy you are very happy. When you are sad, the sunrise does not look the same," Arenui said.

"I suppose that's it. It's a shame I must go back today."

"What is so important in Papeete?"

"My band and I are judges for the Miss Tahiti contest."

"*Le Group Paradise*?"

"You know of it?"

"You are Nick Thomas, the piano player."

"Ayyy," Nick said.

"French Polynesia is a small place," Arenui said with a smile. "*La Dépêche* is delivered to Bora Bora, too."

"Wow."

"You played at Bloody Mary's last night. Is it true that gangster hit Merenui?"

"It's true. I saw it myself. It was very disturbing," Nick replied.

"*Salaud*," Arenui said.

"Bastard, indeed. He's a gangster as well?" Nick asked.

"Yes. He comes here about once a year from Marseilles."

They both looked back at the lagoon. Nick couldn't help but think that Arenui was also taken with his life on Bora Bora.

"So you play the piano," Arenui said.

"Yes."

"Is that what you do in America?"

"No, I was in business."

"Music is better."

Nick and Arenui sat on the sand and talked for more than an hour. They compared lives and Nick, listening to Arenui's stories, wished he had time to go to other more remote islands and see the true Polynesia.

LATER THAT AFTERNOON, NICK AND THE BAND GATHERED with their bags at the shack.

"It is time to bid farewell to Bora Bora, Nick," Maire said.

"I could live here forever. Must we go right away?" He realized he sounded like a little boy and it surprised him.

Maire smiled at Nick like a knowing mother. "Bora Bora has cast its spell on you, Nicholas."

"Yes, I suppose it has."

"The Miss Tahiti Contest is tonight. We need to leave soon if we are to catch the plane," Pierre said.

Nick turned to look at the lagoon. It was sparkling and

clear, with just a ripple flowing from the reef. It made his heart ache.

Pierre came running up. "The boat for the airport is not working."

"Isn't there another we could take?" Nick asked.

"I checked with the local hotel. Their boat is also broken."

Nick looked at the jet skis pulled up on the beach. "Well, I suppose we could...."

IN TEN MINUTES PIERRE, MAIRE, NICK AND THE BAND were splashing along, luggage, saxophone, and guitars lashed to the back of the five jet skis making a beeline for the airport motu. That evening, back in Papeete, Nick found himself seated next to Dewey at the head table watching the dancers and the audience as they listened to the music. There were bottles of good French champagne placed on the table in front of them.

The master of ceremonies appeared. As at any beauty contest, he was schmaltzy, told bad jokes, and laughed too much. But the audience, happy to be entertained, applauded and laughed along with him. After the dancing and singing by the contestants, the judges were called to the final conference. They assembled under a pandanus tree outside the open-air auditorium. The band members stood off to one side. François and Dewey were also off to the side, heads bowed in deep discussion.

It was now obvious to each of the band members that there could be only one true winner, one perfect Miss Tahiti. She was, as they had earlier agreed, Orama. She was beautiful, elegant, poised, and pleasant. She worked in the travel industry and would make an excellent representative for

Tahiti. It was, after all, what the pageant was about. There were more beautiful women, perhaps, but none with so many excellent qualities.

"Are you sure you want to vote for her?" asked Monsieur Dupond, the director of the contest, as he approached the band.

"Well, yes, of course. She is the best," Pierre spoke for them.

"What about Moea?"

"Well, she is beautiful, yes, but Orama, she is clearly the winner."

There were nods of agreement all around.

Dewey stepped forward. "I also cast my vote for Orama. With my vote and François', that makes Orama the winner.

"But Moea, she is so beautiful and dances well...."

"Yes, but Orama is beautiful, intelligent—and she taught the other girls the dances for the pageant."

"Yes, but Moea's father...."

"Ah," said Pierre.

"Ah," said Maurice and Guy. Dewey and Nick exchanged knowing glances.

"Well, I'm afraid her father will have to settle for, say, second place?" Pierre said, looking at the band and Dewey for agreement. They nodded or shrugged. Nick admired Pierre's diplomacy.

"Second place? Oh, ahhh." Monsieur Dupond did not look well. "Second place. Oh, I don't want to be here for the announcement."

"Will there be a problem?" Nick asked.

"Well, she is the crowd favorite..."

"None the less, Orama must be the next Miss Tahiti," Pierre said.

"Oh," said Monsieur Dupond.

"So, that settles it. Orama will be Miss Tahiti; Moea de la Chambre will be first runner up. *C'est bon,*" said Maurice.

Dewey took Nick and the band aside. "It might be in our best interest to leave directly after the announcement of the winner."

"It could get ugly?" Nick asked.

"This is a small place. The coconut telegraph has probably already announced the planned winner. They will not enjoy being mistaken."

"And she is not Moea," Pierre said.

"She is not Moea."

THE BAND FILED BACK TO THEIR POSITIONS AT THE FRONT table. Nick saw Louis Jourdan sitting in the first row of spectators. Nick caught his eye and waved at him before he sat down next to Dewey. Jourdan caught his gaze and smiled.

"What kind of work did you do in San Francisco, Nick?" Dewey asked.

"I started a company that designed solar power regulators. Before that I was in aerospace. Before that I worked as a consultant with companies developing new businesses and expanding their markets."

"Domestic markets?" Dewey asked.

"Domestic, but in this global economy that would be limiting. I considered worldwide markets."

Dewey looked at Louis Jourdan, and then back at Nick. "So, Nick, where are you going after Tahiti? Back to San Francisco?"

"That's a good question. There's no reason for me to go there, except for the return plane ticket I'm holding," Nick replied.

"I do the start-up work for my airline. I go into a market and do all the preparation work before the airline comes in. I could use someone with your talents. How would you like to come to Honolulu and work with me?"

Nick turned to Dewey, eyeing him. "Why me? You hardly know me."

"Oh, I've seen you in action. François has good things to say about you. I have found him to be an excellent judge of character." He gestured toward Jourdan. "You fight the good fight, Nick. That's rare in a man."

Nick looked at Jourdan and back at Dewey. He glanced around at the audience and at the band, engrossed in the goings-on of the contest. He looked at Orama, standing on the stage among the other contestants. She didn't know she would be the next Miss Tahiti. She probably assumed, as did most of Tahiti, the next Miss Tahiti would be Moea de la Chambre. Nick smiled to himself. He turned back to Jourdan, who was clearly observing him. Nick knew his days in Tahiti were numbered.

Damn. I was just getting comfortable. Rejoining the rat race did not appeal to him. Could he live as simply as he had since his arrival in Tahiti? He had few possessions, all of which he could carry with him. What about the work? Was his spirit for work broken? Did he have what it takes? Did he want to move to Honolulu and start over? Did he have a choice? No, he didn't and he knew it. He would rejoin the world and have a new adventure in Hawaii, and he would do it as he always had, fully and completely. He turned to Dewey and smiled.

"When may I start?" he asked.

"How about Monday morning? Your departure from Tahiti is, how shall I say it? Imminent," Dewey said, gesturing to Jourdan.

"Monday." Nick took another look at Jourdan. "You're well informed." Nick took a sip of champagne, "Why not? Monday it is," he replied.

"Good. I'll change your ticket and upgrade you to first class. We can sit together and I'll get you up to speed." They clinked glasses and turned back to the stage.

The noise in the auditorium grew to a fever pitch. The master of ceremonies shouted, "And the winner of this year's Miss Tahiti Contest is," he stopped for a dramatic pause, "Orama Ambleville!"

There was a stunned silence from the audience, followed by a roar of yells and some applause. Orama walked forward and accepted the crown and flowers. Behind her, Moea de la Chambre stomped off the stage.

Nick could see the sweat on Louis Jourdan's reddening bald head. He gave Nick a long cold stare. Nick held his gaze for a beat and shrugged his shoulders.

"It's time to leave, Nick," Dewey said, surveying the crowd and taking a last sip of champagne.

Following Dewey, Nick and the band left the contest and met in the parking lot. All around them there was grumbling and discussion.

"I'm glad we're leaving," Pierre said. "What do you say we continue the evening at Le Club 106?" There was enthusiastic approval among the members of the band, their wives and girlfriends.

"I must get back and finish packing my office," Dewey said. "Good night, gentlemen. I'm proud to be one of the votes for the new Miss Tahiti."

NICK HAD LIVED AS LONG AS HE HAD WITHOUT EVER

drinking a straight shot of tequila. He had been a beer and wine drinker since his college days, and of course, rum. There he was in a waterfront bar in Papeete, trying to pace himself. He pleaded with Pierre to stop pouring after the fourth shot. It was approaching 2:00 a.m., the dance floor was still alive, and he was sitting at the bar with Vahine, one of Maire's best friends. She was a beautiful Polynesian woman with an attractive round face and perfect skin. Vahine, like all the Tahitian women he had met, had a self-assurance about her. She seemed, Nick thought, comfortable in her own skin.

"Nick, Nick," Pierre called, "This is my friend Henri. He is the chief engineer of the cruise ship—*Club Med II*. It's docked on the waterfront. He has invited us to a party on board." Nick shook Henri's hand.

"Let's gather everyone and go," Pierre said.

The band, Maire, Henri, Nick and Vahine walked down Boulevard Pomare to the ship and into the bowels of the *Club Med II* where the officers' lounge was located. Nick found himself on a leather sofa with Maire on his right and Vahine on his left. They were swaying to the music, holding hands and drinking good champagne provided by their host. Nick could feel the heat of the women on either side of him. He was thoroughly enjoying the sensations.

Across the room, the rest of the group was huddled together talking with some crew that had wandered by and joined the party. The champagne, tequila, and more champagne had put Nick in a mellow mood.

"I must go," Maire said.

"Eh?"

"The toilet, I must go. All of this champagne."

"Ah." Nick helped her up and sat back down with Vahine. They talked about Tahiti and Vahine's home on the island of Huahini Nui. Nick realized that he, too, had to go.

He excused himself and left the lounge, following the signs to the toilets. As he approached, he heard murmured female protests and a muffled scream. He tensed and his pulse shot up; he felt sober. He looked around the hallway for a weapon. Nick took a steel fire extinguisher off the wall and approached the door, listening. He heard more protests. He quickly pushed the door open and saw Maire pinned to the sink by two sailors. Maire's skirt was up around her waist. One man was standing between her legs, holding her knees apart, the other had both hands on her breasts under her ripped blouse. The sailors were oblivious to his entrance. She glanced up and into Nick's eyes. She appeared calm, as if resigned to the situation. Nick lifted the fire extinguisher and hit the man standing between her legs on top of the head. As the man dropped to the floor Maire twisted and brought a knee up hard into the crotch of the other man. His eyes glazed and he dropped his hands from her breasts. Nick finished the job with the fire extinguisher to the side of his head. They were both on the floor, one moaning, the other out cold. Nick reached for Maire and lifted her over the fallen bodies.

Maire looked down at the moaning man and shot a pointed shoe into his groin. Nick winced as the man let out a squeal and then passed out. Maire turned to Nick and the anger drained from her face. She reached forward and, taking Nick's face in her hands, she kissed him on the mouth.

"Thank you, Nicholas."

"No problem," he squeaked.

They looked at each other and broke into laughter.

Maire took the fire extinguisher from Nick's hand, pointed it at the bodies on the floor, and pulled the trigger. When it was empty, Nick took it from her and set it down.

"Are we through here?" he asked.

"I still need to use the toilet," she said, checking the mirror and straightening her clothes.

Nick looked at the unconscious men on the floor. He leaned down and checked to see if they were still breathing. They were. "I'll wait for you outside the door," he said, and then left.

"Are you okay?" he asked when she came into the corridor.

"Yes. I'm fine. Thank you," she said. Nick walked with her back to the lounge.

Vahine took one look at Maire's torn dress and rushed to her side, glaring at Nick.

"No, no, Vahine. If it weren't for Nicholas, I would be much worse off."

Nick left them together and moved to Pierre.

"It is time to go, Pierre," Nick whispered to him.

"Nick, it is early, we are dancing, the music is good, the champagne is wonderful, the women are beautiful. I am beginning to like champagne."

"Pierre," Nick said, taking him by the shoulders and staring in his drunken eyes, trying to connect with him. "A couple of sailors attacked Maire in the toilet. It is time to leave."

"Maire? Is she okay?" Pierre turned to see Vahine consoling Maire.

"She is fine, but it is time to leave," Nick said.

"Where are the men? I will kill them," Pierre yelled, looking over at Maire.

Nick put a hand on his shoulder. "They are unconscious, Pierre. There is not much you can do to them. Let's go."

"Oh?" He turned back to Nick. "Thank you. Yes. *Allez*," said Pierre. Among protests, they gathered the group and hustled them up the stairs and out onto the deck.

It was 3:00 a.m. and Papeete was calming down from the contest. Nick, Pierre, Maire, and Vahine sat four abreast on stools at the counter of a food coach on the jetty. The *Club Med II* loomed behind them.

Chatting in French and English, they were eating Chinese food, Nick once again sitting between Maire and Vahine. Maire had ordered the meal in Chinese. To Nick's pleasure and surprise, she was showing no effect of being accosted and had put the incident behind her.

The food was savory and spicy, but the sauce from the noodles got on Nick's hand. He reached for a napkin to wipe it off, but there were none left in the container in front of him. He kept his hand by his side and ate with chopsticks. Maire, without looking at Nick and while talking with Pierre took Nick's left hand under the counter and wiped it clean. Nick was charmed by the gesture. She had a level of awareness that shocked him. He had never met a woman who had affected him so. He looked at Pierre and Maire. They had a comfortable easiness about them, something he yearned for in a relationship but had not yet found. He turned to Vahine who was studying him.

"They are a lovely couple, aren't they?" she asked.

"Yes, they are," Nick said.

The next day the house was quiet until about 2:00 p.m. It had been after sunrise before they got to sleep. Nick opened his eyes and saw on the shelf across the room the Bollinger champagne bottle from his first day in Tahiti, paid for with the last of his money. It stood like a trophy with the cork beside it. He lay there, looking at the bottle, a symbol of the end of his old life and the beginning of his new. It's a better life, now, he thought. Sure, he had fond memories of his past, but it was the past, not to be reclaimed. Now it was into the unknown for him and he was content with that.

He rolled out of bed with a yawn, and walked to the shelf, and took the bottle to the desk in the corner of the room. He sat down, pulled out his notebook, and began to write.

Sometime in life you may decide to start over—
leave it all behind—
the people, the places, the things.

Sometimes in life that is done for you.

If you are lucky enough for it to happen to you, you
may realize what is truly important.

The horizon is waiting.

He tore the page out of his notebook and rolled it up. He looked around for something to tie around the note. There was a coconut husk on the shelf with some shells he had collected. He pulled some thread-like fibers off the shell, tied them around the center of the message and slid it into the bottle.

Leaving the bottle in his room, he padded to the kitchen and found a thin cork to seal the bottle. He put it in his pocket to work on later. But first, coffee. Pierre, appearing as hung over as Nick felt, joined him at the stove.

"Bonjour," Pierre whispered, as he took ice from the freezer and wrapped it in a towel. He put the towel on his head and groaned.

"A little too much champagne, tequila, and rum?" Nick asked.

"*Ouí*. It was a fabulous evening," Pierre said with a smile. "At least until it wasn't," he added.

"How is Maire? Is she okay?"

"Still sleeping. It is not the first time someone has attacked her. She sees you as a hero for saving her."

"Any man would do the same."

Pierre was a great and true friend who had taken him in and clothed and fed him when he was at his lowest rung. On so many levels Nick knew it was time for him to leave Tahiti. He was just glad he realized it before he had done something stupid.

"You are a fine man, Pierre. Maire is lucky to have you."

Chapter Twenty-Nine

While Nick was rescuing Maire in Tahiti, Jody was feeling in need of being saved herself.

"Declined?"

"Yes, Miss. I've run your card through three times."

Jody looked at the card lying on the counter at a dress shop in Covent Garden.

"Well, *merdé*," she said.

"Indeed, Miss."

Jody gathered her bags and her card and left the shop. She found a bench outside, sat down and thought. Her bags were piled around her. She examined the credit card to see if it was damaged. It seemed fine.

She had moved from the Savoy to 41 Hotel, near Buckingham Palace. Jody had been there for two nights since she had checked out of the Savoy. She opened her purse and counted her paper money. She had about 100 euros, and she had put the hotel on that credit card.

She stood up and hailed a taxi to head back to the hotel. She was mad at Lance, really mad.

BACK AT 41 HOTEL, JODY SAT AND SURVEYED HER ROOM. The place was luxurious. The theme was black and white with rich mahogany. There were fresh flowers and fruit, candles, a fireplace, and a complete mini office.

She logged onto the laptop Lance had provided her and wrote him another e-mail. She had passed the anger stage and made an offer to do whatever Lance wanted to get her credit reinstalled. The threats of exposure sure didn't work. Lance did not respond to any of her messages.

She typed away for a few minutes and then stopped and read the e-mail. How depressing. It had been a long time since life had not gone her way. She wasn't sure what to do next.

"Bah," she said to the empty room. She clicked the send button and closed the lid on the laptop.

She read the card on the desk. *Canapés* served in the Executive Lounge each evening.

After a quick freshening up, she took the lift to the lounge. The opulence was spectacular. It was like an English gentlemen's club with a glass roof, chandeliers, more mahogany, and comfortable chairs. There were a few people scattered about.

Surveying the scene, she noticed a man sitting by himself reading a newspaper and made her way to where he was seated. She craned her neck to check his finger for a wedding band. No ring.

She took a seat across from him. He glanced up from his paper, met her eyes and smiled.

"Here on business?" she asked.

"I guess you could call it that. I'm finalizing my divorce."

"Oh, I'm sorry," Jody said, trying to keep the pleasure out of her voice. "My own divorce will be final next month."

"Is that so?" the man leaned forward, smiling and eyeing her up and down. "Allow me to introduce myself."

Chapter Thirty

By their second day of driving, Arthur and Fiona had relaxed and fallen into a comfortable groove. They turned out to be ideal traveling companions. When one of them saw something interesting, they would stop and explore. They continued down the coast and spent the night in Charleston.

After Charleston they slept in a little later and had longer stops for meals. Getting up at seven and out the door at seven-thirty soon became up at nine and out the door after a leisurely breakfast at ten-thirty. They were covering the same number of miles each day, just taking longer to do it. Fiona knew the route and after the first day made a point of showing Arthur her favorite cafés, places to stop for a nice view, and strange little antique shops.

Fiona watched as Arthur drove, ate, and interacted with waitresses and shopkeepers. He was polite, friendly, and left a decent tip. She decided that he really was a nice guy. His story of China intrigued her and he didn't seem to moan about his situation. He was rather matter of fact about it. As they continued to drive south, she grew more comfortable with him. They had chemistry.

It seemed to Arthur that Fiona, like him, was also running from something. He still knew practically nothing about her. He asked small questions and she would steer the conversation back to him. It was frustrating, but she was calmly adamant. He didn't want to irritate her and he was enjoying the trip. So they talked about anything but her. He couldn't help but wonder why she was with him.

By the third day, they had made it as far south as Saint Augustine and the car had started to look lived-in. When they pulled into the hotel parking lot, Arthur cleared out the coffee cups, water bottles, newspapers, sweaters, and jackets. It was 59 degrees when they left Charleston in the morning. It was a balmy 75° in St. Augustine. Arthur was happy they had headed south.

After checking into the hotel they took a post-drive walk and stood below the Castillo de San Marcos at the edge of the Matanzas Bay.

"This place is amazing with history," Fiona said. "The Spanish built it, British took it over, then it returned to the Spanish and then finally to the United States. The US used it as a prison for the native Seminole, Osceola, Apache, and Cheyenne."

Arthur looked at the fort. "That is quite a history, and a sad one." It was a spectacular masonry structure with diamond-pointed corners overlooking the bay.

The next morning in St. Augustine, Fiona was sitting on the bed in the hotel room clicking away intently on her laptop computer. Arthur, who had gone out for coffee, returned with two steaming cups.

"Do you have a passport?"

"Yes. Are we going somewhere?"

"Nassau."

"Nassau? The Bahamas? That Nassau?"

"Well, not exactly Nassau. I know a little get-away."

Arthur considered it. "You know, I'm okay on funds, but I do have a finite amount." He felt embarrassed telling her, and it showed.

Fiona looked up from the computer. "Would you allow me to buy your ticket? I'd like you to come along."

Arthur couldn't help but smile. He wanted to be with her.

"I suppose that would be all right," he stammered. "I mean, yes. Please, and thank you."

Fiona let out an involuntary laugh.

"Great. It'll be fun. You'll love it." She picked up her phone and made a call.

THE NEXT MORNING THEY DROVE TO MIAMI WHERE Arthur bought shorts and light shirts, then dropped the rental car off near the airport. He was feeling nervous about getting on a flight and going through security. What if they have a picture of Lance in the database? How much trouble was that guy in? He had his own identification and he couldn't think of any reason he would be stopped, but it still concerned him. When Fiona hailed a cab and not the rental car shuttle to the airport, Arthur was confused and looked at her quizzically.

"I hate airports. We will take a more direct route."

Fifteen minutes later they arrived at Miami Seaplane Base at Watson Island. A man in a pilot's uniform met them as they drove up. He opened the taxi door and helped Fiona out.

"Jackson, are you flying us today?"

"Indeed I am Miss Fiona. It's nice to see you again. Is it

only you"– he bent down and looked into the taxi at Arthur, "and your friend?"

"Yes, it's just us. This is Arthur. Arthur, Jackson, our pilot."

Arthur scooted over on the seat and climbed out of the taxi. He stood up and extended his hand to shake. The man stood a foot taller than he and had a strong handshake. He could feel the man's eyes inspect, evaluate, and file away his assessment of him.

"Hello, Arthur."

"Jackson. Nice to meet you." Arthur tried to stay composed to the imposing man in front of him.

"Do you need help with your baggage?" Jackson asked.

"No, I can handle it," Arthur said, moving to the trunk.

"I'll need to preflight the plane. I'll meet you on the ramp," Jackson said, touching his fingertip to his hat and walking off.

"Well, he's intimidating," Arthur said.

"Oh, Jackson is a lovable bear. He likes to look out for me."

They took their baggage into the office and then out to the ramp. There was a de Havilland Twin Otter floatplane tied up to the dock.

Jackson walked up to them. "It's just the three of us. I'm ferrying mechanical parts to Nassau." He turned to Arthur, "How would you like to ride up in front with me?"

It was less a question than a directive.

Arthur looked over at Fiona. "Wouldn't you rather be up front?" he asked.

"Thanks. No, I've flown up front a lot. You enjoy it. It'll be fun."

"Okay." Arthur held out his hand to steady her as she got into the plane.

They took their places, strapped in, and put on headsets. Jackson taxied out into the bay.

"Why don't you put your hands on the yoke," Jackson said. "That's the thing in front of you that looks kind of like a steering wheel."

Arthur turned and looked at him then put his hands on the controls.

Jackson spoke into the radio, reached up, and moved the throttles forward. The plane accelerated through the water. Arthur could feel the pilot's feet on the rudder petals, but his hands were in his lap while Arthur's were on the controls.

"Just hold her steady with a slight pull back on the yoke."

"Okay," Arthur said.

"We'll be clear of the water resistance in a moment."

"Right."

"Feel that? Now we're on the step. Now ease back on the yoke and fly her off the water."

Arthur eased back and the rest of the resistance fell away.

"When we get to five hundred feet, make a right turn. That's the altimeter and that's the compass." Jackson pointed to the instruments.

"Got it."

Arthur gained altitude and made a gentle turn southeast toward Nassau.

"You seem comfortable behind the controls. I assume you've flown a plane before."

Arthur had flown before. His college roommate flew nearly every weekend and Arthur often tagged along. While he never was interested in going through the time and expense of acquiring a license, his roommate enjoyed teaching Arthur to fly. He had logged close to two hundred hours by the time he graduated.

"I've flown some. Where's the trim?"

Jackson showed him how to trim the aircraft, which allowed him to fly with less pressure on the controls.

"So does he pass?" Fiona asked over the intercom.

Jackson turned to look at Fiona, "We'll see."

Arthur continued to fly, looking out the window for other planes. Jackson made adjustments to the throttle and mixture. He reached down and flipped a switch on the radio console.

"How long have you known Fiona?"

Having passed the first test, Arthur was feeling more confident talking to Jackson. He made a point of not sounding too cocky.

"Not long. We met in New York and drove down the coast."

"So, what, like a week?"

"More like a couple of days."

"You don't seem like one of those Ivy League boys she usually has trailing after her. West Coast?"

"I guess that must be obvious to everyone I meet," Arthur said.

"Well, you seem different. That's a good start."

Arthur figured being different was the best he would get out of Jackson. He was looking forward to learning about his relationship with Fiona. He was also curious about where they would end up. Fiona wasn't volunteering much and Arthur was happy to go along for the ride. He had nowhere else to go.

They continued in a southeast direction, crossing between the island of Andros and the Berry Islands. Jackson took the controls as they approached Nassau.

As Jackson lined up on final approach he said to Arthur, "Don't worry, this thing has wheels and floats." He reached forward and flipped the switch to lower the landing gear.

After they landed and cleared customs in Nassau, Fiona

and Arthur caught a taxi into town and did some provisioning while Jackson dealt with unloading the cargo. They met back at the plane less than an hour later and continued their flight. Jackson handled the rest of the flying and Arthur sat in the back for the rest of the trip. He could see an animated discussion going on between Fiona and Jackson in the cockpit. His headset was turned off; he couldn't hear what they were saying.

By afternoon Arthur and Fiona were on the north end of Rose Cay. Fiona had Jackson buzz the caretaker's home to let them know they were about to land. Mr. and Mrs. Burrows, a Bahamian couple in their sixties were standing on the dock to meet Fiona with huge smiles and hugs. Both gave Arthur a good look up and down. He smiled at their parental looks, then Mrs. Burrows gave him a hug as well.

"How are you, Jackson?" Mrs. Burrows called.

"I'm fine Mrs. B, how are you?" He came down the dock after securing the plane and received a big hug from Mrs. Burrows and a handshake from Mr. Burrows.

Fiona handed Mr. Burrows his favorite Seven Fathoms Rum from the Cayman Islands. To Mrs. Burrows she gave Cadbury chocolates she had picked up in Nassau. Mr. Burrows loaded them all in an ancient Land Rover and took them down a bumpy road. Arthur sat in the back and watched Mrs. Burrows and Jackson, both with their heads down and talking. They drove past pink sand beaches to the north tip of the island until Mr. Burrows stopped in front of a two-story colonial house.

LATER THAT EVENING, ARTHUR AND FIONA SAT AT AN OLD picnic table on the beach and had a simple dinner of conch salad prepared by Mrs. Burrows. After sunset they adjourned to separate bedrooms on the second floor.

Fiona lay down on the bed and closed her eyes. It was always nice to be back on the island, but this time it was different. She reflected on her time with Arthur—from the first time they met in the coffee house in New York City to his wild story about fleeing for his life after being in the wrong place at the wrong time in Hong Kong. Men before had fooled her, too many times to not be wary. It was a hazard coming from a moneyed WASP family, although her Irish given name confused more than a few. Her mother was a force of nature and insisted Fiona be named after her best friend and college roommate. Back home in Connecticut the men circled her like buzzards and competed for her attention. It was maddening, and after succumbing to the charms of a few suitors, she had had enough. She needed a break. She left, telling her parents she was going to Rose Cay to have time to herself to relax and rècharge.

When she arrived at the airport ,she found her flight cancelled and decided to rent a car. She had only been on the road for an hour when she decided she needed a stop—and a cup of coffee. Now here she was on the island with a man she had known for less than a week. It had been an intense week, for sure, with long hours spent together in different locales in different situations. She had seen Arthur tired without being grumpy, had watched the way he dealt with people, and had been impressed that he accepted and not whined about his past situation. He was a gentleman, that was clear, and he didn't know she came from money. Well, he knows now, she thought. She knew Jackson and now the Burrows were looking after her, but she felt bad for Arthur regarding the scrutiny he was receiving.

Arthur unpacked his suitcase and put his clothes into a dresser drawer. In the second drawer, he found a photo album. There he saw a young Fiona with two people he assumed were her parents. There were also pictures of the Burrows with Fiona and another girl he assumed to be her sister. In the hallways there were photos and paintings, mostly of people. It was clear to Arthur that this island and home had been in Fiona's family for generations.

"Hey, Arthur!" Fiona called from the other bedroom.

"Yes?"

"I miss sharing a room with you."

"Be right there." He put the photo album back into the dresser and headed out the door to Fiona.

Chapter Thirty-One

In Hong Kong, Lance's activities were being watched.

"Diamonds."

"Diamonds?" asked Scarface. They were sitting in the back of the old black Mercedes, in their meeting spot around the corner from Lance's hotel. The green-eyed woman from the casino was sitting across from them. She looked relaxed and elegant, her legs curled up under her. It was no easy feat, as she was wearing her favored attire, a snug-fitting cheongsam, this time in midnight blue.

"Now he's buying diamonds. Just under one carat, VS1 and VS2 clarity, G, H, and I color, unmarked, not traceable." Midas Chan adjusted his tie. He had more than a hundred ties in various shades of gold. He had been buying a new tie a week for the last couple of years. His goal was to have a different gold tie for each day of the year. His girlfriend thought he was out of his mind. He had two black suits and a hundred ties. He viewed it as a sign of his success, and he saw it as his persona. The day he was born his parents won the Mark Six Lottery. His mother had a thing for Greek mythology and she put "Midas" on his birth certificate.

Today's tie was a brilliant gold paisley.

"He's also hitting the hot spots. He was having dim sum at Lin Heung Tea House on Friday."

"Good choice. Have you found where he's keeping his horde?"

"It must be in his hotel room safe. He went into a bank on the island, but he didn't take anything in with him."

"Keep following him. Did you find out who he is?"

"He has a passport from St. Kitts and Nevis in the Caribbean. I checked it out. You can buy a passport there by investing in real estate or their sugar industry."

"Hmmm," Scarface grunted, "get back to his hotel and see what he does next."

Midas got out of the car and walked around to the front of the hotel. Scarface and the green-eyed woman looked across at each other. Finally Scarface spoke. "Xuan, I want you to keep an eye on Midas. I don't like that gleam in his eye when he talks about all that gold."

"All right," she said, unfolding herself in a fluid motion and sliding out of the car. Scarface watched her go. She moved with a grace that always surprised him.

In northern China on the eastern edge of the Gobi Desert about 200 miles from the nearest city lies the small village of Liqian. There it is not uncommon to come across villagers with green eyes and blonde hair. Some scholars have suggested that those villagers with Caucasian traits are descendants of prisoners of the Romans from the Battle between the Parthian Empire and the Roman Republic in 53 BC. Xuan's grandparents were born in Liqian and made their way southeast to Shanghai. Her parents continued the journey south along the coast to Hong Kong. Xuan, Beautiful Jade in Mandarin, was named after Zhou Xuan, an actress and singer from Shanghai who was popular in the 1940s.

Xuan walked around the corner onto Nathan Road past the Kowloon Hotel and slipped on her sunglasses. She walked unnoticed past Midas, who was sitting in the lobby reading a newspaper. In the bar she took a table near the door where she could watch the lobby.

WHEN THE LOCAL GOLD SUPPLY GOT LOW, ONE OF THE gold dealers suggested Lance buy diamonds. Hong Kong had a diamond bourse and although Lance could not buy without being a certified dealer, the gold dealer knew someone who would sell to him for a minimal mark up if the quantity was sufficient. Lance had made the contact, bought his three parcels of one hundred diamonds that same afternoon, and opened a safe deposit box at a bank on Hong Kong Island. On the way back to his hotel he stopped at the shopping arcade at the Peninsula Hotel and looked for a well-constructed carry-on bag that could hold the weight of the gold he had collected. Once he found a bag, he purchased it and walked around the corner to a luggage repair shop and waited while they stitched extra pieces of leather to the straps and attachment points.

Back in his hotel room he spread the gold out on the bed. Some gold was in bars, but most were Sovereigns and Krugerrands. The packaging varied by dealer and resulted in an interesting assortment ranging from boxed and wrapped, to coins in a simple plastic tube in a clear cellophane bag. Off to the side were parcels of diamonds in blue and white gem papers. Lance surveyed his stash. It was the first time he had seen the real spoils from his larceny. Other than his winnings at the gambling table, all the money he had was in accounts he accessed on-line. He had not even seen a piece of paper with numbers on it. He smiled and packed his loot into the case.

He then took the diamond parcels and set them on top of the gold.

The bag full, he added a couple of hotel towels to make it a little more padded. He hoisted it up to test the straps, giving it a good bounce, and found it to be solid. He realized it would appear he was weighed down with a heavy package. Lance practiced walking around the room with the case. He tried several ways to carry it and settled on having the strap across his chest and his right hand under the bag to take some weight off his left shoulder.

He checked his watch. If he left now he could catch the ferry to the island, deposit the gold in his safe deposit box, and be back to the hotel before it was dark. He locked his laptop in the safe, put on a winter jacket, grabbed the bag, and left the suite, leaving the "Do Not Disturb" tag on the door. As he passed through the lobby of the hotel, Midas, still seated by the window, stood up and followed.

It was about two blocks to the Star Ferry Pier. Lance had timed it well. The *Meridian Star* with its kelly green hull and a white roof had just unloaded its passengers. About halfway up there were rows of white life rings on both sides of the boat. The ferry looked old and well used but solid. The boat departed as Lance was taking a seat on one of the simple varnished wooden benches.

THE SUN WAS GETTING LOW AS MIDAS FOLLOWED LANCE onto the Star Ferry and took a seat behind him near the stern of the boat. He watched Lance moving slowly and deliberately; he was holding a bag strapped across his body but it didn't look natural to Midas. When Lance sat down, he dropped into the seat, as if pulled down. It was then that

Midas knew what was in the bag. He licked his lips at the thought of so much gold so close to him.

The ferry steamed into Victoria Harbour and Lance looked around the boat for the first time. It startled him to see the man in the gold tie sitting behind him looking at him. He recognized him from the casino as the man who stood behind Scarface at the baccarat table. He first wondered if it was a coincidence, then felt a pang of dread.

Clutching his bag, he got up and moved to the stern. There, alone, he watched Kowloon fading in the distance. He heard steps behind him and spun around to face the man in the gold tie. The weight of the gold propelled him to the left and the bag caught the outboard edge of the gunwale. He could feel himself lose his balance as the weight of the gold pulled him. Midas saw what was happening and rushed forward to grab him. Lance fell over the rail, catching his leg on a stanchion. The bag hung below him, above the water, tangled in his overcoat. He tried to pull himself up and felt a hand on his free ankle. The ferry hit a wake from a passing boat and the bag of gold swung, dislodging the leg holding Lance above the water. Midas tightened his grip on the ankle, but the torque was too much for him. Lance looked up into the face of the Chinese woman with the green eyes who had appeared at Midas's shoulder. She looked down at him and Lance smiled at her.

Lance heard the bag hit the water before he did. He splashed head first into Victoria Harbour, struggling to get free from the bag of gold. As he descended deeper into the harbor, the dim light from the surface was fading fast. He could feel the building pressure on his lungs. As he continued to twist to free himself, the irony of being killed by his greed was not lost on him.

Midas looked over the side and stared at the fading ripple

left by Lance. He thought about how he was going to explain it to his boss. He wondered if his cousin still had his scuba gear. After watching for a while for Lance to surface, he marked the position of the boat with a GPS application on his phone.

Xuan tapped him on the shoulder.

"Let's go sit down, Midas," she said.

Chapter Thirty-Two

That night in Tahiti, before they left for the club, Nick filled his day pack. He left notes for the band and Pierre and Maire on his pillow.

He grabbed the Bollinger bottle from the shelf. He carved a cork to fit it in the bottle and sealed it with candle wax, keeping the original Bollinger cork as a memento.

Nick left the house through his bedroom door and walked through the backyard, stopping to take a last look at his garden. The change in less than a month was remarkable, he thought. Pierre and Maire had put out a table and chairs and started using the yard. Before Nick arrived, it was ignored and overgrown. He walked out the back gate and walked down the road to the water. He stood on the rocky beach and looked out at the island of Mo'orea and saw the tide was going out. Nick figured the southern equatorial current would take the bottle northwest and toward the Cook Islands. He gave the bottle a solid throw into the water and sat down on the beach. He watched it for a while as it moved away from shore. He felt like that bottle, drifting on a current, rudderless. He stood up. "Time for the next adventure," he said out loud to himself.

At the club, Orama Ambleville, the new Miss Tahiti was in the audience. She made a point of thanking the band for their support, rewarding each with a kiss. Xavier, shy as ever, blushed and stammered. Maurice tried for more than a kiss and happily accepted a slap for his grope.

Maire, Vahine, and Orama sat at a table with François and listened to the music. Louis Jourdan was also in the club, sitting at a table, eating dinner and sipping wine. He had a uniformed gendarme at the table with him. Nick spotted Jourdan from the stage and they exchanged glances. Jourdan gave him a peculiar smile. Nick had a good idea of what was on his mind.

Nick played his best, once again bringing the band up with him, as he had done on the night of his arrival in Tahiti.

After a couple of hours of performing, the band took a break and gathered around the women and François at the table, talking and drinking. Nick looked at Jourdan who was holding his hand to his throat, his eyes glazed. Jourdan rose and walked past him, toward the toilet.

Nick reached out to stop him and said, "Are you all right?"

Jourdan looked at him blankly and continued toward the toilet.

"Say something," Nick said, once again stopping him.

Jourdan pushed him away and continued on his path, making a choking sound as he went.

Nick knew many people died not wanting to make a scene choking on food. He grabbed Jourdan, spun him around, reached across his chest and tugged. The Heimlich Maneuver worked and a piece of unmasticated meat shot from Jourdan's mouth and onto the chest of a French sailor who was passing by. The sailor looked down and watched the meat leave a trail as it slid down his starched white shirt and dropped to the floor. He lunged at Jourdan and connected with a right cross, knocking him out of Nick's grasp. From across the room the gendarme jumped up from the table and ran into the fray, grabbing the sailor, who was joined by his companions. Nick backed away from the melee. The band members dove for cover, taking the women with them. Alain Marchand jumped in and, to Nick's amazement, stopped the fight. It must be a prerequisite for owning a club, Nick thought. Happy to have been in their first brawl of the evening, the sailors were even happier when Alain Marchand offered them each a free beer. Jourdan returned to his table, holding a towel with ice to his head.

WITH *LE PARADISE* CALMED DOWN AND THE HOUR getting late, Nick sat down at the piano and began to play Take Five. He kept the song going, giving each musician a chance to shine. Maurice, Pierre, Guy, and Xavier all rose to the occasion. Nick looked at them, thinking how much he would miss his friends. He looked at these men he had grown to love as brothers, each different, and each a loyal friend. They wound down the song, playing until it faded out with a single piano note. The audience erupted with applause.

Nick stood and gestured for the rest of the band to join him. When they did, he bowed low to the band and then to the audience. The band, looking bewildered, followed suit.

He turned to his friends on stage and shook hands with each of them.

Nick turned to Pierre, "Thank you, Pierre. You are a true friend." He reached down, picked up his day pack, turned, and left the stage. The audience was still applauding.

He reached Maire, who stood as he approached and said, "You were *tres merveilleux*, Nicholas, it was the best I have ever heard you play."

"Thank you, Maire," he said, leaning forward and giving her a kiss on each cheek. "I will never forget you." He held her gaze, taking her in one last time, wanting to remember her as she was, at that moment.

He turned to François and said, "I'll always remember you and *L'Auvent Rouge*."

"Nick, you certainly know how to make an exit," François said with a smile, shaking his hand.

"Vahine, you are a beautiful person," Nick said, "and, Orama, I know you will be a credit to the title of Miss Tahiti."

Nick turned and walked to Louis Jourdan's table. He was holding a towel with ice to his left eye.

"Can you give me a lift to the airport?" Nick asked.

"It would be my pleasure," he said, standing and throwing the towel to the table, exposing an ugly, blackening, eye.

Maire approached the table, followed by the band.

"Nicholas, what is this about you leaving?" Maire asked.

"Yes, what is going on?" Pierre demanded, glaring at Jourdan.

François joined the crowd and looked on with interest.

"My one month visa expires tonight. It is time for me to go."

"But you can have it extended. Everyone knows that," Guy said.

"I have worn out my welcome in Tahiti," Nick said glancing at Jourdan.

"*Allez,*" Jourdan said to the gendarme.

Pierre looked from Nick to Jourdan to François.

"We will see you off then," he said.

"After you," Jourdan said.

AT THE DOOR TO THE AIRCRAFT, NICK WAVED BACK AT the crowd from the club. Many of them had crammed into cars to see him off. They had covered him with shell leis. With regret, he turned and entered the plane. He showed the flight attendant his boarding pass.

"Nicholas Thomas? You were a judge for the Miss Tahiti Contest."

It's a good thing I'm leaving, he thought. "Yes, I'm Nicholas Thomas."

"You were brave to make the right decision. Orama will make an excellent Miss Tahiti," she said, handing Nick a glass of champagne and showing him to a seat in the first class cabin.

"I like your pendant. Did you get that from Tunui on Bora?"

He reached up to his chest and felt the pearl in the silver wave. "I did."

"He's quite a character. Please let me know if I can do anything for you," she said.

Nick settled in and sipped his champagne as the cabin filled. Out the window he could see the baggage handlers loading the plane. The flight attendants did their jobs, seating people and handing out champagne. The seat next to him remained empty. "He's always late," the flight attendant said, topping off Nick's glass.

"Pardon me?" Nick said.

"The man who has the seat next to you, he's always late," she said, checking her watch.

Behind him there was the sound of a late arrival, and Dewey plopped into the seat beside Nick, accepting a glass of champagne as he sat.

"Thanks, Heirani. You're a lifesaver." He turned to Nick, "Hi, Nick. Glad you could make it."

"I see you two are acquainted. Drink up, gentleman. We depart soon," Heirani said, moving on to the next passenger.

"Sorry I'm late. The governor wanted to have one last drink, and I wanted to make peace with him before I left. I did, after all, vote against his choice for Miss Tahiti."

"You had pressure, too?" Nick asked.

"I was given a friendly suggestion. By the way, he was happy with the outcome. He never liked Moea de la Chambre, or her father."

"What a place."

"It is different, isn't it?" Dewey reached into his bag. "Here, this is from François," he said, handing Nick a small box.

Accepting the box, Nick opened it. Inside was his Rolex watch. Nick smiled and put it on his wrist, thinking François must have much deeper pockets than he realized.

Dewey took another sip of champagne. "Ready for your next adventure, Nick? The island drums said you had quite a send off. Did you really deck Louis Jourdan?"

"No, that's not the way it happened."

"Pity. The man is an ass. Well, it's part of Tahitian history now. You're achieving folk-hero status as we speak," Dewey said, finishing his champagne and handing the glass to Heirani as she passed.

"I kind of like that," Nick said.

After a pause, Dewey said, "I heard about your business partner in San Francisco."

"You've been talking to François?" Nick asked.

"Yes. It is a great story. So you lost thirty-two million dollars?"

"Well, I wouldn't say 'I lost it'." Nick sat up and pulled out his pockets to show they were empty. "But I wanted to leave Tahiti as I had arrived."

"Well, you can charge your meals to your room at the hotel. I'll get you a paycheck as soon as I can. You'll earn it, though. The first month will border on madness. We'll be putting in long days."

"I'm ready to do that again," Nick said.

"I thought you might be."

Nick heard a conversation behind him and turned around. Louis Jourdan was standing at the door to the aircraft, his cheek swollen. He handed a note and a small box to the flight attendant and gestured to Nick. He nodded at Nick, then turned and left.

What now? Nick wondered.

The flight attendant brought the box to him. He unfolded the paper. It was on official letterhead:

Direction de la Reglementation
et du Controle de la Legalite

In an elegant cursive hand, the note read:

This package arrived for you today.
Bon voyage.
L.J.

Dewey looked at Nick. "Another Rolex?"

"I don't think so." Opening the box, Nick reached in and pulled out a simple white notecard.

She will be at the 800 dock at the
Ala Wai Yacht Harbor in a week.
We can discuss the details later.
Katherine

Nick peered into the box and pulled out the keys to *Icarus*. He ran his thumb over one of the wings on the fob.

"It looks like I will be staying with an old friend in Honolulu."

About the Author

Patrick Livanos Lester is a writer, artist, and gemologist. He was a flight and ground operations engineer on NASA's space station and shuttle programs and an international business consultant. He knows his way around boats and airplanes and lives with his wife Kim in California and Hawaii and other places with sailboats and palm trees.

Check out and subscribe to Patrick's blog, *The Well Read Sailor* www.wellreadsailor.com. It has book and music reviews, photos and tidbits relevant and not to his books, as well as information and discounts on new releases.

If you enjoyed *Flat Broke in Paradise*, please consider leaving a review on Amazon or Goodreads.

84178387R00192

Made in the USA
San Bernardino, CA
04 August 2018